Goodness Gracious Green

Judy Christie writes such charming characters that I was drawn into their lives. I want to visit Green and meet the mayor and Lois's other friends. This is a perfect summer read!
—Ane Mulligan, Editor of Novel Journey

Take a little time and enjoy this tender tale of small-town drama and triumph. Green is worth the trip, I promise!
—Lisa Wingate, National bestselling author of *Beyond Summer* and *Never Say Never*

Other Books by Judy Christie

GOODNESS
GRACIOUS GREEN

The Green Series

Judy Christie

Abingdon Press fiction
a novel approach to faith

Nashville, Tennessee

Goodness Gracious Green

Copyright © 2010 by Judy Christie

ISBN-13: 978-1-4267-0055-2

Published by Abingdon Press, P.O. Box 801, Nashville, TN 37202

www.abingdonpress.com

Published in association with the Books & Such Literary Agency,
Etta Wilson, 5926 Sunhawk Drive, Santa Rosa, CA 95409,
www.booksandsuch.biz.

Cover design by Anderson Design Group, Nashville, TN

Library of Congress Cataloging-in-Publication Data

Christie, Judy Pace, 1956-
    Goodness gracious green / Judy Christie.
        p. cm.—(The green series)
    ISBN 978-1-4267-0055-2 (trade pbk. : alk. paper)
    1. Women journalists—Fiction.   2. Publishers and publishing—Fiction.   3. Newspaper
publishing—Fiction.   4. Louisiana—Fiction. I. Title.
    PS3603.H7525G67   2010
    813'.6—dc22

                                                                                2010016969

Printed in the United States of America

1 2 3 4 5 6 7 8 9 10 / 15 14 13 12 11 10

To Paul
Love and gratitude for going back to Green with me
and in memory of my dear friend Alisa

ACKNOWLEDGMENTS

Annual Golden Pen Awards Given
from *The Green News-Item*
with many thanks from Lois Barker and Judy Christie

The Green News-Item must thank its fantastic community correspondents, who regularly contribute such great local news to your newspaper.

The Golden Pen Award for outstanding "*News-Item* Community Item" this year was extremely hard to choose with so many friends and colleagues sending in their news. The award is shared by Ginger Hamilton, Freda Jones, Carol Lovelady, Paul Christie, Pat Lingenfelter, Jack Pace, Steve Pace, David Pace, Suzanne Christie Zitto, Tony Zitto, Craig Durrett, Peggy Camerino, Alisa Stingley, Martha Fitzgerald, Monica and Anubhav Tagore, Alan English, Eleanor Ransburg, and Gaye Slomka. Fine reporters, all, keeping you up-to-date on what is happening in Green! Thank you!

In addition, the staff thanks those faithful newspaper supporters—Alisa Stingley, Kathie Rowell and Paul Christie. How could Lois Barker and *The News-Item* have survived this year without them? Many thanks, too, to Etta Wilson and Barbara Scott. What a team it takes to put together a newspaper . . . and a book!

1

A free puppy has turned into a costly venture for Alice Procell. Miss Alice, 84, adopted Rowdy from Animal Rescue. "I chose him because he was hopping all over his pen and asking me to take him home," she said. In the car, Rowdy continued his enthusiastic ways, crawling onto her lap. "I tried to concentrate on my driving, but that little feller wouldn't take no for an answer." As she pulled into her driveway, Rowdy put himself between our friend and the brake pedal. Not wanting to harm her puppy, she drove through the back of her garage. "All that I hurt was my pride. I've been driving for 70 years and this is my first accident."

—*The Green News-Item*

Don't be fooled by the sweater vests.

I looked out the window and saw the Big Boys standing on my porch. They looked like social studies teachers, except for the grimaces . . . and the briefcase.

Of course, in my sweat pants, Mammoth Cave T-shirt, and ponytail, I looked like a high school gym teacher who had fallen on hard times. Maybe I should have chosen the shower over the extra cup of coffee.

I opened the door, loath to start my second year in Green with these men.

"Good morning, Chuck, Dub," I said. "What brings you out to Route 2 so early?" I shivered as a chilly wind blew, and stepped aside for them to enter.

They exchanged a brief look, walked into the warm room, and glanced around the old cottage I happily call home, filled with antiques and a sprinkling of modern art. "Haven't been in here in a while," Dub said. "Aunt Helen loved this place. Lots of memories. You've done a nice job with it."

Chuck frowned at his brother and interrupted in a harsh tone. "Sorry to bother you on New Year's Day, but this isn't a social call. We need to talk to you right away."

"Newspaper business, family matters," Dub said, almost apologetically. "We want to straighten this out before it goes any further."

I motioned to the slip-covered couch and was relieved when they took a seat, giving me a moment to collect my thoughts.

"We've heard some disturbing things around town, Miss Barker. We need to talk to you," Chuck said.

"So you mentioned," I murmured. "I assume you're not here to tell me Happy New Year."

Chuck, the extra-bossy brother, started to stand up, reconsidered, and sat back down. Overweight and red-faced, he breathed loudly, almost with a wheeze. He must have put on forty pounds in the past six months. "We're here to buy back *The News-Item*," he said. "We're prepared to make you a good offer."

"A real good offer," Dub said. A fairly trim man, he was aging better than his older brother. He looked fit today and seemed almost cheerful. He wore his standard khakis and a crisp long-sleeved lilac shirt under a purple-and-gold plaid vest. Dressed like that, he left no doubt he rooted for his beloved LSU Tigers.

"The paperwork's all drawn up, and we'll give you a check today." Chuck clicked open the leather satchel and pulled out files. His brother fished in the shirt pocket under his vest and produced an expensive fountain pen.

"But . . . but . . ." I shook my head. "The *Item* isn't for sale. I own the newspaper. The staff and I own it."

"Of course it's for sale," Chuck said. "Everything's for sale. We heard about that ridiculous little profit-sharing ploy of yours, letting employees have a piece of the action. Won't work." He held out a check and waved it in my face. "This is a generous offer. Take it. Take it."

I stepped back, nearly falling over the ottoman in front of my favorite chair. Like the water moccasins that lived in the pond across the road, Chuck looked ready to strike at any moment. Neighbors who lived closer would be nice right about now.

"I'm not sure what this is all about, but let me emphasize that *The Green News-Item* is not for sale. I have established a partnership with the employees, and we have big plans for this year. End of story."

I walked to the door, as dignified as I could be in my saggy fleece pants. My heart pounded and my hand trembled as I opened the door an inch or two, still facing the men.

"Green means too much to me to even listen to you two," I said. "I'm staying here. You're going."

Before Chuck and Dub could stand, a light knock sounded, and the door swung open further. In walked Mayor Eva Hillburn, carrying her spoiled Yorkie terrier, Sugar Marie.

"Happy New Year, Lois," Eva said. Her eyes narrowed as she looked at the McCuller men, a rare show of what she was feeling. She nodded and stroked her dog's back. "Dub. Chuck. I thought that was your truck out front. Have I come at a bad time?"

"This is a great time, Mayor," I said. I reached around the dog to give her a half hug.

At the same time I leaned toward Eva, Dub moved off the couch, an odd mix of delight and dismay on his face. His jerky motion in the direction of the mayor seemed to startle the little dog, who barked and tried to get out of Eva's arms. Chuck clapped his hands loudly and said, "Hush, you little mutt."

I stepped closer to the mayor, and that seemed to be it for Sugar Marie. She barked again and jumped at me, biting me on the face. For good measure, she nipped my hand. The living room, already tense, became frenzied. Dub hurried forward. Eva turned, hugging the whimpering dog. I reached my hand to my cheek and felt blood.

Maybe year two in Green was not going to be so great after all.

"Sugar Marie, bad girl, bad girl," Eva said, stroking her.

"Oh my word," Dub said, handing me the white handkerchief he always carried. "Use this. Apply pressure."

"Good gosh," Chuck said, snapping the briefcase shut and rising. "It's only a scratch. That obnoxious little fur ball couldn't hurt a fly. She's not a Rottweiler. Come on, Dub."

They moved toward the door, and Chuck turned to look at me as the brothers stepped onto the porch. "This conversation is not over. We'll be in touch."

Stunned, I didn't say a word. I started to offer Dub his handkerchief, but it had blood on it. I held it back to my face, my mouth ajar, as though I had a bad cold and couldn't breathe through my nose. Eva began to examine the bite while I watched the McCullers slam the gigantic black pickup doors, spin gravel on the driveway, and head toward Green.

"I have no idea what that was about," I said and dabbed at my eye, noting more blood.

"Goodness gracious! What a way to start the year," Eva said. "I'm so sorry." The mayor, a normally calm woman with a personality as controlled as her hairdo, shook her head and steered me inside. She apologized again and scolded Sugar Marie.

"I'm thrilled you're staying in Green, and now look at what's happened. We have to get you to the doctor. . . . Sugar Marie, whatever came over you?"

Eva was more flustered than I had ever seen her, even during the final days of the tight mayoral race. "Did she get your eye? Here, let me take another look." She buzzed around me like a hummingbird going for a feeder, her hum of anxiety almost audible.

Sugar Marie, now out of Eva's arms, sniffed around the room. I wondered if the dog would insult me further by peeing on the floor, but she settled for picking up one of my slippers and tossing it about violently. I headed into the bedroom to assess the damage to my face, and the animal growled at me—growled at me—in my own home . . . after biting me on the first anniversary of my arrival in Green.

But Sugar Marie had broken up a very unexpected meeting with the Big Boys. Maybe that was worth a small facial scar. Probably even a doggie treat.

"This needs medical attention," Eva said, back to her take-charge self and only a step behind me as I peered into the mirror. "Face wounds always bleed more. I insist on taking you to see Dr. Kevin. I know she'll meet her best buddy at the clinic, even if it is a holiday."

"I think it'll be okay," I said. "It probably looks worse than it is."

"I've got to take good care of my local newspaper owner," Eva said. "I hear she intends to stay in town for years." She smiled and smoothed her khaki skirt.

"I came over, by the way, to congratulate you on your last-minute decision. Never seen anything like it in all my life. I thought for sure you had sold that newspaper. I had even forgiven you for not selling it to me."

I sank onto the sofa and watched the mayor pace around the room, straightening a stack of magazines, fluffing a throw pillow, and adjusting the shade on a lamp. Out of the corner of my eye, I saw Sugar Marie return to the house shoe and pull at the fleece lining with her pointy teeth.

"Eva, you don't know how happy I am to be in Green today . . . how thankful. I'd hug you again if it weren't for Sugar Marie."

"Green needs you, and I'm among the many who know you made the right choice," she said.

"Obviously Chuck and Dub aren't in that group." I reached up to wipe more blood off my face.

"Those two? Ignore them. If they're not stirring up trouble, they're not happy. Come on. I'm taking you to the doctor." She scrolled through her phone. "I know I have Kevin's number in here somewhere." The dog jumped up onto the back of the couch when Eva dialed the phone, and the mayor patted Sugar Marie and fussed at her in a baby voice, which sounded odd coming from the straightforward, distinguished woman.

"Sugar's never bitten anyone before," Eva kept saying on the drive to the clinic. I tried to keep a little distance between myself and the dog, who curled up in the mayor's lap and whimpered as though I had wronged her.

Kevin pulled into the parking lot in her blue sports car just ahead of us. Dressed like a model in a Ralph Lauren ad, she opened my door and enfolded me with a hug as I stepped out of the mayor's monstrosity of a car. "Lois Barker, you scared the living daylights out of me."

I put my hand to my face. *Was the bite that bad?*

"I thought you were actually going to leave us." She turned to the mayor. "Can you believe this woman? Acting like she was selling that paper and moving back north. She knew good and well Green couldn't do without her." She hugged me again. "And didn't even call her girlfriend till it was all said and done."

"I wasn't sure till the last minute," I said. "I was afraid I would change my mind . . . and afraid I *wouldn't* change my mind. It was crazy."

Unlocking the door to the small, nondescript clinic, she flipped on the fluorescent lights and focused on my face. "Let's see what we've got here." She reached over and scratched Sugar Marie under the chin. "What came over you, sweet girl?"

"I'm the patient here," I snapped. "She doesn't like me for some reason."

"She was startled," Eva said. "She can tell when you're nervous."

"She senses your fear, Lois," Kevin said, washing her hands and poking around my cheek. "Awfully close to the eye. You need a couple of stitches, to be on the safe side. You OK with that?"

I shrugged, my stomach churning, and sat quietly while one of my best friends and the only African American physician in town went into her professional mode. She pulled out a little package of supplies and gave me a painful shot. "Has your dog had her vaccinations?" Kevin asked, glancing at the mayor. "Sure don't want this to get infected."

The mayor acted insulted and squinted at the tag on Sugar Marie's pink collar, nodding and stroking the dog's head again. The dog gave a short, sharp bark.

"I woke up so excited this morning," I said. "Now I don't know whether to worry more about my wound or that scary visit from the McCullers, the files they had, that check."

"Eva . . ." I tried to turn to her.

"Sit still," Kevin said. "It's not that smart to move when I'm working near your eye with a needle."

"Eva," I said again, staring straight ahead. "What were Chuck and Dub up to?"

"No good, no doubt," Kevin said. "What visit are you talking about?"

She tied up her needlework as she spoke, pulling a little tighter than seemed necessary. Her opinion of most of the power brokers in town was pretty low.

"Two of your three least favorite good old boys came to see me," I said.

"This morning, bright and early," Eva said. "The McCullers."

"They sold the paper to me, right?" I asked, confused, my face hurting.

"Yes," Kevin said, clearly not following. "You didn't hit your head, did you?"

"No, but my brain feels muddled. Weren't Chuck and Dub happy to unload the *Item*?"

"Yes," she said again, finishing with my face.

"Things have fallen into place for me here," I said. "Chuck and Dub aren't in the picture anymore. What would pull these two men away from home on a holiday devoted to televised football, their favorite activity in the world?"

"Maybe they miss the power of owning the paper," Eva said. "Or they hope to run you out of town. Could be they're trying to cook up a scheme to make lots of money. That's what Chuck does, him and my brother. Sometimes Dub, too. They look for schemes to make money and don't care who they mow over."

The two men and Major Wilson, Eva's brother, had plagued me since I stumbled into Green as the not-so-proud new owner of *The News-Item*. "They certainly don't approve of how I run the paper. But they've never acted like they wanted it back."

"Don't fret about it," Kevin said. "They can't hurt you. *Wanting* to do something and doing it are two different things."

She straightened up the cubicle. "Why don't y'all come over to Mama and Daddy's for black-eyed peas and cornbread . . . see if we can salvage some good luck for you on New Year's Day?"

"I'd just as soon start this year over," I said. "But I'm not exactly dressed for a party."

"You'll get more sympathy in that outfit," she said and shared what I was sure was a can-you-believe-those-pants look with Eva.

I touched the small bandage and picked up my purse. "I guess there's no point in trying to pay you for this, is there?"

"First patient of the year is on the house," Kevin said.

At that instant Eva's cell phone rang, and I jerked my head in surprise, feeling the stitches pull slightly. As the new mayor of Green, Eva insisted the paper publicize her phone numbers. Her phone rang steadily, despite the lack of decent service in most of the area, but had been quiet today.

She frowned as she took the call. "You're sure? Speak louder. You're breaking up. Downtown?" Eva inhaled deeply. "I'll be right there."

She snapped her phone shut, dropped it into her small, square purse and grabbed her keys. "There's lots of smoke downtown," she said. "Looks like one of the buildings is on fire."

"Is it the paper? Your store?" I jumped up and grabbed my coat.

"You know as much as I do. Fire downtown," she said. "Let's go."

"I'm coming too," Kevin said and flung an array of medical supplies into a black canvas satchel. "They may need me."

As we stepped outside, smoke rose in the distance. Kevin's clinic was at least ten minutes from the paper, and my heart pounded hard for about the sixth time today. My newspaper building sat right in the middle of downtown. So did Eva's department store. And the antique mall owned by my good friends Rose and Linda. And the Cotton Boll Café.

Before we got out of Kevin's parking lot, my cell phone rang.

"Lois, the paper's on fire. . . ." Iris Jo, my business manager and neighbor on Route 2, sounded breathless. "Looks pretty bad. They're calling for help from out in the parish." She was a gentle woman and hearing her rushed tone unnerved me almost as much as her words.

"Slow down," I said. "Tell me everything. Where are you?"

"On my way. I got the call from Stan. The Fire Department notified him. Looks like it's in the press area. Not sure how long it's been burning. Tammy discovered it when she went to handle the obituaries. She says it was smoking then. Now there are flames, through the roof."

"Is Tammy OK? She didn't go in the building, did she?"

"She tried, but the smoke was beginning to seep out. She turned around and called the Fire Department. Stan said she's sitting on the curb across the street, crying."

Flames leapt from the roof when we arrived, and firefighters shot streams of water at the newspaper building and other structures nearby. Tammy sat, with Stan and Iris Jo standing over her. Linda, partner in the nearby antique mall and newly hired assistant office manager at the *Item*, scribbled in a reporter's notebook with a frown. Rose, who ran the antique business with Linda, ran her hand through her hair and shook her head.

The scene made me want to throw up. The mayor and I rushed closer but were quickly scolded. "Hold it right there. No civilians allowed," a young deputy said.

We talked over each other. "I need to get information." "We need to know what's going on."

"I'm the mayor. I want to assess the damage. I'm also a business owner nearby, as you very well know, young man," Eva said. With the demeanor of an angry schoolmarm, she pointed her finger at the poor officer assigned to keep spectators at bay.

"I'm the owner of the newspaper," I said. "How bad is this? What happened?"

Kevin surveyed the area and stepped between the policeman and us. "Dr. Kevin Taylor, sir. Local physician. Available to help as needed."

As she talked, Stan walked up, a somber look on his face. "Miss Lois, Mayor, Dr. Taylor," he nodded at all of us in greeting. "I've got the latest information. No need to put yourself—or someone else for that matter—in danger by getting closer."

I turned, not calm but reassured. Stan was one of those steady people you don't notice until you need them. He made sure the newspaper got printed, no matter what. Twice a week. Every week.

"They got the call about twenty-five minutes ago," he said. "Tammy called first and then someone who was driving by. Both reported heavy smoke. They're close to getting the blaze under control. Looks like it's in the pressroom. Old Bossy may be crankier than ever, after this." Stan's nickname for the ancient press had come about years ago when it had first acted up.

"But what about the damage? How bad?" My stomach roiled.

"There'll probably be more harm from water than fire. They hope to be able to tell us something shortly." He paused as Iris Jo and Tammy rushed up, hugging me and assuring me everything was going to be OK.

I turned to Tammy to make sure she was all right, but she got to me first. "What happened to your eye?"

"My eye?" I had totally forgotten about my dog bite. Suddenly, I realized my head throbbed. I touched the bandage delicately. "Sugar Marie apparently doesn't approve of people hugging her mayor."

"Sugar Marie? You've got to be kidding me," Tammy said. "Sugar Marie?" She almost smiled. "She figured out you're afraid of dogs. Poor little scamp. I bet she's in big trouble now."

"Poor little scamp? I'm the one she bit." I stopped short of arguing, remembering my business was burning. "Do you need to go to the hospital, or have Kevin look you over?"

"I'm fine," Tammy said, waving her hand and rubbing her nose with a tissue. "The worst part is watching it burn. This was going to be our year. I thought I might even make some money from my share. I keep trying to figure out what I could have done quicker."

I patted her arm and hugged her again. Down here in Northwest Louisiana, hugging saved a lot of words. People hugged you to say hello, say good-bye, to share your happiness and ease your sorrow. In the past year, I had become quite the hugger.

"Tammy, you did the best you could. You always do. Now tell me what happened, step-by-step."

She began one of her breathless Tammy explanations, offering details from the type of soft drink she was sipping when she pulled up to her realization that the building was on fire.

"It must have just started when I got here," she said. "There weren't any flames or anything."

She hesitated.

"It was creepy, though. Didn't smell right inside. You know how the *Item* always smells? That sort of ink, paper, musty smell? It was different today. More of a funky sort of electrical smell, like when you forget and leave the iron on."

I had worked in newsrooms for nearly three decades and knew exactly the first smell she spoke of. Newspapers have a distinct odor when you walk in . . . and that varies only slightly from paper to paper. The scent comforted me. I dreaded how things would smell after the fire.

"Then I caught a whiff of something strong and ran back outside, looked up, and saw lots of smoke and called the Fire Department," Tammy said.

During the next few minutes, a mix of paid firefighters and volunteers wearing mismatched uniforms put the fire out, with little damage outside. Linda, obviously taking to her new role on staff, interviewed bystanders and Douglas McCart, the chief of police, a stern, gruff man. He talked intently to Linda and shook hands with her as she walked toward me.

Linda put her arm around my shoulder and gave it a squeeze. "Right when you decide you like us enough to stay," she said, "this happens. I'm so sorry, Lois." She glanced at her notebook. "Not many people downtown today. Tammy saw a car or two—Sunday-driver types. Wish they would have called." Her professional attitude surprised me. With her dark hair twisted up in a clip and her pen stuck behind her ear, she looked like an attractive, experienced reporter, a far cry from the cowed secretary she had been just days ago, working for that lying politician Major Wilson.

A carnival atmosphere sprang up on the street while we chatted, and people rushed to the scene, a common occurrence in Green. As the crowd gathered, someone I didn't recognize served hot chocolate and bottled water from the nearby café, and another person handed out leftover Christmas candy.

"Sometimes I think this town doesn't even need a newspaper," Tammy said, waving to a group nearby. "Neighbors spread the word faster than CNN."

Applause broke out when the firefighters wrapped up, and even the young deputy no longer looked miffed. Hank Harper, head of the Fire Department, motioned for Eva, Stan, and me to come nearer. He handed us hard hats, and I wondered how the mayor would fit hers over her helmet of hair. Tammy, Linda, and Iris walked over.

"We'll go in for a short look, but this is by invitation only," Hank said. "It's not a public viewing. Send your folks on home. We've got it under control, and there's nothing they can do today."

Kevin, who had been busy bandaging a slight burn and getting a big splinter out of a firefighter's hand, asked the three women to her parents' house on the lake. "We all need a bite to eat," she said, "and to catch our breath. Let's go over and see if we can get this year headed in the right direction." Slowly, the crowd wandered off, reluctant to leave the scene.

"We'll be there in a few minutes," I said, wishing I could escape with them. "Keep an eye on Tammy."

As Hank described the damage, I took notes, an old habit and my way of remembering with my brain addled. The power was turned off in the building, and the captain gestured with a large flashlight, almost as though conducting an orchestra.

Stan walked next to him, listening intently and occasionally asking a question. Everything around the pressroom was a complete, soggy mess. We strolled through the smoky building, subdued, squinting to find a clue.

"Here's your problem right here," the chief said, making a clucking noise and shining his light closer. "Looks like that plug caught fire. We'll check that out when the insurance fellow and the fire marshal from Shreveport take a look."

Stan crouched down, frowning, and examined the cord without touching it. "That's strange," he said. "I replaced that cord about two months ago. When we thought Miss Lois was going to sell the paper."

I was surprised and touched by his gesture. I had tried to keep my efforts to sell *The News-Item* a secret, but thankfully that had been a big bust. I was thrilled with my decision to keep it, which struck me as odd, given the circumstances.

Production director, maintenance man, and delivery supervisor, Stan looked closer at the cord, and I leaned in. "Can we get her running by next week?" I asked. "Or should I start making calls to our back-up print sites?"

"If I can't get the old girl up and running, nobody can," he said. "Since we printed our holiday issue Tuesday, that buys us a little time."

With inspections and production questions and suspicions whirling, we all headed to the home of Marcus and Pearl Taylor, Kevin's parents. The light from the windows glowed, and the sound of a college bowl game blared through the front door.

A lively, supportive crowd of Taylor friends was on hand, each person with a theory on the fire. I glanced around, amidst hugs and words of encouragement, but couldn't see the one person I wanted to see more than anyone else.

Where was my neighbor Chris? He always made me feel better. Disappointment hit hard, and my face ached.

Before we ate, we gathered in a circle in the living room and held hands while Mr. Marcus prayed one of his awesome prayers, the kind that soothed me when my edges all felt frayed. "Oh, Mighty God," he said in his deep Southern voice, "I thank you for this New Year and for the blessings of the year past. We beg for wisdom for the months ahead and ask that we may be useful to Thee, no matter what the days bring."

The black-eyed peas tasted good, but I could not fully enjoy them.

2

The jelly jar with 33 arrowheads had been in Richard "Dicky" Diamond's attic for about 40 years. Now those ancient artifacts are in the State Exhibit Museum in Shreveport, purchased for $553 by a museum donor. "They are the best examples of mid-period Caddo Indian flint work they've ever seen," Dicky said. He confesses he didn't find them. "I traded some Lik-M-Aid candy to my 8-year-old brother for them. I wish he was alive to see this. Now I can get my bass boat fixed."

—The Green News-Item

Katy ran out to meet me when I pulled into *The News-Item* parking lot the next morning.

"Lois, are you OK? What happened? Can I write the story on the fire? Can I get up on the roof and see where the firemen made that hole? How long will that tarp be there?"

She was full of the drama of a teenager and the enthusiasm of a cub reporter.

"You're stirring awfully early for someone on a school break," I said. "I thought high-school students liked to sleep in."

"I got here thirty minutes ago but had to wait for someone to let me in. I wish I had my own key. Did someone set the fire on purpose? That's the rumor around town."

"We don't know much yet," I said, making my way up the concrete steps into the building and wishing I had her energy. "I guess it could have been an electrical problem, but newspaper people tend to be suspicious. We all wonder if someone did this deliberately."

"Lee Roy Hicks because you fired him for taking that money? Major Wilson after all those bad news stories about him? Someone else you made mad . . . ?"

Katy's words whipped through me, the names I had been chewing on for the past twelve hours: a former employee, a crooked politician, men who had reason to dislike me. But enough to set fire to the paper?

"Don't know, Katy, but be careful throwing names around in town. Let's keep this among us for now. Hopefully we'll get more details today and can piece it together."

A nervous hum from the staff permeated the building as we entered. An acrid smell filled the air, but the power was back on. Tammy was at the front counter, on the phone, with another line blinking. She held the receiver out with a smile, the other party still talking, and then went back to her caller, saying, "Yes, ma'am. OK. We'll take that into consideration."

Catching Katy's eye, she gave my black slacks and blue sweater a once-over and a thumbs up while she talked, a fairly new habit of critiquing my appearance. Covering the phone with her hand, she mouthed, "Hair. Nice. Wear it down more often."

Only Tammy would focus on how I looked the morning after she had found the building on fire. Sometimes I was jealous of her ability to let things go. A graduate of Green High School, she was proud of her days in the Pep Squad and Future Teachers of America but embarrassed she hadn't gone to college. She carried herself like the sturdy country girl she was, pretty but lacking the polish of many of the young women I had worked with in Dayton. I had grown to think of her as my protector.

As Katy and I walked farther into the building, I surveyed the rest of my staff and felt something relax in my gut. Tom, the copy editor, was making a pot of coffee in the newsroom and waved when Katy and I marched toward the damage. "We'll get 'em, Lois," he yelled. "Don't you doubt that for a moment."

Linda sat at a nearby computer, intent on typing. "Hey, Lois, hope you're OK today," she said and turned back to whatever had her so engrossed.

Intern Molly was laying out a page of classified advertising in the nearby composing room, a skill I did not know she had developed. She ran over to hug me, rapidly covering the short distance into the newsroom. "I'm sorry I missed the fire last night," she said. "I was working my other job. I'm glad no one was hurt."

She looked tired, and I wondered what time she had finished at the Pak-N-Go market. "Her mom is an aide at the nursing home," Katy had said once. "It seems like Molly and most of the other African American kids at school don't have much money."

Stan was already in the pressroom and barely visible under the hulk of a machine. The cavernous area was a stinky mess. Pallets of sodden advertising sections, together with the post-fire odor, made my head pound.

"The press looks pretty bad," Stan said. "Lots of water damage." He got out from under the equipment, covered in sweat and grease. He wiped his hands on a ragged blue cloth and tossed it onto a nearby metal table. "Good thing I like a challenge."

Before I could ask any of the dozen questions in my mind, Iris Jo walked in, carrying a large box of Southern Girl doughnuts and a gigantic accordion file. It didn't surprise me that she would bring doughnuts to cheer us up after yesterday's catastrophe.

"How's that eye today?" she asked first thing. Even though she was not much older than me, Iris reminded me of my mother as she studied my eye, more concerned about me than the newspaper. "Looks pretty good. Does it hurt?" I shrugged and she patted my shoulder before turning to Stan. "How's Bossy? On life support?"

Stan always paid special attention to Iris, and this morning he winked at her and gulped two doughnuts as he talked. "I've been looking things over a little closer. I think we'll be able to get her up and running by Tuesday, but I'm not going to lie to you . . . it's going to be tough. I have the whole weekend, but I'm probably going to need some help from up in Shreveport."

"Whatever you need," I said, trying not to grab a second doughnut out of nervousness.

"What I need is to get started," he said. "The Fire Chief told me not to change anything till their inspector takes a look. I can't wait too long."

"Not work on the press? We can't wait. I'll get that guy on the phone. Talk some sense into him." My impatience escalated.

"Now, Lois, it'll be OK." Iris Jo stopped short of patting me on the head. "Let's come up with a plan, get more information and see what needs to happen. You know we can print down in Alexandria if we have to. I've got all the information right here." She held up the large file. "Insurance policies and agreements for emergency print sites."

"Amazing," I said. "You're the most organized person I know." Iris Jo, longtime bookkeeper and a distant, poorer relative of the McCullers, held *The News-Item* together day in and day out. Even though she had divorced more than a decade ago and lost her teenaged son in a car accident within the past two years, she had a peace about her that made me want to be like her.

"You've already pulled all that together?" I asked, reaching for the file. "Did you spend the night here?"

"I keep all of this at home. I've always figured if we had a problem, I'd need a backup of my paperwork." Iris Jo lived down the road from me, and it pleased me to think of her rummaging around for the newspaper's most important papers.

"By the way, Chris called this morning," Iris said. "He's over in Tallulah at his aunt's house. Took his mama up there yesterday. He called to remind me to feed his dogs. He was upset when I told him about the fire. Said we should have called him. Wanted to make sure everyone was OK, especially you."

Chris and I were not dating or anything, but he was another of my Route 2 neighbors and a good friend. My feelings had been hurt—OK, crushed—when he did not show up at the fire or call afterward.

"When will he be back?" My attempt to sound only mildly interested sounded weak, even to me.

Stan was back under the press and obviously not paying attention. Katy, who had been propped up against the metal table, snickered and wandered off. Iris Jo smiled. "I think he's probably rushing his mother right now. I got the impression he was going to cut their trip short."

Her words eased my nerves, and once again I felt happy I had decided to stay in Green.

Questions and plans filled the rest of my day, pushing Chris to the back of my mind. Everyone in town had kicked into crisis management mode, from banker to insurance agent to community correspondents. My urgency to have *The Green News-Item* printed in-house must have been contagious, and no one wanted to see us bogged down in bureaucracy.

"Don't let the pencil-pushers beat you, Lois," said food columnist Anna Grace when she stopped by with a loaf of fresh banana bread. "A tradition is a tradition."

Bud, the agriculture correspondent, brought me a sweet potato casserole his wife had made, complete with tiny roasted marshmallows on top. "We've never printed anywhere else," he said. "Not once."

Their attitude renewed my zeal. "*The News-Item* is always printed in Green," I said to the fire marshal in Baton Rouge after a nice woman in Shreveport suggested I bypass the regional office. "You have to get your people here sooner than Monday."

"We can't turn it around that quickly, Miss Barker. I'll have somebody there first thing next week," the state official said. I slammed the phone down and muttered under my breath as Katy sauntered into my office with a notebook and long list of questions.

"There's no rush to get your story done," I said. "We don't seem very high on the fire marshal's priority list."

That afternoon, to my great surprise, an inspector showed up, minutes after the insurance adjustor. Leaving the newsroom, I found him, in uniform, hugging Katy in the lobby.

"What's going on here? I didn't think you could come till next week." I took the tone of the snippy city editor from Dayton. I had used that voice much more frequently when I first moved to Green, but now it hit my ears as rude and inappropriate.

"Power of the press, ma'am," the inspector said with a smile, reaching out to shake hands. "I'm Katy's uncle, Ricky Coffey. She called and told me we needed to get here quick. Said we were interfering with production . . . and she wanted to ask me some questions. Sorry for the delay." He winked.

Katy cut her eyes in my direction. "I need to get to work on the story, if you're going to let me write it. I have questions, Lois, good questions. I called Uncle Ricky and asked him if they could get down here quicker. I hope that's OK. Tammy's cousin works in the insurance claims center. Tammy called to tell her about the fire and, well, maybe, sort of get them in gear, too."

Living in a small town for a year had taught me many things, one of which was that everyone knew everyone. Knowing people always got things done. Friends in the right places made life easier. Sometimes the interference disturbed me, but certainly not today.

"Sorry if I was rude," I said. "Let me show you what we've got." I led him over to Stan, who was studying a blueprint of the press in the cluttered production office.

By afternoon, Ricky was still poking around every inch of the pressroom with a clipboard and measuring tape. I finally tired of watching and went back to my office to face more than a dozen voice mails and a stack of messages delivered by Tammy and Iris Jo.

"Wanted to make sure no one was badly hurt," the hometown writer from Ashland said.

"I'm praying for you, Lois. Call me if you need anything," Pastor Jean, from the little church down the road from my house, said.

"I'll be over as soon as I finish delivering the mail," Rose, who owned the antique mall, said. "I want to hear all the latest."

Rumors swirled that I had been hit in the face by falling wood and required numerous stitches. A few of our regular crazy callers, as we referred to them, suggested conspiracy theories about terrorist groups bombing newspapers, or government plots to silence us. One person said I had no business running the paper and should go back where I was from, "wherever that is."

Kevin phoned to check on my dog bite, and Chris left a brief message that he was headed home and would drop by later. I listened to the message twice before feeling foolish and deleting it.

Three messages from my best friend, Marti, in Ohio were interspersed with the fire calls. "Where are you?" her first excited message said. "Why haven't you called me back? I have news."

"Call me, quick," she said the next time.

"I'm headed into a news meeting," said the next call. "You better have a good reason for not calling me back."

I had been so frazzled the day before that I had not even thought to call and tell Marti about the fire . . . nor had I remembered to return her call earlier that day. In my first days in Green, I pestered her so much she practically stopped taking my calls. How things had changed.

"I'm *engaged*," she shrieked when I reached her at her desk in the features department at *The Dayton Post*. "Gary proposed to me late yesterday afternoon and gave me a gorgeous ring that belonged to his grandmother. Oh, Lois, it was all so perfect. He told me he wanted to start the New Year knowing he'd always be with the love of his life. Can you believe it?"

"Wow, congratulations, Marti!" I said, feeling an unexpected urge to cry.

"I wanted you to be the first to know, but half the *Post* knows, and my best friend is just finding out. Why didn't you call me back? You sound a little weird."

"Oh, I'm fine—other than getting bit on the face by a dog and having someone set fire to my newspaper."

"Lois, what are you talking about? What's going on down there?"

"The stitches hardly hurt . . . and there's absolutely no proof it's arson." I sounded like Katy on a grumpy day. This was Marti's big moment, and I felt decidedly sorry for myself.

My friend sighed loudly. "I hoped you were going to have an easy year this year, a good year."

"Remind me to stay clear of dogs that people carry in their purses." I paused. "Enough about all that. When's the big day?"

"Probably during Gary's autumn break at seminary," she said, nearly giddy. "I want you to stand up front and wear a horrid dress for the occasion. Be my maid of honor, like we've always planned."

"That sounds great . . . especially the yucky dress part," I said. "Please, no pastels, preferably no florals or ruffles, and find a good-looking, single best man, will you?"

I had met Marti's boyfriend and liked him a lot. She had dated a host of real losers through the years, but Gary was a great guy. However, I had secretly hoped I would get married first. Who wants to be the oldest never-married person in town? Was I officially a spinster?

The mushy story of the proposal thrilled me and made me envious, a very distasteful feeling to have when it involves your best friend. Her year had gotten off to a considerably better start than mine.

As I hung up, I told myself I did not have time to worry about romance. I had other things on my mind, and my life was going in an interesting, different direction. I had a press to fix and a newspaper to run—and a possible crime to solve.

I laid my head on my desk, wincing when the dog bite touched the wood.

Thankfully I had recovered somewhat when Stan slipped into my office, the smell of smoke coming from his jumpsuit, and a grim look on his face. Iris Jo followed.

"Lois," he said, dropping the habitual "Miss," "I don't think the fire was an accident. Someone sabotaged the press."

The fire marshal backed up Stan's assessment, a frayed cord in his hand. His white uniform shirt was smudged, and he had a large black spot on the right leg of his tan slacks. "The fire almost certainly started as a result of vandalism," he said. "It was arson all right, one way or the other. I've notified local authorities."

All day, despite words of support from dozens of people, I had been unable to get the nagging worry about enemies out of my mind—politicians, a former employee, and an assortment of others in Green. Katy's guesses that morning had already been written in my brain, and I knew others had similar thoughts.

"But why? Why would someone want to mess with the press?" I reached out to inspect the cord.

"My guess is they wanted to get our attention, keep us from printing next week," Stan said. "They knew we'd be off for the holiday, and maybe hoped to catch us napping. Looking at what they did, I don't think they meant to start a fire. I think they meant to bust Bossy."

The small staff, part owners of the paper for less than a week, gathered in my office as Katy's uncle and Stan reported their findings, word spreading quickly through the close-knit crew. They leaned against the bookshelves, sat on the edge of my desk and pulled in a couple of chairs from the conference room. Katy sprawled on the floor, a reporter's notebook and purple felt-tip marker in her hands.

I was tired. I touched my face and frowned. Tammy left the room, returning with two Tylenols and a bottle of water.

"I'll get back to you early next week," the inspector said. "It's OK to do whatever you want back there." He walked out, shaking hands with Stan and giving his niece a hug. No one else in the room moved.

"I've got a few thoughts," Linda said.

"Me, too," said Katy and Molly at the same moment.

"We've got to talk about the press run Tuesday," Stan said. "And we've got lots of building repairs to take care of."

"The mayor dropped off sandwiches and said to call if you need anything," Iris Jo said.

Their support-and-conquer mode lifted my spirits.

"Let's move into the conference room," I said. "The time has come for a serious conversation."

I could think of nowhere I would rather be.

3

Suzy Futrell entered her famous cherry pie in the Green Neighbors Fair again this year, and did it make a splash! After hastily pinning the Blue Ribbon on the delicious dessert, all three judges fell terribly ill. Suzy claims her pie is not what made the judges sick, but when we asked her daughter about the incident, she said, "Mama hasn't made a pie in over three weeks!" Tony Boyd, John Stratton and Karen Chaffin are all expected to make full recoveries.

—*The Green News-Item*

Chris pulled his pickup truck into my driveway not five minutes behind me.

I smiled as he strode up to the porch, his three dogs right at his heels. He was a good-looking man . . . and clearly he had been waiting for me to get home.

Opening the door before he could knock, I was not quite sure what to expect.

"Are you OK?" he asked and grabbed me into a fierce embrace, holding me tight against his wool jacket, which smelled like wood smoke and hay. "Why didn't you call me about the fire?"

He stepped back and gave me a close look. "Your face is hurt. Iris Jo didn't tell me you were injured."

His dogs barked, demanding my attention, and then began their routine check of my yard, sniffing trees and chasing unseen creatures. Mannix, always the leader, corralled Kramer and Markey, and they tussled with each other as Chris shut the door.

"Welcome back, neighbor," I said. "It's been a crazy couple of days."

"What happened to your eye? Did something hit you from the fire?" He stepped further into the living room and gently touched my face, avoiding the bandage.

"Sugar Marie."

He looked puzzled. "Eva's dog?"

"Yep. Bit me. Got me on the hand here, too. Totally unrelated to the fire, although it certainly spices up the talk around town."

"What about the paper?"

"Looks like someone wanted to sabotage the press, not burn the building down. Basically the press needs repairs, there's a hole in the roof, and the production area's a huge mess, but I hope everything's going to be pretty much back to normal by tomorrow."

"Normal?" Chris said. He shrugged out of his jacket and perched on the arm of the couch. His brown hair had grown out over Christmas break and was messy and cute. He rolled up the sleeves of his flannel shirt, adding to his charm.

"Stuff may happen like this every day where you come from, but it's a big deal in a little place like Green. You have to keep your eyes open. We need to get to the bottom of this."

His concern both touched me and put me off. Everyone in town had an opinion on the fire. I did not need one more person telling me what to do, not even this handsome catfish farmer/coach. On the other hand, people cared about me and my safety. My head spun. I chose the chair a few feet away from where he sat.

"I wish you had called me," he said. "That's what friends are for."

Ahh, friends. That's what we were. *Was he giving me a not-so-subtle message? A sort of "I'm happy you're staying in Green, but this is not a romantic deal" hint?*

"We're neighbors. Route 2 folks stick together. Why didn't you call me?"

Hmm, neighbors, part of the Route 2 group that looks out for one another, day and night. Next thing I knew he'd tell me he put me on the prayer list at Grace Community Chapel.

Truth was, I did not know why I had not called him. We were in some sort of odd middle ground where the rules were not clear. During the past few months, we had gotten closer, but I had planned to leave town. My decision to stay in Green, keep the paper . . . well, that changed things. And he had lost a beloved wife to cancer. That complicated everything.

"It was a madhouse around here," I finally said. "When I got home, I fell into bed. I knew you would hear it from someone. News travels fast in Green, as you well know."

"I didn't want to hear it from just anyone. I wanted to hear it from you. I can only imagine what a zoo it was. We don't get a lot of New Year's Day arson action in these parts."

"It was probably a fluke, maybe kids or a vagrant," I said. "How was your trip?"

"In other words, mind my own business, right?"

He settled on the couch with a slight smile and propped his scuffed work boots on my primitive flea-market coffee table. "I took Mama over to see her brother and sister. Ate too much."

"Isn't that what usually happens around here? I've never seen a place where people like food so much."

"It's because the food's so good," he said, seeming to relax. "Have you noticed when Southern families get together, they heat up the grease and then decide what to fry?"

I laughed, glad to talk about something other than the fire. We chatted easily, the glow of my lamps and the space heater making the room warm and inviting.

"My friend Marti's getting married," I said. "I get to be her maid of honor and wear an ugly dress."

"Well, congratulations. On the honor business. Not on the dress. I hope I get to meet Marti one of these days now that you're here to stay."

"Maybe I'll invite her and Gary down. Depends on how bad my dress is."

"You should have seen the tux I wore at my wedding," Chris said. "It looked like something out of a John Travolta movie." He spoke the words casually, and they did not sting as much as they might have.

"Tell me it wasn't powder blue," I said.

"Don't ask. Don't tell," he said, grinning.

It was the closest we had come to weaving Fran, his dead wife, into our conversations. A tiny door that had been nailed shut cracked open.

"Speaking of your friend's engagement, my uncle Wendell over in Tallulah has a new steady girlfriend," Chris said. "Ouida. She's seventy-five, eleven years older than him. She makes him go outside to smoke at his own house. Seems to have pretty much taken over."

"Maybe Uncle Wendell needs to give Katy a call," I said. "She took control of the paper today, got the fire marshal down, assigned herself the lead story. She could set Ouida straight."

"Ouida could probably give Katy a run for her money," Chris said. "That woman was pretty much the talk of the trip . . . with one exception."

"Let me guess. They were more interested in how your Rabbits did in basketball."

"Nope."

"Where the new highway is going to wind up?"

"Not even warm."

"OK, I give up."

"You."

"What?"

"You. You were the other hot subject."

"What do you mean, me?"

"My mom spent half the trip telling people about you. She's glad you decided to stay in Green. Not half as glad as I am." He picked up his jacket. "On that note, I'd better round up my mutts and head home."

He was leaving after that beautiful sentence?

As he got up, he gave me the second hug of the evening, his arms wrapped tightly around me, his body warm and solid. "Next time someone tries to burn your newspaper down, you call me right away," he said, his chin against my hair. "I want to be there to keep an eye on you."

He headed off my porch, a serious look on his face. "Latch your screen door." The dogs jumped into the back of the truck, tails wagging, and Chris waved as he backed out onto the road. I stood at the door until his taillights disappeared.

The phone rang a few minutes later, and I picked it up quickly, sure it would be Chris, following up on that "glad you stayed" business.

Instead it was Stan at the newspaper. "You can sleep easy tonight, Lois. I got her running," he said. "We're back in business."

Crawling into bed, I pulled the comforter around my shoulders and felt certain I had made the right decision about staying in Green.

All would be well.

I hoped.

I turned over to the left and then to the right. I threw the covers off and pulled them back on. I thought of Chris and his sweet words, then pictured him marrying Fran, powder-blue lapels flapping as they left the church.

I daydreamed about my cozy condo in Dayton, its central heat suddenly appealing. I imagined my friend Ed in his managing editor's office, and the corporate owners ready to jump in to solve problems and run the show. They would know how to handle a fire. If Ed had not died and left me the *Item*, he would own the paper and be dealing with this chaos. I put the comforter over my head, making a safe, dark cave, and wondered if anyone else in the world had such mixed emotions.

A smaller than usual—and that's pretty small—edition of *The News-Item* came out right on schedule Tuesday.

Katy, yes, a high school student, wrote the lead story about the fire with a short sidebar by Linda, who had been a journalist for all of a week. Tammy, a clerk, got the photo credits. Alex, our one experienced reporter, pouted because he was visiting his parents when the fire occurred and had been scooped by Katy. He managed to scrape up a feature on the youngest and oldest volunteer firefighters.

I was exhilarated by their work. *The News-Item* had been printed on our own press, and the staff was pumped. We had won another battle with this most motley group of soldiers.

"Fire Damages Local Newspaper, Arson Blamed" was the headline splashed across Page One. "We have no suspects" was the official statement from the police.

"*The Green News-Item* is a strong newspaper in a vibrant community," I said for the record. "We will not be intimidated by cowardly bullies." My hidden feelings were not as optimistic, since we had no solid clues about who could have done such a thing.

We gathered again that afternoon and drew up a long list of possible villains.

Tom, who loved an editorial cause, looked like an aging superhero in a bright blue T-shirt, pounding his fist on the table. "We dig out dirt for a living," he said, looking fierce with his gray hair sticking out from under the old-fashioned green visor he always wore. "They won't get away with this. They've messed with the wrong people this time."

"I wish we had something definite," Molly said, fresh off the school bus, huge backpack thrown on the floor behind her chair.

"We ought to look back at other fires," Katy said. She had come in slightly behind Molly, stopping by the newsroom fridge to grab a soft drink. "Maybe we can find a link."

"Or keep this from happening to someone else," Molly said.

"We should keep our eyes open and act calmly," Linda, newest to our team, said. "We won't let this draw us off course."

I wished I had said that.

"Linda is right," Iris said. "We can't lose our focus on putting out a good newspaper."

"A good community newspaper would investigate this," Alex said. "We've got to jump on it."

I couldn't get a word in edgewise at my own meeting. Another strange mix of feelings flowed through me, pride at their ownership of this situation and fear that they didn't need me anymore.

"What do you think, Lois?" Stan asked, easing my mind. "Where do we go from here?"

"We seem to be on the right track," I said. "We stay focused. We investigate to find out who sabotaged our press. But we don't neglect other stories, and we don't spread rumors."

The staff left the room discussing plans for the next edition. Alex thought he had talked himself onto Page One with the roundup on local fires in recent months. He and Katy huddled together for the next two afternoons, even making a chart to see if they could find a connection between our fire and others.

Early Friday morning, he scurried into the newsroom in his usual beat-up tennis shoes and worn-out jeans. Never in my wildest dreams would I have seen him as my ace reporter, but last year he had come up with an outstanding exposé on local corruption and had won a statewide award. He proudly told everyone I was his mentor and his tormentor.

"I've got a great article for today's paper," he said. "Remember that story we had at the end of last year? The one about the family in that terrible house fire? A baby was badly injured, and his mother and sisters were killed. The kid's about to be turned over to foster care. His elderly grandfather is still in critical condition, may not live."

"At this time we are making arrangements for the child," a state official told Alex. "We will monitor this situation day by day."

I called Tammy in and asked her to try to take a photo of the child. She scurried over to the hospital, but was turned away by an administrator. "Absolutely not," he said. "No photographers allowed in my hospital."

Discouraged, she returned, stepped into the newsroom, and said, "Wait!" She held up her hand, said, "I'll be right back," and rushed out. Within thirty minutes she was back with a small portrait of the child, the kind taken at department stores for holidays. He wore a cute little white suit with a bow tie, an adorable, oversized look for such a tiny tot.

"I went over to the neighborhood, got this from a woman who used to babysit for the family. Isn't he precious?" Tammy's face was red from the cold and animated as she showed the picture.

Together we laid out the page, and I edited Alex's story. Molly went to the composing room and put the other pages together without my asking. She smiled shyly when I thanked her and quickly went back to work.

The Green News-Item was definitely in business.

⸎

Kevin practically pounced on me when I walked into her office later that day for a check of my stitches. She was holding the newspaper, looking beautiful as usual in a tailored skirt and blouse, partially obscured by her lab coat.

"Did you see this?" she asked. "That poor little baby has nowhere to go. I've got to do something."

I was caught off-guard by her intensity. I hadn't seen her this worked up since the day she told me she was buying twenty-five houses in a poor neighborhood because she wanted to provide decent family housing at a fair price.

"Are you going to buy him a house?" I asked.

"No, Ms. Smart Aleck, I'm going to adopt him. That's what I'm going to do. I'm going to adopt him." Right before my eyes she decided to change her life—and that of a hurting toddler. "Will you help me?"

"Kevin, are you sure? This is huge. A baby's a big responsibility." I stopped, embarrassed. I was lecturing a very good doctor about the challenges of raising a child.

"I've been looking at this little guy every time I make rounds," she said, "Playing with him. Taking him toys. Lois, he is so cute. And he's so alone. His granddad is not doing well at all. I can't believe this hasn't hit me before."

Kevin sat down in the one chair in the exam room. "I won't be able to live with myself if I don't try to make this happen. I have so much to offer a child . . . and he needs someone who will love and care for him."

I scooted off the end of the exam table and hugged her.

"Go for it . . . and be prepared for some major spoiling by Aunt Lois."

"I need to get my ducks in a row. Probably should contact a lawyer, get in touch with the state. Better go tell my parents first. They won't like it if they hear this from someone else. Wonder if your friend Walt might help with the legal stuff?"

She motioned for me to get back on the exam table, a position that always made me feel like I was about to hit the floor. "Your eye's going to be fine. It wasn't half as bad as it looked. You may have a little scar there, though. Want me to refer you to a plastic surgeon?"

"Plastic surgeon?" I looked in the mirror hanging next to shelves full of cotton squares, swabs, and thin rubber gloves. "I don't think so." I looked closer. "But can you do anything about these wrinkles?"

As I drove back to the paper, my selfish thoughts took over. Kevin with a baby would shift my life again. We already were so busy our friendship sometimes slipped between the cracks. Now she'd be even more tied up. And she would have someone special in her life, to love and take care of. I was edging awfully close to forty. The thought of adopting a child had never even crossed my mind.

At that moment I admired Kevin and did not think very highly of myself.

Pulling into the paper, I looked up at my baby—a one-hundred-twenty-four-year-old, twice-weekly newspaper that used community correspondents for lots of its news and seemed to be constantly under attack by someone—powerful political leaders, good old boys who did not like change, the prior owners, and even an angry former employee.

I walked through the small lobby, let myself past the latched swinging gate, and barely waved at Tammy, who was taking information about a fiftieth wedding anniversary.

In my office, once shared by Chuck and Dub McCuller, I dug around in the huge stack of yellowing newspapers in the corner. I found the story about the house fire that injured the baby. I laid it next to today's paper.

Little Asa Corinthian Thomas.

Poor guy. He looked so sweet in the photo. Kevin could change his life again, this time for good. I hoped it would all work out.

As I read through the articles, Tammy walked in, a cross between apologetic and breathless. "You have a guest in the lobby. That cute lawyer from up in Shreveport. I told him I didn't know if you were seeing people today or not."

Tammy, always a bit on the excitable side, seemed extra hyper.

"Walt? Sure, Tammy." I headed toward the front of the building. She usually called to let me know when someone came in to see me. What was with this nervous walk into my office?

"Mr. Walt, Miss Lois will see you now," Tammy said, sashaying behind her counter in her short skirt. *Was she flirting with him?*

Walt, as close to a former boyfriend as I had had for the past few years, thanked Tammy and gave me a brief hug. He looked like a big-city attorney with his gray suit, striped tie, and bookish glasses.

"What's with that eye?" he asked as we headed into my office.

"It's nothing. What brings you here?"

"Usually when a client has a business burned down by a suspected arsonist, they give me a call. Courtesy, you know." Taking one of the two somewhat comfortable chairs in my office, Walt frowned, a sort of exaggerated, aggravated look. "I've been in Dallas on business or I would have been here sooner."

He pulled out a legal pad. "It appears we have some sort of injury claim, too, by the looks of that eye."

"This wasn't from any arsonist. It was from that blasted Yorkie that Mayor Eva calls a pet."

"You were attacked by the mayor's dog? Hmmm." A dramatic sneer appeared on his face. "Even better. Win-win in the world of lawyers."

He was joking. Or at least I hoped he was.

"You know I'm not suing the mayor . . . or anyone else for that matter. It's good to see you, though. Kevin and I were just talking about you. ESP, I guess."

He turned slightly. "Have you changed your mind about not dating me anymore?"

I rolled my eyes in mock dismay.

"I'm plowing old ground, aren't I?" he asked.

"Walt, Walt, Walt, what am I going to do with you? Or I should ask, what would I do without you?"

"You're still not interested in dating me, are you?"

"No, but I wish I were. I couldn't have figured out how to keep the newspaper if it weren't for you, and now you show up to check on me. Kevin needs to talk to you about a legal issue. Maybe we can round her up for supper, if you're not in a hurry."

"Maybe she'll want to date me," he said, smiling.

"I wouldn't count on it. She doesn't seem to have time for a man."

I stood up. "This fire thing is a bit of a mess. Want to take a look?"

4

*The Bienville Parish Activity Center will offer Cajun
dance lessons, starting Tuesday night and running for six
weeks. A second six-week class will be scheduled later if
there's enough demand, said Paula Beckman, instructor,
talented dancer and native of Evangeline Parish, where
Cajun dancers are more common. "Pay according
to what you can afford," Paula says, "and come
cut the rug with us."*

—The Green News-Item

An odd cracking and creaking sound awakened me. Someone was breaking in! Maybe the person who set the paper on fire nearly three months ago . . . or someone was trying to set my house on fire. I grabbed the wooden baseball bat propped by my bed and fumbled for the black rotary-dial telephone left by Aunt Helen.

I dialed Chris's number. He was close and strong. No bad guy in his right mind would take on Chris. But I couldn't bring myself to complete the call. I was not a big baby. I could take care of myself.

The noises continued, like something out of a horror movie, with a big thud every now and then. "Who's there?" I yelled.

"Who's there? Don't come any closer. I'm armed. I'm calling the sheriff right now."

Maybe I should call Iris Jo—

I heard the sound again and sat frozen, holding the bat as though ready to swing at a fast pitch.

I tiptoed over to lock the bedroom door, sliding the bolt. A handyman from the church down the road had installed the lock when I first moved in, nervous about living in the country alone. At first I had locked it every night. But months had passed since I had been fearful in my home.

Suddenly I recognized a more familiar sound—hard rain on the roof. I padded over to the window, pulling the telephone cord, baseball bat in hand, and peeked through the ancient Venetian blinds.

Everything was covered with ice.

Pine tree limbs snapped right and left, bowed by the weight. They made a weird creak as they broke, and I could tell now they were hitting my roof. Laying the baseball bat down, I walked to the front of the house and opened the door to a blast of cold, wet air.

A buried recollection of life in Ohio hit me—the bitter, gray days of winter and the chore of de-icing my windshield. A freaky wintry front had moved in overnight, and memories of my old life and the routine of my new life crashed together. Shivering, I recalled the hassle of a bad-weather day as the city editor at *The Dayton Post*.

The sleet turned to snow as I watched. Huge flakes sounded almost like rain as they hit my yard.

While I made a pot of coffee, my first call of the day came. Tammy chattered breathlessly about the bad weather as soon as the receiver got to my ear. "Since I won't be at work, who's going to cover the phones? Should we leave the night recording on?"

I couldn't wait for the coffee to finish brewing before grabbing a cup, half listening. Finally Tammy slowed down, and I jumped in. "Why aren't you going to work? It's Wednesday. You always work on Wednesdays."

"We shut down when it's icy," she said, sounding annoyed. "Not that it happens very often, though. Not even in *North* Louisiana."

"Shut down?" I ignored her joke. "We're a newspaper. Why would we shut down? Last time I checked, we cover the news every day, with the possible exception of a holiday or two." We printed two days a week, but I wasn't about to mention that.

"Lois, have you listened to the radio? The roads are treacherous. The police say to stay at home unless it's absolutely necessary to go out. Schools are closed. Most businesses won't open."

"For this little storm?"

Tammy took the tone she used when she was put out with me. "You obviously have forgotten that this is Green, Louisiana, not Dayton, Ohio. It's not expected to get above freezing all day. We don't get much snow and ice down here. We don't know how to drive in it."

I needed more coffee. "Let me give Iris Jo a call and see what our bad-weather policy is. I'll call you right back."

Iris confirmed Tammy's worries. "Most folks don't get out in weather like this, Lois. Not unless it's the day the paper comes out. We usually work a skeleton crew. Stan has a four-wheel drive, and he can pick me and you up, if you'd like."

"Not necessary," I said. "I'll go in and assess the situation. You call the staff and tell them to hold off till mid-morning. Then we can decide about their schedule. Ask Tammy to take pictures in her yard. See if she can get at least a few shots in the neighborhood. I'll snap some, too. And tell Katy to call her friends and see what they're doing since school is out. Get details for the main story."

My planning, which I was so proud of, accomplished little.

Tammy pulled slowly into the newspaper parking lot ahead of me. As I suspected, the possibility of taking snow pictures overcame her fear of winter precipitation. I waved and took the turn too fast, sliding into our newspaper rack and knocking it over.

"Nice driving, boss," she said with a smirk and walked up the steps to unlock the door.

My condescending attitude about the weather smacked me in the face. The spring storm caused more excitement and consternation than I had seen since the downtown festival the previous July. People were drawn together in their quest to stay off the roads and play in the snow.

Despite my attempt to be blasé, I had fun. I dodged when Tammy let a big snowball fly in my direction. I chased her and clobbered her with one of my own, calling upon years of expertise. At the end of the day, I admitted I was wrong and accepted Stan's offer of a lift home. My little house seemed more welcoming than ever when I climbed out of the monster truck, waving to Stan and Iris, and wondering again about their relationship.

"See you in the morning, eight o'clock sharp," I said.

"Hey, Miss Lois," Stan yelled from the truck window when he was almost to the road. "Next time, holler at me for a lift. It's a lot easier than fixing that rack."

I laughed and staggered to keep from slipping on the driveway. Yep, I was indeed the resident cold weather expert.

Not allowing myself time to think about it, I picked up the phone the moment I entered my house and dialed Chris. I was still keyed up by the wild day.

"Want to go for a walk?" I asked.

"Are you crazy? It's freezing out there. Where did you grow up anyway?" He laughed and seemed pleased to hear my voice.

"Look at it this way, Coach. We won't be bothered by mosquitoes."

"I'll be right down. I'll bring vegetable soup Mama made. It's in the freezer."

We walked for almost an hour, all bundled up under a clear sky covered with stars. The gravel road was not too slippery, but from time to time Chris reached over and took my hand, as though to steady me. Our soup supper capped one of those days when you feel thrilled about life, as if the whole world is humming around you and you're part of it.

"I had a great time," Chris said as he left. He leaned over and gave me a swift kiss. "I've missed our walks."

I smiled and leaned against the doorframe as he headed to his truck. This man, born and reared in the Deep South, had no trouble keeping his footing. So much for my Midwestern honor.

By the time the newspaper came out two days later, the temperature was in the high sixties, and spring had returned with a vengeance. "Say It Ain't Snow," the headline read in large, bold letters, sitting over Tammy's photograph of a gargantuan snowman on the courthouse lawn. "Green Turns White For A Day," the subhead said.

I liked the headlines so much I volunteered to buy Tom lunch at the Cotton Boll.

"Come with us, Tammy," I said. "My treat for being such a pain when it snowed. Besides I need your ideas on our profit-sharing plan. We've got to figure out how we proceed from here."

The fire, ice storm, and tedium that sometimes went with getting the paper out had taken the shine off my dramatic announcement about employee ownership. The grand gesture now had everyone from Katy to Tammy throwing out wild suggestions, and I carried the burden of deciding how to use the good ideas while reining in the outlandish ones.

"We love being partners, Lois," Tammy said as we ate, "but we aren't sure what we're supposed to do. Nothing's really changed."

"That's good," Tom said, "because people don't like change."

"We need change," Tammy said. "Otherwise we get set in our ways."

"In the year I've been here, Green has changed a lot," I said. "We've got to show that."

"We need ideas from you, Lois," Tom said. "We're all much better at pointing out problems than coming up with solutions. We've always been like that."

The lunch with Tom and Tammy propelled me into our first employee-owner meeting on Saturday morning, on the heels of the big storm. The unexpected foul weather seemed to have led to foul moods, with the tiny staff arguing over how we should have handled the special report, noting that the news was old by the time it was printed. Their playfulness had melted with the snow.

"Excuse me," I said, using my firmest publisher voice. "Could I have your attention?" My attempts at formality seemed ridiculous since we were gathered in the newsroom, drinking coffee out of Styrofoam cups and eating low-fat blueberry muffins that Iris Jo had brought in a sudden effort to get us to eat healthier. Watching her arrive with Stan, talking softly as they came into the building, had been the best part of this meeting so far.

"Pardon me," I said louder.

Alex and Tom kept sparring, and Linda raised her hand, as though in class. In her previous job for Major Wilson—local politician, Realtor, and bully—she mostly sat quietly, served coffee on demand, and took care of the endless details of his business with little credit. I couldn't figure out her ambitions at the *Item*, but this employee-owner meeting seemed to be an opening.

"Let's get focused," I said with the tone I had hoped to avoid. "We've got a lot of ground to cover today. You've all been great helping after the fire, and it's time to move forward." I casually pointed to Linda. "You get us started."

"I'm learning the business," she said, "but we need to find a way to get the word out more quickly when something big happens like this storm. It was already warm again by the time we told people about the snow."

Tom jumped in defensively. "We got it out as quick as we could. Tuesdays and Fridays. That's when we print. What do you want us to do? Call everyone in town?"

"That's a funny idea, Tom," Katy said, laughing. "Or we could text everyone." She held up her pink cell phone with colorful jewels pasted to it. She was seldom without it, despite weak service throughout Green. "I have two hundred numbers right here, and Molly has about the same in hers." Molly was absent from the meeting, working at the grocery store, but sent a note with a list of ideas that included putting news briefs on our website several times a day.

"Two hundred numbers? What are you talking about?" Tom, her writing coach, never snapped at Katy, but he seemed close at the moment.

"Come on, Tom," Alex interrupted. "We all know newspapers are a thing of the past. We have to find a faster way to get news to people."

Once again everyone talked at the same time, including Iris and Stan, who mostly were a quiet pair. In my fantasy, everyone shook hands, celebrated the first official gathering of employee-owners and laid out a strategy for the year ahead. Instead I had an argumentative group dressed in sloppy jeans and wrinkled shirts about to get in a fistfight. I deliberately sat back and watched, somewhat callously wanting my co-owners to see how hard my job was.

Walt stood off to the side, on hand to answer legal questions about the profit-sharing plan. He wore his usual pressed slacks and crisp long-sleeved shirt, carrying off his friendly, professional look and keeping quiet.

When I glanced at him, he took his glasses off and cleaned them slowly on his shirt, a sure sign he was collecting his thoughts. Then he smiled at me and winked at Tammy, who loved drama and clearly enjoyed the staff spat. She adjusted the clasp on her necklace and winked back.

"Good morning, everyone," Walt said. His courtroom voice caught the group's attention, and slowly the noise died down. "Everyone has a say in this meeting, but we'll make more progress if we agree on a method for commenting."

"What a wonderful idea," Tammy said, tossing her hair back and fidgeting again with the clunky silver chain she wore around her neck. "Why don't we let Walt walk us through a mature way to talk about this?"

"I thought we were going to discuss a plan for the future," Tom said, muffin crumbs sticking to his shirt. "How to do a better job with this newspaper, how to cover our community. What role each of us is to play."

"That's what we're talking about," Alex nearly shouted. "Covering the news better. That includes the Internet. We can't have a newspaper that doesn't utilize technology. Our website looks like something my sister put together when she had her first baby."

"I have all the respect in the world for you, Miss Lois, but I don't like the direction we're headed," Tom said. "More than half our readers don't even use the Internet. I bet most of them don't even have a handle."

"A handle?" Tammy's voice came out in a shriek, her sophisticated demeanor of moments ago replaced with an outraged tone. "We're not talking about CB radios here. What century are you living in?"

My head ached.

"What's a handle?" Katy asked.

"Let's get on with this," Tom said. "I might need to go out and shoot some video of a car wreck or something."

"Tom, is that attitude necessary?" Linda asked. Her sharp tone startled me.

I bit into my healthy muffin and wished for a doughnut. I glanced at Walt, and he gave a small shrug. I suspected he was rethinking volunteering to come to Green on a Saturday morning.

"Most people in Green don't even have a computer," Tom said. "They're thankful to have electricity."

"You're living in the past," Alex said.

Tom slowly pushed his chair back from his desk, which looked like a cross between a landfill and the public library. "Young man," he said in a tone I had never heard him use, "newspapers have been in business for centuries. They are the only business protected by the Constitution of the United States of America."

He started fishing for something on his desk, and for a moment I thought he might produce an original copy of the historic document. "This is Katy's first front-page byline in *The Green News-Item*. Clipped and saved. That is something you can hold onto. That means something."

"Thanks, Tom," Katy said, clearly touched. Then she looked at me. "Maybe you could tell us what you have in mind.

Seems like we need both the regular newspaper and online stuff, too."

Katy, in the second semester of her junior year in high school, was the voice of reason in a meeting filled with so-called adults. She and Molly and Alex represented the future of this crazy business, as eager and energetic as I had been twenty years ago.

"Good point, Katy," Alex said suddenly. "Let's get on with it, and figure out how readers can help us."

"Help us?" Tom repeated.

"Yeah, you know . . . E-mail more press releases, so we don't have to type them in. Plus, we get more stories. And they can send in more pictures."

Tom labored with this turn in the discussion. "Are you telling me we're going to get people out in Ashland and Martin and Robeline to be *computer correspondents*? Our personal touch is what sets us apart. That's what you always say, Lois."

Having been through this conversation a few thousand times at *The Dayton Post*, I knew this would not be easy. "We absolutely do not want to lose our personal touch, Tom. But if we can combine new options with our old-fashioned news-gathering, think about what can happen."

Always the bottom-line person, Iris Jo spoke up. "Heaven knows we have to do something. We're seeing our business dwindle by the month."

"Little newspapers are going strong," Tom said. "All the industry experts talk about is local news this, local news that."

"The economy in Green is not that strong," I said. "The new highway is spooking people, and at least three of our steady advertisers are going out of business."

"Plus we shut down Major Wilson's real estate business with our stories, and that cost a lot," Alex said. "We did the right thing, though. I admire you for that, Lois. Hope you'll remember that when it comes time for layoffs."

"No layoffs," I said. "We'll figure something out."

My world, which shifted on a regular basis, changed again in that meeting. I recalled similar discussions at my former paper and could still see my friend Ed stomping out of the room, muttering under his breath.

The unexpected winter storm had brought my two lives together in more ways than one. Like it or not, *The News-Item* was going to have to make changes, the very changes I had happily left behind in Dayton.

"Good job," Walt said as I walked him to the front door after the gathering. "Don't forget—if this were easy, everyone would do it."

A couple of weeks after the contentious planning meeting, Katy tapped on my office door and hesitated. Usually she rushed in, full of whatever joy or outrage was on her mind at the moment. A born journalist, the girl did enjoy a good story.

"Got a second?" she asked, almost timidly, holding a large manila envelope pressed against her black T-shirt. A retro pin, a giant flower, sat near her shoulder, and large sparkly earrings swung from her ears. Katy could pull together a burlap bag and pajama pants and look fashionable.

"I always have time for you," I said and meant it wholeheartedly. I pushed aside the spreadsheets that taunted me and moved to a chair on the other side of my desk. "What have you got there?"

Katy plopped down in the chair next to me and dumped the envelope's contents onto her lap. "Tom and Alex think it's possible that I could get this," she said. "Molly's not so sure."

Thoroughly confused, I craned my neck to see what she was talking about. "My mom and stepdad say they'll have to think about letting me go to New York for a whole summer. I wonder what you think." She handed me a stack of materials, with a glossy brochure about a magazine internship on top. Underneath lay a multi-page application, partially completed. "I hope you'll write a letter of recommendation and edit my essay. But it has to be there day after tomorrow."

Katy not only had the inquisitive spirit of a journalist, she had the knack for putting everything off until deadline. Overnight delivery was one of my favorite modern inventions, along with sticky notes and rolling luggage. She would, I felt assured, follow in my footsteps.

As I digested her information, Katy stood up. A pen and pencil rolled out of her lap and under the desk, and a copy of a magazine fell to the floor. "Oh, never mind. It's probably a dumb idea anyway. Molly's being a jerk about it. She thinks I'm too young to get it. She won't say it, but she doesn't want me to go."

Getting down on her hands and knees, Katy scrounged for her supplies. As she stood, she pulled at the legs of her tight jeans and fidgeted, shuffling from one foot to the other, slipping in and out of her bright flats. "Maybe I'll work at the *Item* this summer."

I thumbed through the enticing brochure, pained by her doubts. Through the years I had honed that awful ability not to get my hopes too high. I hated seeing it in Katy.

"It's just that . . . I thought it might be fun," she said. She had collected her materials and her composure and now doodled on a piece of notebook paper. "Can you imagine three months in New York City? They probably don't even know where Green is. And I'm a junior. They usually take seniors."

"Of course you should give it a shot," I said. "This looks so great I may apply." For a moment I wished I *could* leave everything behind and have an urban adventure, no strings attached.

"If it doesn't work out," I went on, "you can always look at a newspaper internship around here, maybe even up in Shreveport."

Katy snatched at the paperwork. "You don't think I can do it. You're like the others."

Sometimes I forgot how tender the emotions of a teenager could be. "Katy, Katy," I said, sounding like a Green politician warming up for a campaign speech. "I know you can do it. They'd be crazy not to choose you. You're a rock-solid young journalist. I fully expect you to be running this place one day."

"Really?" she asked, picking at the bright nail polish she wore, once again easing her foot in and out of her shoe.

"You're more comfortable in public than most adults around here. You're a born leader."

"Uh, Lois . . ." she shifted. "It's all right with you if I try for this? It won't hurt your feelings or anything?"

"Scoop, you know I'll miss you, but I'll be so excited for you. This internship's a great idea. That's how I got my foot in the door at *The Dayton Post*."

"You called me Scoop," Katy said. "That sounded like something out of the movies."

"That's what my friend Ed called me up in Dayton. You've earned the name. I'll talk to your parents about the internship. Now, let's look at that application."

After Katy rushed back to the newsroom, re-reading the essay she had begun days ago, I felt oddly off balance. I understood her parents' fear and knew *The News-Item* would seem dull without her smart mouth and endless energy.

The job would change her. What if she decided to go to college up north? In my mind, I was already saying goodbye to the teen journalist who had become so dear to me.

I picked up the budget numbers again and winced at the expenses required to clean up after the fire. Revenue did not keep up with the cash flowing out the door. The advertisers who had gone out of business in the past few months had hurt us badly.

I made notes in pencil, filed a stack of forms that had accumulated, and tried to reach Marti to hear how wedding plans were coming.

"I have a new appreciation for bean counters everywhere," I said on her voice mail. "I take back every mean thing I ever said about Zach. Maybe he isn't such a bad editor after all." When I worked under a corporate editor, I thought he was obsessed with numbers, but now I saw how much money it cost to print the newspaper and how tenuous advertising was, especially in a small market.

I shoved the budget folder into my desk drawer and headed out to the lobby, disappointed to find Tammy away from her desk. I needed some of her down-to-earth opinions.

I stuck my head in the newsroom, but all was quiet, except for the crackle of the police radio.

5

*The annual Route Two Art Show is planned for next
month, so dig out your arts and crafts, and get ready.
A new regulation this year is that all animals (cows and
pigs included) must be leashed or haltered while at
the show. Many of you may recall the events that led
to this decision. Sally Ann Morgan's pet hog, Rufus,
attended last year's show unaccompanied, and
proceeded to eat young Ruby Fields' prize-winning colored corn art picture. Then Rufus tried to join
the Daffodil Dance Line. The four- and five-year-old
dancers scattered with most of their costumes intact,
except for the flowered headgear.*

—The Green News-Item

The McCullers waited four months to pay their second visit.

Not enough time had passed to ease my jitters about what they were up to. Just enough time had passed to hope their New Year's Day call had been a fluke.

Walt had not heard any *News-Item* gossip at the courthouse in Shreveport or in Bouef Parish, other than the occasional wild tale of the paper burning down and the owner being scarred for life trying to save "her people." The Fire Department had not identified my arsonist. Linda told me she heard at the antique mall that Chuck and Dub and their buddies had gone on a golfing trip to Florida and were enjoying retirement.

My life in Green was not exactly calm, but it was beginning to have a good rhythm, largely shaped by the demands of put-

ting out a newspaper twice a week. My participation at Grace
Chapel, high on my to-do list for my second year in Green,
was not gold-star quality, but I had smugly made it to Sunday
school a handful of times. Chris and I visited regularly, and we
were even making a little progress in the romance department.
My friends continued to look out for me, weaving themselves
more tightly into my life.

Staying in Green seemed increasingly like the right
decision.

That changed quickly when I came back from lunch one
day to find the Big Boys sitting in my office, as though it were
still theirs. Tammy had been away from the front counter, and
I was blindsided.

"Miss Barker, nice to see you." Dub spoke first. I jumped
and dropped the slice of strawberry pie I was carrying. A blob
of whipped cream flew from the plastic container right onto
my phone, and the container tumbled toward the floor, as
though in slow motion. I grabbed for it, succeeding in turning
it upside-down on the carpet.

"Cotton Boll pie, I see," Dub said. "Strawberry's my favorite,
too."

Chuck cleared his throat. He had not said a word. He sat in
my chair, tanned and wearing a pastel golf shirt with a palm
tree logo.

"This is a surprise," I said in a voice that encouraged me
with its strength.

"We're here to follow up on the details of taking back ownership of the *Item*," Chuck said. He made it sound as though we
had already come to terms and needed to wrap up a few minor
issues. "Had some out-of-town meetings to tend to or we'd
have been here sooner." When he said the word "meetings," he
pretended to swing a golf club and smirked.

"I beg your pardon?"

Walking around the pie, I moved behind the desk, until I was so close Chuck finally stood. I squeezed past him and rolled the chair slightly, giving me enough room to sit down. I tried to look imposing, although the sticky pie filling on both hands hurt my effort.

"We have everything ready," Dub said. "Chuck, do you have the check?"

I shook my head, scarcely believing my eyes as Dub's brother picked up his briefcase, took out a check and held it up in the air, as though it were a prize I had won.

"Chuck, Dub, I have no idea what you're talking about. As I told you on New Year's Day, this newspaper is not for sale. That has not changed in the past four months."

When I did not take the slip of paper, Chuck laid it on the desk and made an elaborate show of wiping his hands with his handkerchief, as though he had gotten pie on them. He fished around in a pocket, pulled out a small knife and started cleaning his fingernails. *Was it too much to hope that the man could use nail clippers like a regular human being?*

"We want the paper back," he said. "We are prepared to give you a generous price for it. This paper has been in our family for decades, and we are voiding the sale mistakenly made to you a year ago. Our attorneys have spent the past few weeks getting details in line."

I stared him straight in the eye, trying not to show the fear collecting in my gut. "Are you forgetting you sold my friend Ed the paper? That you sought a buyer and chose him? That he died, and I took over the sale? That you approved that?"

It took all that was in me not to add, "Are you crazy?"

Dub jumped in, almost apologetic. "Your friend was a fine newspaperman. We hope you understand, but we should have backed out when he died . . ."

"You don't know how to run a newspaper," Chuck said, interrupting. He gave an almost imperceptible shake of his head, looking at his brother. "Employees were not intended to be owners. And this is a hometown paper, not some big investigative operation. That's not the way things are done around here."

"How *The Green News-Item* is run is not your business any more," I said. "For the record, I bought it, and I chose to start a profit-sharing plan with the employees. Maybe you should have tried being a little nicer to them all those years."

"None of that matters," Chuck said, shifting his briefcase to the side. He spoke with a certainty born of years of getting what he wanted. "Our lawyers have reviewed the contract. You are not living up to the terms of the deal, and we have legal grounds to take it back."

"You're not from around here," Dub said. "You don't have any people in these parts, never wanted this paper in the first place. Take our offer. You can go home with money in your pocket."

"*This* is my home," I said, amazed at how good it felt to utter those words. "In case you don't know, I intend to stay in Green and run this newspaper."

"You've done nothing but stir up trouble since the day you got here, Miss Barker," Chuck said. "We're ready to accept our mistake, settle up with you, and move on. Frankly, this has taken much longer than we expected. Forget the delay tactics." His voice had risen almost to a shout.

"Delay?" I felt as though I were in some sort of alternate universe.

"The fire sidetracked the deal," Dub said. "But we want to get on with this."

"We can file suit, of course, but we hope that's not necessary," Chuck said.

I stood up and crossed my arms, bluffing at how brave I felt. I had tried to get rid of this newspaper only months before, but I was prepared to fight for it now. Sometimes I was unsure in my life, but this I knew. This mattered.

"Let me tell you one more time that the *Item* is not for sale," I said. "You cannot waltz into my office and try to take it over when you sold it to me."

Iris Jo walked through the door as I made that pronouncement. My relief was so great that I took a deep, shaky breath and felt my legs tremble.

Not acknowledging her former bosses, also distant cousins, Iris walked to my desk, sidestepping the pie with a curious look. "Lois, I hate to interrupt, but you have an important call. Would you like to take it at my desk, since you have guests?"

"Call?" I said with a croak. She never came into my office to tell me I had a call.

"Yes, Lois, a call, on the phone."

"Certainly. Thank you, Iris." How I loved that woman!

She spoke to me as soon as we got out of earshot of the two McCullers. "What is going on in there? Why was Chuck shouting?"

"I'm not quite sure. They seem to believe they have the right to take back the paper." I glanced around. "They don't, do they?"

"Good heavens, no," she said. "At least, not to my knowledge."

"Why don't you go back in there, Iris, and make sure they don't touch anything? I'll try to reach Walt, see what he thinks I should do."

She turned to walk back into the office. "And, Iris," I said, "thanks. You saved my life."

Walt instructed me to escort Chuck and Dub off the premises, and he scheduled a meeting with their legal group, a high-profile firm from Baton Rouge.

"You will not win this one, Lois Barker," Chuck said, snarling as he slammed through the gate in the lobby. "This paper is ours. Was ours. Is ours. Will be ours. You might as well get that through that Yankee skull of yours."

From behind him, I could see Tammy, her eyes wide.

"Yankee?" My anger spilled over. "Take a geography lesson, Chuck. I'm from the Midwest. Let me say it again. Green is my home now. I love it here. I have a house, friends, a church, and a great newspaper. My newspaper."

"It is not your newspaper. The bank owns most of it, and you've diluted what little bit you did own by giving shares to the employees. Whoever heard of such a thing?" he shouted again. "And Aunt Helen was obviously senile when she left you that house."

"Get *this* through those good old boy skulls of *yours*," I said. "I have no intention of going anywhere. And do not dare say a word about Helen." I turned to walk away. "Tammy, show these men out."

The clerk, with the bearing of a warrior queen, strode to the door. "Chuck. Dub," she said, pushing it open. "Our lawyer will be in touch."

A relieved grin came to my face, and I sank down in Tammy's chair. She turned from the door, her face looking as though she had witnessed an ax murder. "I have never in my life . . ." Her voice trailed off.

"Our lawyer will be in touch?" I repeated.

"Well, won't he?" she said.

Iris came through from my office and put a hand on my shoulder. "That was certainly unpleasant. Want me to get Walt on the phone again or give Chris a call?"

"Not right now," I said. "I need to collect my thoughts before I speak to anyone." I walked back into my office, listening to Tammy and Iris talking heatedly. Words like "legal action" and "morons" floated through the door.

I cleaned the pie off my phone and floor, washed my hands, and walked back to the lobby, where the two women sat, joined by Stan and Tom.

"I'm going to step out for a few minutes," I said. My voice quivered, much to my dismay.

"Don't you worry about a thing, Miss Lois," Tammy said. "We'll hold down the fort."

The others nodded, and I practically hurtled through the door, eager to be in the spring air, away from the scene of that horrible confrontation. In the parking lot, I decided on a walk to shake my fear, and grabbed my shoes out of my car.

As I tied the laces, the school bus rounded the corner with its usual after-school noise, and dropped Katy and Molly at the curb across the street, an afternoon ritual that I looked forward to on most days. Before I could escape, Katy spotted me and practically danced across the street, Molly trailing glumly.

"I got it, I got it, Lois, I got the internship," Katy yelled, waving a sheet of paper in the air.

My hand stung after Katy high-fived me with the enthusiasm of a college basketball player who had dunked the winning basket. "I'm going to New York," she sang, skipping around Molly and me.

My McCuller gloom lifted, and I smiled at the two girls. "I never doubted you for a minute. But we're going to miss you around here, aren't we, Molly?"

Molly was somber, and her brown eyes glistened. "It's going to be a long, boring three months."

"I'll be back before you know it," Katy said.

I grabbed Molly's hand and squeezed it. A heavy girl, Molly wore jeans and loafers and an orange shirt with brown flowers. Katy told me her friend bought many of her clothes at a local thrift store, and Molly always looked cute if not flashy. Thankfully she had not taken up Katy's habit of smoking cigarettes, an act that bothered me no end and resulted in occasional arguments among the staff. Molly and Katy became best friends after the death of Katy's boyfriend, who was Iris Jo's son. The two girls, white and African-American, spent most of their time together, sometimes earning frowns from conservative old-timers in town.

"Molly, I hope you'll be able to help us out at the *Item* again this summer," I said. "We're going to be hurting without Katy's coverage; I'll be depending on you."

She stared at me with the solemn, gentle look she often had, and then dabbed at her eyes. "I'm looking forward to it," she said. "I'm not letting Katy get ahead of me."

Katy pulled Molly's hand away from mine and practically dragged her friend up the steps to the paper. "Let's tell the others. Enjoy your walk," she said, pointing to my shoes with a grimace. "Thumbs down, Lois. Next time let me help you pick those out."

I strolled through downtown, smiling at a few familiar faces but not stopping to talk. My thoughts wavered from fear from Chuck and Dub's visit to excitement at Katy's upcoming adventure to regret for Molly, who seemed to struggle so hard for everything she got.

I meandered over to the vacant, rundown ice cream stand, its old Dairy Bar sign still standing, and carefully sat at one of the broken tables. Green looked charming and inviting with the shine of spring. Bayou Lake sparkled across the street, although its surface was marred in places by a greenish plant unlike its usual lily pads.

Restless, I wandered across the street to the lake and down to the tiny city park, with big shade trees and a pretty walking trail that had recently been cleaned up by our Green Forward downtown group.

Slowly I made laps on the path.

What should I do? Would everything in Green always be a fight? Disheartened, I turned back to the newspaper, stuck my head in the lobby, shouted "good-bye," and drove home, desperate for the peace that usually overtook me as I turned onto Route 2.

<hr />

Late that night we had the second fire at the newspaper.

The first call for help came from an anonymous person driving by. My notice came from Mayor Eva, whose voice was full of regret when I answered from a surprisingly sound sleep.

"Lois, I don't want to have to tell you this, but the paper's on fire again."

I sat up, groggy.

"What did you say, Eva?"

"The paper's on fire. Doesn't look big, but you better come on downtown."

I felt clammy as I called Iris Jo and pulled on jeans and a T-shirt.

"I just heard," she said. "Do you want me to pick you up?"

"I'll drive myself. Can you give Tammy and Tom a call, maybe Alex and Linda, too? I think they'll want to know. I wouldn't bother Katy and Molly, though."

As I headed for my car, I realized I should have called Chris. But it was the middle of the night—a school night at that. No point in getting him out of bed.

Turning onto the main street, I immediately saw a crowd already gathered. I smiled, despite the fear that gnawed inside me. Glancing at the newspaper building, I could see little activity, no sign of flames or smoke.

I wheeled up to the curb and stopped, parking behind the mayor's hideous oversized car, a twenty-year-old model that suited her hairstyle and her personality. Sugar Marie, securely inside the vehicle, barked and then whined when I walked by, trying to get out through the small crack in the window before curling up on the seat.

Katy, already on the scene, had a notebook out and was interviewing a deputy sheriff, who did not look much older than she was. Molly looked over Katy's shoulder. Those kids never missed a thing. Alex was also taking notes. Katy's stepfather stood near the group, wearing a warm-up suit, his hair sticking out in all directions and looking like he'd rather be having a root canal. I figured Katy woke him up to bring her downtown.

Iris Jo was talking to a small group that included the mayor, Stan, Tammy, Linda, and . . . was that Chris? Even Pastor Jean was there, sporting another of her souvenir sweatshirts.

Each person listened closely to Eva, each with a solemn expression. Chris was the first to spot me and turned with a small smile. "Here comes Lois," he said, a bit loudly. The others rushed to hug me, but I had that weird feeling they had been talking about something they did not want me to hear. Chris lingered by my side, his arm snugly around my waist.

"Don't you people ever sleep?" I asked, a bit more sharply than I intended.

"Not when someone keeps trying to burn the paper down," Tammy said. She had a small camera in her hand and snapped my picture. "For the files."

"You might want to use that thing on someone who's newsworthy," I said.

Everyone talked at once, until Eva held up her hand. "Lois," she said, "we're worried about you. These sorts of shenanigans do not happen in Green, and we want to get to the bottom of this."

"Shenanigans?"

Iris put her hand gently on my arm. "Someone set fire to the files on your desk. Most of your paperwork was damaged, but there doesn't appear to be any serious loss. Hank and his guys say the fire was set deliberately and was intended to warn you."

"Warn me?"

Within a moment, I saw Linda chatting with the Police Chief, and they approached us together. "The chief agrees it was arson combined with a nasty dose of vandalism," Linda said.

"No doubt about it," the officer said. "Someone broke in through that back entrance. You probably need to add another light back there."

"Someone has it in for Lois," Tammy said. "I hardly think a light is going to solve the problem."

The Fire Chief walked up, dusting his hands off and looking weary. "Miss Lois, Stan, I can let you inside now if you're ready. The rest of you better head on home. Morning's going to come mighty early. Someone will have to talk to the fire inspector again and have the insurance adjustors in."

"Guess I'd better get Molly and my stepdad home now," Katy said, giving me a quick hug. "I'll have my notes to you right after school tomorrow."

Alex was interviewing bystanders and gave a wave to the two girls. The car doors slammed, and the taillights went out of sight. I wished I could slip away, too, escape from the fear the fire had reignited.

"I'm going inside with you," Tammy said, as I moved toward the building. Chris, Iris Jo, Eva, and Linda followed her. Alex scurried to catch up. Hank started to say something, and then shook his head and fell in with the group, gripping his fire helmet.

"Oh, my," Tammy said, as we entered the office.

It was a disgusting mess, and I felt tired to the bone. My desk was charred, and the paperwork molded into a pile of gooey ashes. Tammy took enough pictures to fill a coffee table book, mostly dark shots of the soggy trash on my desk. Alex scribbled notes as he wandered around the room.

The chief took notes, too, and threw a handful of questions at us. "Who was the last person to leave? Did anyone see anything out of the ordinary?"

"Lois usually shuts the place down," Tammy said, "but since she was upset, she left early. I was the last to go."

"Upset?" Hank said. "What was she upset about?"

"The McCullers had . . ." Tammy started to say.

"I'm standing right here. I can answer my own questions."

"Sorry," Hank and Tammy said at the same time.

"Chuck and Dub came in," I said, "and things got heated. They're trying to take back the newspaper. Even though it's been over a year since my friend Ed left the paper to me, they've had second thoughts."

I ran my fingers through my messy long hair and sat down as far away from the desk as possible.

"It's going to be OK," Chris said, walking up beside me. "Do we have to go over all this tonight, Hank?"

"We can pick up the discussion tomorrow," the chief said. "We're going to need to call the regional arson squad and consider the pattern here."

"Pattern?" I asked.

"Two fires, same place, short time frame. It's likely a pattern. We'll dig around and see what we can come up with."

"We'll get it all cleaned up as soon as you give us the go-ahead," Stan said.

"Let's get Lois home," Iris Jo said. "I'll figure out what we lost first thing in the morning."

I shook my head and walked outside. If I tried to say anything, I knew I would burst into tears.

Chris followed me home and walked me to the house. His dogs, in his fenced yard, barked fiercely when he drove past, and I almost expected to see them come charging down the road.

"Out of curiosity, Chris, how in the world did you and Pastor Jean get downtown before me?" I asked as we walked onto the porch.

He took my key to open the door, and his face was somber. "I was a little peeved you didn't call me after the first fire, so I asked Iris to call anytime she thought you needed me. She called Pastor Jean, too. We're all worried about you, Lois. We have to stick together to figure out what's going on."

I stared back at him, my face also solemn.

Chris stroked my hair, briefly, and kissed me lightly on the lips. "Get some sleep. I'll check on you tomorrow."

It took all my resolve not to grab him and pull him into my house, to beg him to watch over me and not to leave me at the mercy of this scary world. But I knew that was more than Chris could offer.

Overwhelmed by the same misgivings that had swamped me when I first moved to Green, I once more whispered, "Help," but it sounded lame to my ears. "God, help me," I said again, a prayer in earnest.

This path—staying in Green, making a difference in the community, having faith—was supposed to be easier.

Doubt and fear battered me like the water from the fire hose. The sneering voices of Chuck and Dub ran through my mind again and again.

6

Michelle LeBleu has announced her resignation from a
25-year position as secretary of Green High School, and
will soon be moving to Detroit, Mich., to marry
C. W. Jones, a senior law partner with Smith, Jones, and
Hamilton. Michelle revealed that she met her new fiancé
online. "The registration fee for that dating service is the
best investment I ever made," Michelle says. Students
and faculty sent her off with a lovely cake and
best wishes for a happy-ever-after.

—The Green News-Item

The bell jingled when I pushed open the heavy old door at
the Holey Moley Antique Mall, a familiar sound that always
cheered me. Rose looked up and smiled.

"Lois Barker, you haven't been in here in a month of Sundays."
She walked around the weathered wood counter to greet me.
"I thought you'd come over all the time when you decided to
stay in Green. My profits are in the dumps without you."

"Join the club," I said. "The *Item* doesn't even know the word
profit these days. I need a cheap antique fix—and an attitude
fix while you're at it. Between the fires and the drop in advertising and everything else, it gets worse and worse."

Of late my moods shifted all the time, sometimes by the
minute. The early arrival of unbearably hot weather had caused

any happy spirits I had to evaporate. "Hot and dry," said the weather page, and that went for my heart as well.

Rose reached under the counter. "I have just the thing to cheer you up. I found this at a garage sale last week. A souvenir of your encounter with Sugar Marie."

The chipped green piece of pottery, exactly what I collected, was shaped like a playful dog. Reaching for it, I put my other hand up to my face and smiled. "This is much more agreeable than the real thing. I feel better already. How much?"

"For you, free. For other customers, two bucks." She laughed and wrapped the little dog in an old copy of *The News-Item*.

I sat down on a stool, salvaged from a shed at Rose's parents' farm on the edge of town, near where the new highway was scheduled to be built. "That's way too cheap," I said. "You won't listen to my sales advice, will you?"

"Lois, this cost a quarter because of that crack on the ear. Looks like someone glued it back on. We've got a trade—your marketing advice for a twenty-five-cent dog. Let's call it even."

Rose was a hard-working woman in her early fifties who juggled her precious antique mall, her rural mail route, and a farmer-husband who was quite a bit older than she was. She loved gossiping about the people on her route, and I'm sure she violated every postal rule in the book. The nosy journalist in me relished the tales.

She was among a core group of people who had first made me love this clumsy little town. Her business was one of my favorite places, and she delivered my mail. I scarcely made a move that someone in Green didn't notice, and Rose could win a Pulitzer Prize with her reporting on my life. She pulled two bottles of water out of the little cooler she carried on her mail route every day and offered one to me.

"Stirred up a little trouble out your way today," she said. "I fussed at Mr. Elmo for subscribing to *Penthouse* magazine.

Told him he should be ashamed of himself, him a deacon in the Baptist church and all." Rose grinned. "Then he pulled the brown paper back, and I could see the whole title—*Paint Horse* magazine, a subscription from his grandson."

"Rose, maybe you should keep your nose out of other people's business."

"Not like you and that staff of yours don't earn a living sniffing around people's business," she said. "Y'all do everything short of digging in trash cans. And I wouldn't put that past you."

"Good point." I raised my water bottle as though in a toast. "Although it's not much of a living these days."

"I'm about to poke into your business now," she said.

"I'd much prefer to hear you talk about other people."

"You've seemed a little out of sorts the past few times I've seen you. You're not having second thoughts, are you?"

"Second thoughts?" I repeated. "A few."

I stood up and walked over to a display of Depression-era glass, carefully studying a pale pink plate. I needed to send something special to Marti, and this might be nice. I stalled, hesitant to answer Rose's question.

"This year hasn't gone smoothly. When I stayed, I thought everything would work out. That's what everybody told me . . . that's what I told myself."

I put the plate back in place and sat down on the uncomfortable stool.

"Things always work out, but that doesn't mean they're easy," Rose said. "You've had setbacks. You couldn't have known you'd have two fires and half a dozen businesses in town would shut down."

"It's too much. Those fires frightened me, Rose. The budget's killing me. I'm going to miss Katy when she goes to New York. She talks constantly about this bistro or that boutique she's found online, a bus route she'll take, all that big-city stuff. Everybody already seems quieter, just knowing she'll be gone . . . and fretting about arson. Tammy doesn't seem to have much to say, other than flirting with Walt. I'm sick of fooling with Chuck and Dub and always wondering when they'll show up next."

"You do have a lot on your mind," Rose said. "And you haven't mentioned that boyfriend of yours." She acted as though she couldn't recall Chris's name, but she knew it, first, middle, and last, and very likely his social security number.

"He's not my boyfriend, Rose. In fact, we seem to be headed in the other direction. He invited me over to his parents' house for Sunday lunch, and I backed out at the last minute. I told him I wasn't ready for that."

"Ready for what?" Rose asked. "Since when have you had second thoughts about lunch?"

"That's pretty much what he said, and he hasn't come around quite as much since."

Rose rearranged a stack of receipts on the counter. "Every unmarried woman in Green has a crush on Chris Craig. They're looking for reasons to bump into him—at church, ball games, even out around his catfish ponds. The co-op owner says he's never had so many volunteers to haul feed out there. If you don't snap that coach up, some other woman will."

A sharp, unpleasant feeling of jealousy leapt into my chest. "Maybe Chris likes one of them, is, you know, interested."

"Quit being ridiculous," Rose said. "Everybody except you and Chris know that you and Chris have something going on. You better not play hard to get for too long. Men in Green don't go for that sort of thing."

"Hard to get?" Quite certainly this was the first time anyone had used that term to describe me.

"You know what I mean, Lois. Always independent and half the time looking like you've got one eye on the door to somewhere else. You jumped into the ocean. Now quit acting like you don't know how to swim."

Where did she come up with these things? I thought, as I left the building.

I scuffed my feet against the pavement as I walked back across the street to the paper, butterflies in my stomach. I tripped on the curb, and my sweet pottery dog flew out of my hand and smashed on the sidewalk. When I pulled back the newspaper padding, it was shattered.

That little fellow had survived decades, and I had ruined it.

I looked over my shoulder to make sure Rose hadn't seen, and tossed it into the trash can in our parking lot.

Perhaps *I* was the one who was supposed to be living in a big city up north, wearing sophisticated clothes and taking the bus or train to trendy cafes. Maybe unrealistic dreams of the perfect little town, perfect job, perfect man had led me astray.

I trudged up the steps to the newspaper and stopped to read the long list of death notices painted on the window, a *News-Item* tradition that daily made me pause. When I first arrived in Green, the names meant nothing to me, but more and more I knew the people and tried to send a card or go by the funeral home.

That, I discovered, was a major social event in Green, and the number of people who came to your loved one's visitation a point of honor. "Why, you couldn't even get close to the coffin. The line was out the door" was praise of the highest sort.

Today on the list was an older woman from the downtown Baptist church, a sweet lady who had brought me a jar of dewberry jelly when I moved to town. I also noticed a man Iris had mentioned who had battled emphysema.

Dejected, I stepped into the lobby. Tammy's loud voice interrupted my thoughts.

"Lois, look!" She hopped over the swinging door in the lobby, a trick she had perfected after only one pulled muscle. Most days it amused me, but today I was irritated.

"Be careful there, Tammy," I said. "You're going to break your neck."

Immediately her attitude shifted. I'd seen that look before. She was deciding whether to hit me with a nasty comeback or slink back to her desk. She opened the gate and pointedly held it for me.

"After you," she said, tossing a pile of five-by-seven photos onto the countertop and picking up the ringing phone. "*News-Item*, may I help you?"

While she took information on an upcoming wedding, I flipped through the photos, wondering who had shot them and why Tammy had been so excited.

Slowly the images registered, pictures of Mexican migrant workers in Green, in the fields, gathered for prayer at the services Jean had started at Grace Community Chapel, and at a grocery store that promised "cheap phone cards." Dozens of worn faces looked back at me.

Tammy hung up the phone and wrote on a sticky note with one hand, rummaging in her bright green-and-white purse for a piece of gum with the other.

"I'm sorry," I said. "I know I was snippy. I had something on my mind."

She slowly unwrapped the stick of gum, and rolled the foil into a ball. An aggravated Tammy was a scary thing, and I had become fairly comfortable apologizing to her the past year or so. A cheerful Tammy made eating crow worth it.

"Who took these?" I asked. "They're fantastic."

"You think so?" she asked, beaming.

One thing about Tammy. She could change in an instant. I envied her that.

"I took them," she said.

"You? I didn't know you were working on a photo essay."

"I wanted to see how they came out before I said anything." She picked them up one at a time and studied them, fidgeting with her hair with her other hand. "I carried a disc to the drugstore and got prints made, so I could look at them closer. I read online that's the way to get better with portraits."

Tammy was studying photography online?

I prided myself on being observant, but I had sure let a lot slip by me. When I stopped to think about it, she had contributed a string of great pictures to the paper the past few months, starting with the first fire. Her snow pictures had been fun, and her shots of the end of school brought numerous requests for reprints.

"These . . . these are fantastic," I said. "They show a side of Green we rarely have in the paper. You have a great eye." My brain whirred with thoughts of how to play the photos. "Let's plan a spread for them—maybe next Friday or the Tuesday after. We can start on Page One, write some copy to go with them. What do you think?"

She hesitated. "I love these pictures," she said, now toying with the top button on her bright pink shirt. "But they will make people mad."

"Mad?" I moved them around on the counter, arranged as they might look on a newspaper page.

"Lois, you know as well as I do that some people think there are too many Mexicans in Green. They want them to work in the fields for cheap, but they don't want them around town. Those readers don't like to see Mexicans in the newspaper."

As editor and publisher of the paper, I butted heads with residents on this issue at least once a month. "Put more local folks in the paper," one caller said when we ran a feature on a restaurant owner who sent money to his family in Oaxaca. "Play up the good things about Green."

Several community leaders and even certain church members continued to criticize Pastor Jean for her Spanish prayer service. "We have other ministry priorities," a deacon told her. "If they want to live here," a member of our downtown association said, "they should learn to talk English. This is the United States."

A few days earlier, I cringed when an older man in the grocery store called a worker at the meat counter a derogatory name, trying to get the employee's attention. "He can't hear you over the freezer noise," I said.

The man threw a package of bacon into his basket and nearly knocked me over as he steered the buggy away. "It ain't the noise that's the problem," he said. "It's that he can't understand plain English."

Tammy's photographs captured this change that had come to Green.

"Your work can make a difference," I told her. "*The News-Item* will introduce people to their new neighbors. Show them there's nothing to be afraid of."

She shuffled through the photos, as though they were a deck of cards. "You know why I like to take pictures, Lois?"

She picked one up and tapped it with her index finger. "They show real people. Everyday life. Look at these guys." She pointed to men loading hay out of a storage barn onto a big, old truck that looked like something out of *The Grapes of Wrath*.

"They're just like us in their own way," she said, so softly I could barely hear. "They have a longing."

I turned to go back outside, wondering if I could retrieve the broken dog and glue him back together. While I was at it, I'd work on the pieces of my life.

7

The youth choir at Fellowship Christian Church had to
withdraw from the singing competition at the regional
choir festival after five of its members lost their voices
from participation in a crawfish eating contest. With
puffy lips and barely audible voices, two tenors said they
realized the spices were too hot while they were eating,
but the food was so good they couldn't stop. The choir
director is disappointed, but said all things happen by the
Lord's will, and the choir needed more practice anyway.

—*The Green News-Item*

Paperwork snags and red tape delayed Kevin's efforts to adopt
a son, but she seldom let on that she was bothered. She had
fallen in love with Asa Corinthian and was willing to do whatever it took to help him.

"It's a slow process, Lois," she said over supper one night.
"I knew that when I went into it. Daddy keeps reminding me
it will happen in the fullness of time. I still hope to have Asa
home before the end of summer."

She dug in one of her designer purses, which I tried hard
not to covet, and pulled out her phone. "Look at these pictures," she said, scrolling through the digital images. "Isn't he
the cutest thing you've ever seen?"

"He's beyond adorable," I said. "Are you still seeing him every day?"

"Wouldn't miss it," Kevin said. "Morning and night. And I check in with the nursing station a couple of other times a day. His burns are much better. I slept over there last night. That rocking chair isn't as uncomfortable as it looks."

State officials first said they would keep Asa in the hospital until he was placed in long-term foster care or adopted. Then they said they would place him in short-term foster care with a couple who only kept infants. "We appreciate your interest, Dr. Taylor," they wrote in a letter, "but we must follow procedure."

"I wish they would let me take him home with me," Kevin said. "I don't want him to go with another family and then get moved again."

"Poor little guy," I said. "It doesn't seem right even to consider putting him somewhere else."

She clicked open another image and leaned across the table. "Here's his grandfather, Papa Levi. He has taken a slight turn for the better, although he's got a long way to go." The older man looked gaunt, but he smiled, with his bony hand raised, almost waving at the camera. The house fire had taken much from him, and a deep sorrow had settled on his face.

"He needs at least one more surgery, maybe two," Kevin said. "He told me the other day that sometimes he wishes he had been called home with his daughter and Asa's sisters."

"Asa needs him," I said. "Life's hard enough. A grandpa can help."

Kevin conceded a small smile. "I suspect that's why they've both made it this far."

A few afternoons later I stopped by the hospital to see Kevin and check on her soon-to-be-son with my own eyes. Stepping around the information counter, which I had never seen actually staffed, I nearly ran into Katy.

"Hey, Lois," she said. "Checking up on me?"

I gave her a small hug, a far cry from the way I used to greet reporters in my previous life. "Sure thing, Scoop," I said. "What hot story are you working on?"

"Tammy told me about a ninety-five-year-old hospital volunteer who sings to patients," she said. "Nice woman, but she can't hear a thing. I asked her why she started volunteering. She nodded and said, 'fine, doing fine, and you?'" Katy opened her notebook. "I got two quotes I can use."

"You didn't see Dr. Kevin around here, did you?"

"You mean Iris Jo? Just saw her." Katy pointed down the hall. "She was going to some sort of doctor's appointment."

"Iris? Must be her checkup. No, I'm looking for Kevin. I'm visiting her and the little boy burned in the fire. Did you know she's adopting him?"

"No kidding? How cool is that." Her sixteen-year-old attitude burst through on a regular basis. "Can I do the story?"

"It's not a done deal yet, so we're holding off," I said. "Want to come visit?"

When we walked into the room, we found Kevin holding Asa, whispering into his tiny ear, stroking his curly black hair. The boy had a bandage on his stomach, and his body was dotted with marks.

"Oh, Dr. Kevin, he's adorable," Katy said in a hushed voice. "Hey, little man." She touched Kevin's hand. "He's so lucky to have you."

"I'm the lucky one," Kevin said. "This child blesses me in ways I never expected. I thank God every day."

I couldn't keep myself from touching his soft cheek and felt tears in my eyes.

"He's perfect," I said. "Look at him watching you, Kevin."

While we visited, Katy made funny noises and played peek-a-boo. Delighted, Asa Corinthian seemed to know Katy was not another grown-up. He giggled and fidgeted in Kevin's arms.

"I guess I'd better get back to the paper and write my story," Katy said. "Bye, Asa. Get well soon."

"Have a great time in the Big Apple," Kevin said. "Take lots of pictures, and don't forget your friends in small places."

When I left the hospital room, I kissed both Asa and Kevin on the cheek. "It'll all work out."

"I know," Kevin replied. "I was meant to be Asa's new mother."

The Friday before Mother's Day, Kevin received a certified letter from the State Department of Child Welfare, "an update on the status of your case." The bureaucratic letter said they had located a cousin who might want to keep the child, and guidelines had to be followed.

"Let's go for a walk and talk about it," I said when Kevin called. The letter had punctured her balloon of patience, and she was a woeful mix of angry and tearful.

"I can't stand it," Kevin said. "I don't know what I'm going to do."

Stopping briefly at the newspaper's front counter, I filled Tammy in and wished her a happy weekend. I had a hunch she had a date, but she was not forthcoming about her plans.

Kevin had been crying when I met her at the park.

"A distant cousin," she said. "She has never even called the hospital to check on Asa. She doesn't care about my baby."

Kevin walked so fast I could only just keep up. The late afternoon sun prompted a trickle of sweat down my chest.

"I already feel like his mother," she said. "I talked to the caseworker. She thinks the cousin wants money, knows she'll get a monthly check if she takes Asa." Kevin stopped abruptly. "She can have the money. I don't care. I want my baby."

"Kevin, it will be OK. You know that." The words sounded feeble, but I could not bear to think the boy might be sent off to someone else. Someone he didn't know. Someone *we* didn't know. "You are his mom now, and he'll be home with you one day soon." I hoped my optimism was not misplaced.

The small grove of trees provided shade, and we slowed our pace. Two hummingbirds fought over a mass of honeysuckle next to the path. Kevin patted her face with a Kleenex, and I picked up a candy-wrapper someone had dropped nearby.

"I wanted him home by Mother's Day," she said. "I wanted to take him to church and let him know how much I love him. Mama and Daddy were going to come over for lunch. I prayed so hard and was so sure it would work out."

Tears once more ran down her lovely face. I depended on Kevin's serene joy, a constant in my life, and for a moment I wanted to run. I felt ill-equipped to speak to her deep doubts, to calm her fears.

"You know things work out for the best," I said tentatively.

"I'm beginning to wonder," she said. "Why is it so hard to do the right thing? Sometimes I wish I had gone to Dallas when I had the chance, taken that practice with the family doctors' group, gotten away from Green, not fallen in love with this child."

Instead of my heart sinking, I could almost hear the voice of my late friend, Aunt Helen, pushing me to say the right thing. She had died of heart problems months into our friendship, but she had taught me much. She also steadied me when I wrestled with my decision to stay in Green.

"Kevin, you could no more have gone to Dallas than I could have sold the *Item*," I said. "You are meant to be in this town. You know there's a plan for you." I stumbled over the last words, well out of my league. "I can't say how this Asa situation will play out, but I know one thing. That baby needs you, and you can't give up."

Kevin bent to shake a pebble out of her shoe, holding my arm to steady herself. As she straightened, she looked in my eyes, her calm restored.

"You're absolutely right, Lois," she said. "I will fight for this. I will use every dollar I have and every ounce of energy. I will not let that little boy grow up in a world without someone to love him, to teach him about faith and family."

Silently we walked a few steps, and Kevin wrapped her arm around my back in a Laverne-and-Shirley kind of move. "Thanks, Lois. You are a dear, dear friend."

Contentment washed through me, and I said a silent "thank you." I wasn't sure if it was directed at Aunt Helen or God. Or both.

As we relaxed, a car whipped into the parking lot, barely visible from the shadow of the trees. A woman got out, not pausing to close the door. She ran toward us, yelling, her arms flopping like a rag doll.

It was Tammy, moving faster than I had ever seen her move.

This could not be good news.

"Lois, come quick!" As we rushed to meet her, she kept yelling breathlessly. "Hurry!"

I gulped to catch my breath and marveled at how out of shape I was. My nightly walks with Chris had decreased with baseball season, and I found plenty of excuses to sit on my porch and read.

"Your house is on fire," Tammy said. "My cousin, the volunteer firefighter out on Route 2, called me. A passerby reported it. Your house is on fire."

"Oh, my Lord," Kevin said.

The trip took nearly twenty minutes. My stomach rolled over and over as Kevin drove my car, Tammy following. The scar on my face throbbed for the first time in weeks.

"What am I going to do?" I asked. "What about my things? And Aunt Helen's house? She gave it to me to take care of. It was part of her. It's part of me."

"It's going to be OK," Kevin said, echoing my words to her from moments earlier. "The Fire Department is good. They'll take care of it."

"Nobody's out on Route 2 at this time of day. Half of them are probably still at work. It's so isolated, and that house is old and wood."

"Take a deep breath," Kevin said, going into doctor mode. "You don't want to be hysterical when you get there." She took a hand off the steering wheel and patted my knee. "Deep breath."

I sat qui   and sucked air in and out. Digging fo   s Jo's house, then Chris, and Pastor Jea   onnections were weak, and I reached

"Har   nutes," Kevin said.

"Sor.   ie," I said, hating the tremor in my voice. "Who: to hurt me? First the paper. Now this."

When we pulled up to my cottage, it was not on fire. But the garage was completely gone.

A dozen pickups lined the road, and the old fire truck that was usually parked in a shed around the corner was in my driveway. I could make out the melted skeleton of my new yellow-and-black riding lawnmower, the one Iris said I "buzzed around on like a bumblebee."

Stunned, in relief and grief, I jumped out of the car and rushed toward the debris, halted by a cluster of sweaty firefighters. I recognized some from church but could not call them by name. Other than Pastor Jean, my usual group of close friends had not made it yet. I had little doubt they would show within minutes.

"Sorry for the mess, Miss Lois," one young guy in jeans and a sooty gray T-shirt said. "It was too far gone by the time we got here."

I walked with him back to where the pile of ashes smoldered. Pastor Jean joined us, linking her fingers between mine, but saying nothing.

"Looks like it started over here," the boyish firefighter said. "Wind picked up, and it went up like this." He snapped his fingers. "A wonder it didn't jump to your house."

Turning slightly, I noticed Chris whip into the driveway, all three of his dogs in the bed of his truck. The vehicle had barely stopped when he and the dogs jumped out and rushed toward me. The animals sniffed around my house and growled.

"What in the world happened?" Chris asked. "You OK, Lois? Everyone OK?"

The weirdest things go through your mind at the oddest times. At that moment I noticed Chris's wedding band, scratched and gold, on his left hand. I had wondered how much time would have to pass before he quit wearing it. But the sight of it today seared me in the same way my poor garage did.

"Lois?" he said again.

Dazed, I tried to clear my thoughts. "That garage was about to fall down anyway. I guess now we won't have to tear it down." I stepped into Chris's arms and groaned. "Three fires this year. What am I going to do?"

Kevin walked up and gave Chris and Jean a quick hug. "We were at the park walking. Tammy came to get us. This is what we found."

"Let's go inside where it's cooler," Chris said. "We'll figure this out." Another vehicle pulled up. "There's Iris Jo and Stan. They'll help."

Over the next couple of hours, people came and went, the phone rang endlessly, and I answered dozens of questions, with a female firefighter writing official notes on a yellow tablet on a clipboard. The casserole brigade from church arrived with enough supper for the entire Fire Department, friends, and curious passersby. Neighbors huddled in small groups, murmuring and looking tense. Every now and then I caught a snatch of conversation that included "third fire this year" and "pure meanness."

"Someone's out to get her," I heard a church acquaintance saying as she took plastic wrap off a large fruit salad and searched through my drawers for a spoon.

"It's a crying shame," another woman replied, sticking rolls in the oven and running a sink full of steaming hot water. "Where do you think she keeps her detergent?"

I settled into a chair in the living room. Everyone insisted on waiting on me hand and foot while I stared into space, trying to figure out what had happened and what to do about it. My kitchen was probably cleaner than it had been since I moved in, and Iris was even sweeping the porch.

"Lois, we'd better let you get some rest," Pastor Jean said. "Time for us to head out." Her attempts to give me a little peace and quiet were blatant. Tammy scooted out first, most of the others following.

"Before you go, Jean," I said, "will you walk back here for a moment?" I steered her to my bedroom, pulled the door shut, and sank onto the soft comforter. "Would you say a prayer for me? Like you did that time at the church, that day I was so confused about whether to stay in Green?"

She clasped both my hands in hers and bowed her head. I closed my eyes and listened to the sound of voices down the hall. The front screened door slammed, and one of Chris's dogs barked. A whiff of lingering smoke touched my nose, and the ceiling fan blew my hair. I tried to believe it was the touch of God. We sat in silence for a several seconds, an urgent longing for calm coursing through my body.

". . . Walk with Lois through the valleys," Jean murmured, squeezing my hands. "In Thy holy name." She reached to hug me. "We can talk later. Anytime, Lois. Call or come by."

As my friend and, now, pastor, left, she offered a ride to Kevin and Iris Jo, who were still fussing around the kitchen, looking for lids that fit odd-shaped plastic containers filled with leftovers.

"We'll get to the bottom of this," Kevin said as she headed out. "Evil will not win."

Within minutes, only Chris was left, and he stood to hug me as I waved to the two. "You are so brave," he said, shutting the door and turning me into his embrace. "You handle a crisis better than anyone I've ever seen."

I savored his strong arms around me. "I'm a big chicken at heart. I can't even think what this is about. Why does someone hate me so much? How did they know someone wouldn't see them? Are they watching me?"

Chris pulled me onto the couch, sitting close. "I want to kill whoever is doing this to you," he said. "To wring their lousy necks." His voice sounded so different from his usual laid-back manner.

We sat silently, snuggled close. I felt safe.

Chris's dogs, closed up on my screened-in front porch, interrupted the moment with frenzied barking. Someone knocked at the front door, and I could hear a male voice murmuring quietly to the dogs.

Chris pulled the door open, while I sat on the couch expecting another cake or pie.

A deputy in a beige, polyester sheriff's uniform stood on the porch. "Wayne, hey, come on in," Chris said. "Someone call you about the fire? The others have left."

"I heard you had some trouble out here," the deputy said. "But I'm not here about a fire. I'm here to see Miss Lois."

The deputy ambled over to where I sat, and held a clipboard out with an apologetic look. "I'm sorry I'm running late, Miss Barker. Things downtown got kind of backed up. Will you sign here, please?"

I glanced down.

The paperwork said, "McCuller versus Barker, d/b/a *The Green News-Item.*"

I was being served notice of a lawsuit, courtesy of my old buddies Chuck and Dub.

8

Homer Raines, area biologist, says the white perch should be spawning in the next couple of weeks up Ditch Bayou, as water temperatures reach the upper 60s. Don't forget annual fishing licenses expire at the end of this month, and wardens will be enforcing the cutoff. More than four dozen of you were caught fishing with expired licenses last year, so don't get hooked again this year.

—The Green News-Item

Pastor Jean opened her aluminum back door within moments of my knock. An elastic headband held her hair, and she wore a pair of pastel plaid shorts and a knit shirt. The casual look suited her, made her look younger than her late forties.

"How's the intrepid journalist this morning?" she asked. "I was beginning to think you were avoiding me." She gave me a one-armed hug, trying not to spill the cup of coffee in her other hand. Two weeks had passed since the garage fire, and Jean had left multiple messages.

"I should have returned your calls, but I couldn't work up the energy to talk to anybody. I thought I could get through this, investigate, pray about it. You know the drill."

For reasons even I couldn't identify, I had kept to myself at work, dealing with endless insurance and fire department paperwork in a distant way that I could tell bothered Iris and Tammy. I had Alex chase every possible fire tip, but asked for his reports by e-mail. I avoided Chris, who despite being tied up with his team and catfish, tried to visit and told me several times on the phone how worried he was. With the investigation at a standstill, every part of my life felt immobilized.

"Are things better?" Jean asked.

"Nothing's burned this week, so I suppose that's something. But I need your help. I'm floundering."

Jean turned to the coffeepot, reaching into the painted cupboard for one of my favorite pottery mugs, bright yellow. "You want sugar and cream with this advice?" She poured the coffee and pulled out one of the ladder-back chairs for me.

As we sipped her thick-as-mud dark roast, I was embarrassed when tears filled my eyes. I dabbed at them with a paper towel and set my cup on the kitchen table.

"Not only has my newspaper caught fire twice and my garage burned to the ground, but the McCullers are suing me to take the paper back. Someone anonymously faxed the suit to my former boss in Dayton, the editor of the big paper where I worked. He called, acting like he wanted a comment for a news story, but he was just rubbing it in. He's still mad that I left the company. Oh! And let's not forget Sugar Marie leaving me this lovely little gift." I pointed to the pink mark under my eye.

"I read about the lawsuit in the *Item*," Jean said. "Can't say I'm surprised." Her matter-of-factness annoyed me, as though she were a therapist, waiting for me to discover my hidden issues. Still, I could not stop talking.

—⚬⚬⚬—

"I thought I had it all figured out, that I was doing what I was supposed to do. Now look at me."

"What do you mean?" she asked, refilling her cup and adding two teaspoons of sugar. She cleaned the table with a paper towel; her house was always spotless. A row of bright tomatoes, likely from her small garden, sat on the kitchen windowsill.

"Did I make a mistake, Pastor Jean?"

Jean pondered, neither smile nor frown to let me know which way she was headed. She seldom spoke off the top of her head. Today her silence unnerved me, and I could not wait for her to respond.

"I listened to you, to Aunt Helen, to so many good people. Now it looks like one big mess. I slip in and out of church like some sort of feral animal that has to be approached with caution."

"I've seen plenty of your species," Jean said with a smile. "Everyday living takes faith. Even stubbornness—although that's probably not the biblical term for it."

"I'm stubborn. I *thought* I had faith, Jean . . . feeble, but faith nonetheless. My fresh faith feels pretty stale right now."

"You act like you're the only one who can't get it right, like some sort of cosmic Rubik's Cube with the colors out of whack. You're way too hard on yourself."

"I expected this to play out more clearly." I rapidly tapped a spoon on the table. "Here's how it was supposed to work: A) Listen for guidance. B) Find my path. C) Go along my merry way, reaping blessings."

Jean laughed, then tugged the spoon out of my hand and laid it aside.

"That's a little simplistic," she said. "Haven't you heard of a course correction? Just because you have to stop and get your bearings doesn't mean you've totally lost your way."

"Do you do that?" I almost whispered. I felt as though I were sitting on the front row at church.

"Of course I do," she said. "When I became a minister and moved to Green, I felt ready to save the world. Then Don decided to keep his job in Baton Rouge and visit on weekends. The highway department wants to tear down the parsonage. The church council complains about my new Spanish prayer service, and the all-knowing church fathers push the produce guy off the church parking lot."

She leaned back on two legs in the kitchen chair. "Everyone has challenges, Lois, those worries that wear thin in a hurry. Some days I tell God I'm not getting out of my chair until I get a clear direction. I've sat there longer than I care to admit."

"I'm not nearly as sure about all of this faith stuff as I thought I was," I said. "I assumed it was going to be easier."

"Lois, you're not a person to take the easy way."

"I like easy. I want easy."

"You wouldn't take easy if it hit you in the face. You're smart and brave and need to do something that matters with your life."

"How can you say that, Jean? I'm a wreck. Those fires and that lawsuit . . ." My voice trailed off, and I rinsed my cup, put it in the sink, and patted her shoulder.

"Lois, I don't understand why all this is happening to you, but I have never doubted for one minute that you were sent to Green to make a difference. These problems don't change that."

I felt encouraged when I left her house, and I promised to be at church the next day. I made a U-turn out of her driveway, and cut through the church parking area. A slight movement caught my eye.

In the tiny church cemetery, I saw a man kneeling, one hand placed flat on the front of a granite stone. A second look was not required to know it was Chris, visiting his wife's grave.

A large knot in my stomach replaced the calm. I felt sad—for myself and for Chris. How hard it must be to lose someone you loved so much . . .

Despite Pastor Jean's words, my brain told me I must have gotten the signals wrong when I kept the paper and stayed in Green. My car turned toward the newspaper, although my thoughts were back at the cemetery. Speeding as I made the turn at the intersection, I hit the shoulder, throwing rocks. The produce man, the one Jean had mentioned, had set up shop on a bare patch of land near the corner, and he jumped back when I swerved, taking cover behind his dented minivan.

"Sorry," I yelled, and waved.

He waved back, and, in my rearview mirror, I saw him wipe sweat from his face with a large red bandanna.

Slowing, I put my blinker on and turned around in a nearby driveway, drove back, and eased off the road. I stepped out of the car, struck by how hot the month of June was.

"I'm sorry I came so close," I said. "I wasn't paying enough attention."

"Crossroads tricky," he said, his voice thick with an accent.

Crossroads? I looked around and glanced back at Jean's house and the little church. I couldn't see the cemetery from this angle. "Yes," I said. "Crossroads tricky. How's business?"

Not understanding, he picked up a plump red tomato and smiled. A tattered cowboy hat shaded his wrinkled face, and he pointed to the signs with prices. "Sale today. You want?"

I pointed to a small basket of tomatoes, and picked up six ears of corn, frustrated by my inability to communicate with him. He put the vegetables in an old grocery sack and wiped his brow again with the worn bandanna.

"I saw you leave church," he said with his heavy accent. "Christian?"

"I beg your pardon?"

He pointed to Grace Chapel. "Christian?" He smiled and crossed himself.

"Un poco," I said, holding my thumb and index fingers about two inches apart. "Small Christian. Tiny Christian."

"Grande," he said, shaking his head and smiling. "Grande. God's love is grande."

Not up for another talk about faith, I dug around the bottom of my purse and pulled out a wad of small bills. "Please take what I owe you," I said. He carefully counted out the money and closed my hand around my change. His wrinkled brown hand was calloused and scarred, almost stained. The way it looked shamed me for some reason.

"Lois," I said. "I'm Lois Barker."

"Miss Barker," he repeated. "I am Joe. Joe Sepulvado."

I shifted my produce and stretched my hand out. "Pleased to meet you, Mr. Sepulvado."

"Kind to meet you, ma'am."

As I drove toward the office, I groaned. "Un poco?" The only thing I might be worse at than religion was Spanish. I committed right then to learn the language. More and more Spanish-speaking people lived in Green, and I needed to connect. While I was making promises, I decided to try to pray more. That was the best I could do at the moment.

Turning at the newspaper parking lot, I did my second U-turn of the morning. Suddenly, sitting at my desk did not appeal to me in the least. Instead of heading back to Route 2, I veered off towards the little town park near the lake, remembering how much I had enjoyed my recent walks there.

Relieved to see the parking lot empty, I parked and walked briskly, one loop and two, three, and then four. Every few steps, I looked at the sky, wondering what I was supposed to do. "*I am at a crossroads. What path should I take?*"

The emotional seesaw of the morning escalated. My prayers mixed with angry ideas of revenge on the Big Boys and anyone who sought to hurt my little paper. Worry about the profitability of *The News-Item* surfaced. I recalled thoughtful gestures and kind words in recent months, the encouragement to make Green my home. My mother and father's faces popped into mind, and I felt the piercing sorrow of Mom's early death and the pain of my father, who smoked himself into an even earlier grave. I scarcely remembered him. The sight of Chris in that cemetery lurked in each of my thoughts.

"I thought that was you!" A jovial voice made me jump, as the shadow of a hawk darkened my path. "Why did you park way over there?"

Major Wilson, town scoundrel, walked toward me, wearing tennis shoes, blue overalls, and a red baseball cap with his real estate logo on it. He looked like one of the guys in a movie who sat around the front of a feed store, not his usual businessman self. He walked briskly as he came nearer.

"Long time no see, Miss Barker." He started to pat me on the back, and I flinched, and then tried to act as though I had stumbled.

"I didn't know you were a walker, Major."

"Doc says it's good for me. Need to take care of that high blood pressure you gave me with all those articles you ran." His tone was joking, but the look on his face did not match his words. "I'd appreciate a follow-up, by the way, now that I'm reformed." He made the last word into two distinct syllables and grinned big, his teeth yellow like those of a smoker.

"We're always happy to update the news, sir," I said and glanced around. I did not like being alone with this man. I resented the way he had kept Kevin and other African Americans from buying houses in his developments, and I wondered again if he had set my fires. Because of the newspaper's reporting, he had been arrested for a variety of crimes.

"There you go again, calling me 'sir.' Plain old Major's fine." He turned to look at me as we made our way around the path, me intent on getting away and him appearing to want a heart-to-heart.

"I pleaded guilty this past week to two misdemeanor charges," he said. "I want to let the good people of Green know I am making up for my past. That was all an ugly misunderstanding. I wasn't discriminating against anybody, no matter what your newspaper said."

"I didn't realize you were in court," I said before I could stop myself. "Was that something last-minute?"

"I still have a friend or two in this town. You might not know quite everything that's going on. Some people are willing to help me out when I ask."

Point taken. He had sneaked it through. I should know better than to underestimate Major Wilson, federal investigation or not.

"We'll be happy to do a story in Tuesday's edition," I said. "I appreciate your letting me know." I walked faster and felt the sweat trickling down my forehead.

"I want to do something more than let you know."

"You do?" I swallowed as I spoke, making it sound somewhat like a burp. Thoughts arose of strangling, choking, and other forms of murder, with his hands and my neck.

"I owe you an apology, lady. I was mad because you were out to get me—you and that newspaper of yours burned me pretty good."

Burned him? My heart pounded even faster than it usually did when I exercised.

"I'm sorry for the trouble I caused my sister Eva, especially with her running for mayor, and the other folks of Green. I'm going to work hard to get re-elected to the police jury and restore my good name."

"Re-elected?" My voice was pitched high.

"Election's coming up this fall, and I'm hoping for a full pardon. With this mess behind me, I can go back to serving my constituents. I hope *The Green News-Item* might endorse me. If you can find it in your heart—and your editorial board—to forgive me. I intend to make amends however I can."

He sounded sincere, but bitterness tightened my heart. Surely this guy was joking. Getting off with misdemeanors was downright insulting to the people of Green.

"Well, I've done my time for today and had better get going." I said and then winced. "Didn't mean that the way it sounded. I'll have Alex give you a call."

I scurried toward my car, happy to put a comfortable distance between us. Once more I had no idea what that meeting was about. What had happened to nice little situations where I was in control?

"Lois, is that you over there?"

The female voice that called to me was more cheerful than Major's. Katy and Molly entered the park on foot, near my car, and I was relieved to see their smiling young faces. Katy carried a colorful gift bag with a balloon tied on its handle, and Molly held a large stuffed animal of some sort. I couldn't tell if it was a dog or a horse.

"Is that Major Wilson in those overalls?" Molly asked. The two girls giggled, amused at the sight.

"What's he up to?" Katy asked. "He hasn't been around much lately."

"He wants us to endorse him when he runs for re-election," I said.

"Endorse him? You must be kidding," Molly said. "I heard he pleaded guilty to some crime this week. Something about not letting us black people live in his houses on the lake. My mama says he's a slumlord."

"A slumlord?" Katy and I said at the same time.

"Doesn't take care of his rental property, makes people live in shacks," she said. "My cousin doesn't even have indoor plumbing, and one of Mama's co-workers uses buckets to catch the water from leaks. You won't endorse him, will you? He's a jerk." Suddenly Molly looked as though maybe she had said too much. She glanced over my shoulder, and I realized Major was approaching.

"Howdy, girls. Good to see you," he said with a wave and walked around the corner to where his car sat, hidden by a large bush. Uneasiness ran down my spine.

"What're you doing in town today?" Katy asked me as Major drove off. "Don't see you over this way much on weekends."

I let out a short breath, still anxious from my encounter with Major. "I was getting a little exercise. I like this path. But that walk sort of knocked the wind out of me."

Molly laughed. "Exercise always has that effect on me too. Not on Miss Skinny Minnie here, though." She pointed at Katy, a slender girl who was at least thirty pounds lighter than her friend. "She likes to exercise. Especially now that she quit smoking."

I had not seen Katy with a cigarette in days but did not know she had stopped. Her smoking habit had worried me since my first days in Green. "You finally stopped? That's great news."

"Thanks for bringing that up," Katy said, giving her friend a playful shove. "You'd like exercise too if you'd try it."

"You wait till you get back from the big city," Molly said. "I'll be firm and fit and leave you in my dust."

"In your dreams," Katy said.

A week remained until the teen flew off to Manhattan. She would spend three months shadowing reporters and doing in-house clerical work. The magazine editor had liked Katy's application and phone interview so much that she chose Katy enthusiastically. We'd planned a small going-away party for Tuesday after the paper came out.

"Your parents still OK with it?" I asked.

"If by OK you mean nagging me over every detail from remembering to brush my teeth to keeping my hair out of my eyes at the office," she nodded. "They're making me come home in July for Grandma's birthday. They say I can't miss her eightieth, but I think they can't stand the thought of not seeing me for twelve weeks."

"You'll be glad to see them, too," Molly said. "You begged them to let you come home from church camp three summers ago, and you were only gone a week."

"I wasn't homesick," Katy said. "I was allergic to all that dust in the bunkhouse. You know that place is nasty."

"Never been there," Molly said. "I'll take your word for it."

"So," I jumped into their bickering. "Where are you two off to so bright and early?"

"We're going to see A.C.," Katy said. "Molly's got to work her other job this afternoon, so we had to get going early."

"A.C.?" Sometimes I had no idea what Katy was talking about.

"Asa Corinthian. A.C. The coolest kid in town."

Asa might just be the coolest kid in town—certainly one of the most beloved.

Despite Kevin's best efforts, the boy had been placed in temporary foster care with a family who kept babies until adoptions went through. The state insisted this was the best route. Since she knew almost everyone in Green, Kevin found out immediately who had Asa and promptly visited. Before long, Kevin's parents and Katy went, too.

"My son will never doubt I loved him from the beginning," Kevin said the first day she dropped by. "I don't care what rules I have to break to see him. The foster parents are wonderful. They want what's best for him. They say I can come anytime."

The girls chattered on for a few minutes and walked off, turning down my offer of a ride. Katy talked loudly, and Molly nodded. My nerves calmed as I watched them laugh, nearly losing the balloon and grabbing it by its ribbon.

The encounter with them had erased part of the morning strain.

Determined to take off the five pounds I had put on since moving to Green, I pulled a cap out of my car and made another round on the track, my thoughts a jumble of Chris, Major, Katy and Molly, Mr. Sepulvado and the new language I meant to take up. I moved quickly to the shady part of the track.

Everything looked so green, the bright green that had given the town its name more than a century ago. A shadow crossed my path again, and I looked up. Two hawks circled, their nest resting high in an oak tree on the edge of the park.

How I longed for my nest here in North Louisiana, no shadows, no predators.

9

Chicot School Principal and fireworks enthusiast Dan Thorn was injured when his entire neighborhood show exploded at the same time, throwing him onto the street. After the brief disruption and confirmation that Principal Dan was okay, Greg Bostick, 5, was named winner of this year's Shetland pony giveaway, an annual event in the neighborhood since 1955. However, according to Greg's father, "That horse bit a plug out of me and is going to the glue factory." At last report, Greg and his mother were seeking a good home for the horse and ask you to let them know if you're interested.

—*The Green News-Item*

Marti and her fiancé chose the worst possible time to visit Green.

"Why don't you wait till fall? It's so pretty then," I said.

"Lois, you know the wedding's in the fall. This is our only open weekend. We can use frequent flyer miles and come cheap."

"You should have come in the spring. It's beautiful here then. You would love the azaleas."

"Lois Louise Barker, save your breath. We are coming, like it or not. I want to see where you live, meet these people you talk about, give that guy Chris a once-over."

"First of all, you know my middle name is not Louise. Secondly, I told you that Chris and I don't see as much of each other these days. And third, Green is not that . . . well, appealing . . . in the middle of summer."

"We're coming anyway. I'll let you know when our flight gets in. You'd better be there."

Old friends have the weirdest way of taking care of you and annoying you at the same time. With the Friday paper printed and the carriers on their way, I sped up to the airport in Shreveport, excited and nervous. The trees along the interstate looked parched from the mid-July heat, and the sky didn't have a hint of rain. The grass in the median was brown and straw-like.

What if Marti and Gary didn't like Green?

What if they were different now that they were engaged?

What if it was . . . uncomfortable?

The airport parking lot was so hot you could fry an egg on it, as Rose liked to say. I feared my friends would melt when we made our way to the car.

The moment they stepped into the baggage-claim area, I knew nothing had changed. Marti practically sparkled as she flashed her engagement ring at me, and I enveloped her and Gary with a hug. "So, this is Louisiana," Marti said, stopping to look at a casino ad and pointing at a beautiful photo of sunflowers, posted above the conveyor belt where the luggage landed.

"Home sweet home," I said. "We're less than an hour from Green."

The cute couple wilted before my eyes when the automatic doors slid open, and we stepped onto the sidewalk. "It feels like a sauna," Marti said. "Not to hurt your feelings, but a sort of stinky sauna."

"Tried to tell you not to come in the summer," I said, helping Gary load their luggage into the trunk. "Wouldn't listen, would you?"

Gary sat in the back seat and patted Marti on the head as we jabbered on our way home. "Now, children," he said when we argued over whose life was the most stressful.

"Honey, I told you Lois makes me crazy," Marti said, twisting around and making a kissing noise. With the air cranked to high and blasting moist air into her face, she commented nonstop on the sights, from cypress trees and a swamp that was green and slightly scummy to the crawfish hut where we exited the interstate. "Is that a bait stand?"

"They sell crawfish there in season, boiled by the pound," I said. "Or you can buy a whole sack, live. They eat them around here by the truckload. People go a little crazy if you buy the ones imported from China."

"Eat them?" Marti asked. "As in food? They're raising them? Imported? What have you done with Lois?"

Marti and I had been best friends for years and spoke a language others sometimes could not follow, but I had added Green to my stories. She had added Gary. More than the landscape had changed. We had changed. For some reason, the thought made me happy. It was time.

"Marti, girl, you ain't seen nothing yet," I said in my best Southern drawl, eager to get to Green. "Katy says she misses fried crawfish more than anything, other than her friend Molly and Miss Poodle, her dog. I can't wait to see her. . . . Katy, I mean, not Miss Poodle." I glanced back at Gary. "She's in New York this summer, but Marti might have told you she'll be in this weekend. I can't wait for y'all to meet her."

"Y'all?" Marti and Gary said at the same time, and we all laughed.

"I can't believe I said that. Am I out of the wedding?"

I promised to show them *The News-Item* later, and we drove toward Route 2, where it looked as though someone had cued the locals to come out. Things I didn't notice anymore had Marti and Gary pointing and asking questions. Near my church, a tractor inched along the highway, carrying a large garbage can in its front-end scoop. The elderly driver, Mr. Warren, gave me the customary wave, lifting his hand and moving it slightly, almost like a friendly salute.

Mamie Davis, the woman who lived in a trailer immediately before our turn, put the finishing touches on gray, green, and black stripes on her mailbox, an apparent attempt to replicate camouflage. She waved without looking up. Her purple and gold four-wheeler, with a trailer hitched to it, was parked next to her.

Mr. Sepulvado sat in a webbed lawn chair, his hat pulled down over his eyes, a pile of watermelons in the back of his van and a gallon jug of water on the ground. Rhonda, the roving hot tamale woman, was parked as close to the Grace Chapel parking lot as she could get without in fact being in it, a sign taped to the windshield of her car.

"What're 'Zwolle tamales'?" Gary asked, doing a fair job of getting the pronunciation right.

"Skinny tamales, corn meal and some undetermined meat," I said. "Very tasty but spicy, even the mild ones. Zwolle's a town south of here. That woman is in that spot every Friday— 'rain or shine, sleet or snow, Rhonda's tamales are on the go.' If you miss her here, you can catch her downtown on Tuesdays and Thursdays. I fully expect to see her on the Food Channel one of these days."

I turned around in Iris Jo's driveway. "I'll grab a couple dozen," I said. "One of many culinary experiences you'll have while you're here. Don't mean to rub it in, but the food down here shames that stuff they call food in Ohio."

"How soon she turns on us," Marti said to Gary, grabbing his hand and pulling him out of the car to inspect a trio of ice chests filled with small foil-wrapped packages.

My transaction was nearly complete, and Rhonda was explaining her weekly route in painstaking detail when Chris drove up. "You having regular, hot, or very hot?" he asked us, rolling his window down. "I'm telling you, a tamale's not a tamale unless it's very hot."

He got out of the truck, wearing his Green Rabbits football team jersey, blue jean cutoffs, and an old, stained pair of running shoes. "Chris Craig," he said, extending his hand. "Welcome to Louisiana. Lois insists I tell you this is not the best time of year to visit." He shook hands with Gary and got caught in the awkward shake-or-hug move with Marti. She quickly recovered and went for the hug.

"So this is Chris," she said without a shred of subtlety. "You can't begin to know how happy I am to finally meet you."

"I've heard a lot about you, too," Chris said. "Lois says you taught her everything she knows about stirring things up."

"I'd say it's the other way around," Marti said. "She's the leader. I follow and try not to get caught."

Chris's battered pickup and plain mobile home down the road suddenly jarred me. I felt self-conscious and then guilty for feeling self-conscious.

He touched me on the arm and winked before he drove off. "See you at the cookout tomorrow," he yelled. "Sorry I can't make the downtown festival."

"Man, he's cute," Marti repeated for the third time, as we lugged their suitcases into my house. "What's the deal, anyway? I saw that look he gave you back there at the tamale place."

"Not quite sure," I said. "Maybe you can figure it out while you're here."

"I'm on the case," she said, putting her quilted tote bag and tiny purse on the floor in the living room and strolling through each room.

"What a darling house. Are these real live houseplants? You have an African violet in bloom?" She touched a leaf and moved down the hall. "Oh my gosh! Gary, she made her bed. I told you she was settling down."

My laugh sounded like a snort. "I pulled out all the stops. Didn't want Gary to think I was a slob. Can you believe Aunt Helen gave me this house?"

I pulled the framed note from Helen off the wall over my bedside table. "She knew before I did that I wouldn't sell the *Item*. She was an incredible woman. I wish you could have met her. She didn't mince words, and those McCuller nephews of hers didn't push her around. She wouldn't have let them push me around either."

Marti handed the note to Gary. "Look, mom, no mortgage! How's that for a gift from a friend? Oh, Lois, it's so good to be in Green. I miss you so much."

"Ditto," I said, hugging her fiercely. "Who would have thought our lives would have turned out like this?"

"But we've got to get this thing with Chris moving. Why are you dragging your heels?"

"I told you Chris is busy. He's teaching summer school, and they've started early football drills, and he has to take care of the catfish ponds, and he's driving down past Lafayette tomorrow to get some sports equipment."

"I need to get to know him better," Marti said. "You've been seeing him for a year. I want more action."

"*I* only started getting to know him about ten months ago." I threw Gary an apologetic look, but he didn't seem to mind the girl talk. "You know how wild that was, the paper up for sale and me about to take that editor's job in North Carolina. Life's been crazy. Neither one of us is in a hurry."

"Moving too slow, if you ask me," Marti said, something she regularly told me by phone.

"His wife died. He loved her. He's not ready to date yet. I'm enjoying being friends for now. Just because you're in love doesn't mean everyone else has to be."

"Looks to me like he's plenty ready," Marti said. "Now, let's go see your newspaper."

The weekend reminded me of the pleasure of old and new. Marti and Gary fit right in, putting on shorts and Green Forward T-shirts and serving ice water at the second annual downtown ice-cream social. Katy, home for her visit with a wild new haircut, burst into the lobby of the paper Saturday morning, nearly knocking me down with her hug.

"Is this hot or what?" she asked, twirling around and running her hands through her red-and-blue dye job. "I had it done for a Fourth of July party in the city."

Tom rushed out of the newsroom when he heard her voice and lifted her off the floor. I was shocked his back didn't give out. "What in the world have you done to your hair?" he asked. "Are you in a parade today?"

"Very funny. To think I've been bragging on what a great writing teacher you are. Although I notice you haven't been editing my blog."

She was blogging for *The Green News-Item*, something that still shocked me. Not that Katy was blogging. That the little community newspaper embraced it. The "New York Katy" pieces had evolved from yet another feisty staff conversation.

Tammy, leading newspaper tours for the festival, showed a small group out and came back to hug Katy and meet Marti and Gary. She jumped in. "Your news posted from Manhattan is so fun," she said. "Did your coworkers really take you to an Ethiopian restaurant for your birthday? How *did* Cameron Diaz look when you saw her on Fifth Avenue? How did she have her hair cut?"

"Did you see the photo layout I did of your pictures?" Tom asked. "Gave you almost all of page five on your New York scenes."

Tammy turned to Marti and Gary. "Sorry for talking shop."

"Makes me feel right at home," Marti said. "We have that blog conversation a dozen times a week in Dayton. Usually not quite so civilized."

"Katy's stuff is a big hit with kids in town," Molly said. She stuck close to Katy's side, relieved to have her home for the weekend. "They think it's the best thing the paper's ever done. They can't believe the *Item* is social networking."

"Social networking my hind leg," Tom said. "Nice to meet you, Marti, Gary. I've got to get the obits done."

The one cloud on this day was running into Chuck. He stared at the *Item* and sauntered around to the loading dock, then came back to the street and waved to a couple of men from the bank.

"Might as well get this over with," I said to Marti and Gary, and led them the few feet to where he stood.

"Chuck McCuller," he said, reaching his hand out to Gary immediately. "Longtime Green resident and former owner of this paper." As the introductions to Gary and Marti progressed, Chuck put on his super polite Southern manners.

"Miss Barker, I hope you don't mind me looking around the place while I'm downtown today," he said. "I was reminiscing about all the papers that have gone out through the years under the McCuller name."

"Don't miss the festivities down the street," I said, practically shooing him along, but he would not budge.

"I hear you're a journalist, too," he said to Marti. "I should have torn this building down when I had the chance and built one of those modern, new plants. Maybe one of these days."

As he walked off, I looked at Marti and Gary with a frown.

"I can see why he gives you the creeps," Marti said. "I'd do my best to stay away from him."

At the cookout at my house that evening, the encounter with Chuck put away, the couple visited with the crowd as though they had known them forever.

"I'm so happy to have my two girlfriends here together," I said, squeezing into the porch swing between Kevin and Marti. "And thank goodness for ceiling fans!"

"I thought you were exaggerating when you told me how hot it is down South," Marti said.

"You call this hot?" Kevin said. "You're a lightweight. Wait till August."

"It looks like some sort of advertisement," Marti said, as we watched guests grab hot dogs and hamburgers as quick as they came off the grill. "A soft drink commercial where everyone is friendly and happy."

I glanced around, taking in the people I liked so much. Tom, wearing a lightweight sage green jumpsuit, chatted with the mayor and Kevin's parents, Pearl and Marcus, near the dessert table. Even Sugar Marie was on her best behavior and looked cute with a red, white and blue striped bow on her topknot. I made it a point to pet her and slip her a small piece of meat.

Linda, wearing a sleeveless white shirt and khaki cargo shorts, chose a folding chair next to Chris, but turned to visit with Jean and her husband, in town for a rare weekend. A piece of conversation about college football wafted toward me, Gary and Chris arguing good-naturedly about one conference versus another. Tammy, Walt, and Alex stood nearby, chiming in. Stan handled the grill tonight, and Iris Jo kept coming and going, bringing him a Coke, more buns, and then a plate overflowing with food.

When swarms of mosquitoes descended in full force, most of the crowd scattered, shouting their thanks as they drove off. Chris lingered, sitting on the screened porch as Marti and Gary asked questions about raising catfish and growing up in Green.

"Why don't you ride up to Shreveport with us tomorrow?" Marti asked. "Lois is taking us to the airport about noon, and we're having brunch somewhere on the way." I squirmed but was glad she asked.

"I'm due at my parents' house for Sunday dinner," Chris said. "My nephew's back from football camp over in Georgia, and I'm expected to hear the full report."

Gary shook hands firmly when Chris left, and Marti gave him another hug.

"Super nice guy," Gary said as Chris backed out of the driveway.

"Marry him," Marti said.

"At least go out on a date with him," Gary said.

The farewell on Sunday was not as hard as it might have been because of excitement about my upcoming wedding visit. "Marti promises we're going to have a great time that entire weekend," Gary said, hugging me goodbye.

Marti squeezed me tight.

"Lois, I love your new life in Green."

I put my arm around her shoulder and tried not to cry.

"So do I. So do I."

10

*A disturbing garden incident has stricken a local woman,
who wishes to remain anonymous but is one of a handful utilizing organic practices here in Green. While
harvesting tomatoes, she was traumatized by the death
of a large lizard, trapped by netting used to keep her
overenthusiastic golden retriever from pulling the large
green tomatoes off the plants. "He thinks they are tennis
balls," she said. "I was unable to pick the remainder of
my tomatoes and had to call my son at Louisiana Tech to
come and get the dead lizard out of the garden."*

—The Green News-Item

Little Asa came home to Kevin's in late summer.

I waited on the front porch to welcome the baby, eager to show love and support. Pearl and Marcus sat inside, watching from the window with Asa's Papa Levi, whom they had picked up from his burn rehab unit for the afternoon.

All of a sudden, Mr. Marcus, usually so dignified, burst out of the house, followed closely by Miss Pearl. "There they are!" he shouted as Kevin's new SUV pulled into the driveway. "They're here!"

The three of us rushed to help as my dear friend pulled her son from his car seat and carried him up the steps and into his new home. Her smile was huge. "Mama, Daddy, Lois," Kevin said softly, tears running down her cheeks, "my son is finally here."

She took the boy over to Levi, whose burned hand trembled as he touched Asa. "Thank you, Lord," the old man said. "Thank you."

We all cried, except little Asa, who wiggled to be put onto the floor and then crawled around the living room, grabbing one toy and another.

"He knows this is home now, don't you think?" Kevin asked, snatching tissues out of a box on the end table.

"I'll say he does," I said. "He clearly knows who his new Mama is." Every few moments Asa would scan the room for Kevin, catch her eye, crawl over to her or just make sure she was nearby.

"Look," Miss Pearl said in a loud whisper. "He's pulling up."

Sure enough, Asa Corinthian pulled up, turned to look at Kevin and took a small step. Then he sat down abruptly, acted as though he might cry and turned to the bright cloth blocks I had brought.

A few days later it was Molly who suggested we have a shower for Kevin now that Asa was home. When we had tried to do it earlier, Kevin politely turned us down, afraid, she said, "to get too attached before things are settled."

This time, when Molly and I stopped by her house, she agreed enthusiastically. "Sounds lovely. My son and I will be there with bells on."

My new Country Club membership provided the perfect site for the afternoon party, which was filled with conversation and laughter. The formerly stuffy room looked like it had shed fifty years. Even the carpet seemed newer.

More than one hundred people—from church friends decked out in dress clothes to neighborhood men in their jeans—turned out to greet Asa and bestow their blessings on him and Kevin. Gifts spilled over into the hall and finally into the dining room.

Pastor Jean showed up late with three little boys she now cared for regularly, Mexican children who lived in a ramshackle house on a cutoff road behind the church. I had first seen them with her more than a year ago playing at the downtown festival and now saw them often at church or her house.

"Sorry to bring the kids," she said, pulling them into the room in a red wagon with a bow on it, "but their mom is working today. I wanted to be here for Kevin and Asa."

The children, sometimes a bit dirty, shone. They wore obviously new outfits, shorts and T-shirts with different farm animals on them. Instead of pouncing on the punch and cake, they stood quietly in the corner, speaking to each other in Spanish, while Jean and I chatted.

Chris, who did not quite fit my picture of a baby shower guest, walked over, squatted down, and said something to them. The three boys smiled, took each other's hands, and followed him to the refreshments.

"That man is something else," Pastor Jean said. "Guess I had better go to his rescue."

"I didn't know Chris spoke Spanish," I said before she could move.

"He's learning. He can get his point across. He helps with the Spanish prayer service, mostly greeting, that sort of thing."

As the afternoon wore on, it seemed as though everyone wanted to say something publicly to the new mom and her son.

Pastor Jean read a scripture verse from Isaiah about how God goes before us, making the crooked places straight. Members of the Lakeside Neighborhood Association led the group in singing a rousing version of "Victory in Jesus."

The neighbor who had called 911 when the house fire broke out spoke of how God works all things for good. "Thanks to the generosity of Dr. Kevin Taylor and this community, our neighborhood is being fixed up. At least six houses are good as new." A church friend asked for prayers for Mr. Levi's continued healing.

An older woman from Miss Pearl's Ladies Circle led the group in "Jesus Loves Me," a touching rendition that seemed ever more real that afternoon. One of the three Hispanic boys pulled Asa and the two other boys around in the wagon while attorney Walt, who had vigorously helped Kevin through the adoption paperwork, made sure no one fell out.

Katy sent Kevin a picture by cell phone, a photo of the young journalist standing in Times Square holding up a sign that said, "I ♥ AC." Molly scooped the little guy off the floor and held him out in front of her. "You are blessed of the Lord," she said and then quickly sat him down. "Whew. And I think you may have just stunk this place up."

The crowd laughed, and Kevin left the room for one of her many new frequent activities. "I'm not afraid of a stinky diaper," she said as she left.

While she was gone, Tammy moved near me, taking pictures with one of *The News-Item's* two new digital cameras. In our monthly employee-owner meeting, she had insisted on the purchase. "We must start running bigger and better images," she said. "Readers love to see pictures, especially photos of people they know."

She had passed out copies of an article from the Internet explaining how digital equipment could be used effectively. "Plus, we can run online photo galleries and even do videos."

The part-time photographer, who had worked at the paper a few hours a week for nearly a decade, left the room in a huff that day, quitting as he went. "Consider yourself without a photographer, Lois," he said. "I'm out of here. I would rather shoot weddings any day than put up with this."

Tammy quickly turned into a much better newspaper photographer than he had been, and I wondered if ego was part of the reason for his departure. But I also knew change was hard, and we still had hurdles to cross.

"Say cheese," Tammy said loudly, and snapped my photo. "Oh, look, it's a great one." She turned the camera for me to look at what was a pretty good picture.

"Fun party," Tammy said. "What a wonderful day." She nodded to the corner where Walt, Chris, and several other men stood, looking oddly charming holding dainty glass punch cups. "Great bunch of guys, eh?" She held the camera up and took a shot.

"That Mr. Chanler is something else," I said, teasing. Benjamin Franklin Chanler was at least eighty, if not older, and an active member of Mr. Marcus's Sunday school class. He held the attention of the entire group of men.

"Oh, be serious," Tammy said. "Walt and Chris are plenty cute, and you know it. . . ." She paused, seeming almost nervous. "By the way, has Walt mentioned to you that we're dating?"

"You and Walt?" *Tammy and Walt?* "As a matter of fact, he hasn't." She seemed a little young for him, close to twenty-five to his near forty. "Congratulations. That's great," I said and felt proud of myself for meaning it.

Walt needed a good woman and someone to spice up his life. Tammy needed someone who saw beneath her sometimes-ditzy surface to the jewel of a woman she was. Perhaps his influence was behind the changes I saw in her these days, including her studious approach to photography.

"I owe it all to you," she said. "First, you broke up with him." She laughed. "Would have been kind of hard to go out with him if he was in love with the boss. But you know what else?"

She seemed to wait for an answer, although I thought the question was rhetorical. "Walt wouldn't have given me a second look until I met you. You made me see myself as something more than a dumb clerk at a country newspaper." She tinkered with the camera. "How do I say this? The world got more interesting."

Tammy stopped talking, stood next to me, and held the camera up in the air, facing the two of us. "Smile, Lois. I want to take lots of pictures of my friends. One of these days I'm going to put them in a big scrapbook."

After she took the photo, she hemmed and hawed again, something else obviously on her mind but not rolling out, unusual for Tammy.

"There's more?" I asked.

"I was sort of hoping," she said, "that you and Chris might actually start dating, step it up to the next level. You sure spend a lot of time together not to be a couple."

My friends, from Ohio to Louisiana, were matchmakers through and through. They could not bear to think of me single and living alone. A thirty-seven-year-old woman who had never married was somewhat suspect in their minds, peculiar, as my mother would have said.

"We visit quite a bit," I said and left it at that. I did not want to give Tammy any gossip ammo for the coffee gatherings in the newsroom or her next bunco night.

"I guess he's still not over Fran," she said. "I know I'd miss Walt if anything happened to him, and we just started dating."

"Probably so," I mumbled, an answer that seemed to cover the Fran comment and the Walt remark.

"I was sort of surprised when I heard Chris had supper with his in-laws this week," Tammy continued. "Didn't think he saw much of them anymore."

Her words hit me right in the heart. "I'd better see if Jean needs a hand with the boys," I said, trying to find an excuse to walk away. "I'm real happy for you and Walt."

After the party, I went by the office, my fallback position when I was unsettled. Work was plentiful and would keep my mind off couples and babies and my empty house out on Route 2.

Still a little uneasy since the fires, I seldom was alone in the building at night. I turned on all the lights, taking a quick look in each area. I sang loudly to show any criminal I was not afraid. I unlocked one of the new filing cabinets, installed after the second fire, and pulled out the binder with Aunt Helen's typewritten history of *The News-Item*.

I sat at my new desk, picked out by Tammy, and read more of the tale, including extra notes in Helen's flowery, old-fashioned script, determined to finish sorting through her papers in the next few months. Absorbed in her words, I glanced up to see a man's face at my office window, his hand raised. I screamed and jumped up, sending my chair crashing into the wall.

"Lois, it's me," Chris yelled when he caught my eye again. "Open the front door."

I banged my leg on the swinging door in the lobby and frowned at Chris as I unlocked the door, my body quivering. Chris frowned back, his hands gripping a cardboard box.

"You scared me to death," I said, practically screeching. "As Aunt Helen used to say, I'm shaking like a leaf."

I leaned back on the counter to steady nerves on high alert from fright and pleasure. He looked so handsome in his slacks and short-sleeve knit shirt, the same thing he had worn to the shower. *What was he doing here?*

"I knocked, but you didn't hear me," he said. "What in the world do you mean coming down here on a Saturday night by yourself?"

"I wasn't planning on staying. What brings you downtown anyway?"

"Miss Pearl took some of the leftover flowers for the altar tomorrow and sent you the rest. I volunteered to deliver them and thought I'd see if you wanted to grab a bite to eat."

He showed the contents of the brown cardboard box, including two white sacks and a couple of large plastic cups. "When you weren't home, I was a little antsy. Wanted to talk to you. Came to the Cotton Boll. Saw your car."

He held the box toward me. "Supper," he said. "You got plans?"

"Not a plan in sight." I motioned him toward the conference room and locking the front door. "Other than recovering from the coronary you gave me."

"I'm sorry about that. I don't like you coming down here by yourself. I mean it, Lois. We still don't know who set those fires."

"I'll be careful," I said. "Can we eat now?"

We spread the food on the conference table, and I scrounged around and found a candle. "Festive," I said. "Fancy table. Big chairs. Huge burgers." I stuck a straw in the cup and took a big drink. "Cotton Boll sweet tea. If I had known about this, I would have moved to Green years ago."

"Definitely uptown," Chris said. "Why don't we bless the food, greasy though it might be." We held hands and bowed together, although I sneaked one look at him, thrilled by his visit.

"Lord, God, Creator, we thank You for this food. We thank you for little Asa and Kevin and ask your special touch on their lives together. Thank you for Lois and her life and work here. In Thy name. Amen."

"Amen," I added, amazed that I had prayed with a man I was interested in romantically. *That* had never happened before. Most men I had known weren't into saying blessings before eating.

I wished I could write his prayer down. It was so . . . thoughtful. Something I wanted to remember.

"Great party today," Chris said. "What a crowd. Everyone loves Dr. Kevin, don't they? That little guy doesn't know how good he's got it."

"I told Kevin she ought to bring him out to one of your games, get him used to football nice and early," I said. "With a name like Asa Corinthian and that chunky little body, I think he has a future on the team."

Our suppertime chatter continued with a range of topics that went from the Spanish ministry at church to Chris's dogs.

"I'd like to see the Spanish services branch out," Chris said. "I don't think we're doing enough. I don't quite know how to go about it, though."

"It's not the most popular topic," I said. "I even overheard some of the older African American men at the shower today talking about it, complaining that Mexicans are taking all the jobs. I've been trying to think of something *The News-Item* can do."

"Maybe we can come up with something together," Chris said. "We're a community here, always have been. Some of the weirdest people you'll ever meet live here. I sure don't see a problem in taking in a few more folks."

He reached over and dabbed a spot of mustard off my face.

"On a lighter topic," he said, "have you seen what that crazy Mannix is doing?" I had rescued Mannix after an injury about a year before. The incident led to my frequent walks and talks with Chris. "He climbs over the new fence like a mountain goat. He gets up to the top, teeters there, and then jumps over. I don't know what I'm going to do with him." Chris made a choking gesture with his hands and laughed.

"When I turn my truck onto Route 2," Chris continued, "he looks up, races me down the road, climbs back into the yard, and stands at the gate, panting, as though he has been there all day. Markey and Kramer stand there looking at him like he's the smartest thing around."

We laughed more. Then suddenly the conversation lulled, and the hamburger set heavy on my stomach. I coughed.

"You OK?" Chris asked.

"I heard you had supper with your in-laws the other night," I blurted. "Everything OK with them?"

Chris looked surprised and nodded in the slow, deliberate way he had.

"Everything's fine. I invited myself over for pork chops and mashed potatoes." He paused. "Or did someone tell you that too?"

"I didn't get the menu. Someone at the shower happened to mention that you'd been over there."

"It must be mighty easy to be a journalist in this town. There's not one secret, not one single little secret." He ran his fingers through his hair, which stayed on the shaggy side. I suddenly noticed he was not wearing his wedding band.

"Did your sources happen to mention why I went to see the Millers?" he asked. "Other than the home cooking?"

"Nope. No agenda. No menu. Merely a sighting." I was definitely frazzled.

"No agenda, huh? Well maybe there is a secret or two still to be had. You got some coffee somewhere in this joint?"

Impatient, I made a pot of coffee in the newsroom carafe, once clear but now the color of the water in Bayou Lake. Chris cleaned up the food containers and napkins and carried them over to the large bin in the newsroom. Making the coffee and getting settled kept us from having to talk, but I knew this discussion was headed somewhere. The minor chores felt sort of like a scene in a play, where two people are about to have a big fight or fall into a passionate embrace.

Chris sat on the small, scratchy tweed settee, probably bought about the year he was born. I took my favorite chair, the one at Katy's desk, propping my feet up on a fake leather stool that Tom swore had been there longer than he had.

"This is kind of hard for me to say," Chris said. "I went to see Fran's parents to tell them I have met someone. I didn't want them to hear it through the grapevine. They've been part of my life for a long time." He shifted, causing the settee to make a weird noise.

"I can't believe how nervous I am," he said. "I feel like one of my players threw a Hail Mary pass with the state championship at stake . . . and I can't tell if the receiver caught it or not."

He took a gulp of coffee. "I told Fran's folks I'm pretty serious about this woman already, even though we haven't had a real first date yet. . . . Would you *say* something for heaven's sake?"

I had wanted this moment for months and should not have been surprised that it happened in the newsroom, where most of my life's big moments seemed to occur. I reached for his hand and smiled.

"You sure better be talking about me," I said.

11

*Bouef Parish Health Administrator Timmy Barnwell
reminds everyone to be careful when swimming in Bayou
Lake because of the presence of new plants and possible
parasites. "You might want to pick you up a pair of those
plastic shoes to keep worms from getting into your feet,"
he said. A spot check of local stores found many styles
and colors to choose from.*

—The Green News-Item

The lawsuit against the paper would not go away. Walt and I met at least once a week, wrestled with the McCuller legal team, and worked every source he had––to no avail.

Today we were in his downtown Shreveport office, a masculine, studious place with marble halls and original Art Deco touches. I volunteered to meet there because I hoped a fresh perspective would help me find some clarity.

"They are dead set on moving forward," Walt said from behind his desk, looking through a stack of files that had grown since last week. "I can't figure out what they're up to. There is no legal precedent for this. And they're not frivolous suit kinds of guys."

"What should I do next?" I asked, wandering around his office while we talked, enjoying his memorabilia, most of it handed down from lawyers in his family through the years. My favorite was a framed letter, written in his grandfather's hand, about a summer visit Walt had made as a child.

"Lois, look at me," Walt said gently. I turned but still stood by the back wall.

"I have to ask you again: Do you want to try to settle?" He almost winced as he asked the question. "Or consider taking their offer?"

My hesitation surprised me.

"I expected to say no without even thinking," I said. "Green has taught me that questions seldom have simple answers. *The Green News-Item* is not exactly a cash cow, and this year has been trying in ways I never imagined. The fires are never far from my mind, and I thought the economy would be better by now."

I sank down into one of his upholstered chairs, my yellow print dress looking perfect against the brown fabric. I engineered little moments of distraction when I wanted to ignore a problem. "The Big Boys are waving around real money, and I could use it. The staff could use it. We need money to pay off the fire clean-up expenses. It's hard to utter those words, but that's what my head tells me."

"We could always try for a compromise," Walt said. "Maybe bring them in as co-owners. That would get you some operating cash."

"You can't mean that," I said. "I wouldn't work for those two if my life depended on it."

"That's our answer then," Walt said. "Head overruled by heart." He pretended to hit his desk with a gavel. "Case dismissed."

"If it were only that easy," I said.

"We must choose a line of attack. We can wait for their next move, but we need to know what we're doing and why."

"Walt, do you pray?"

"Pray?" he asked incredulously. "Lois, we need to focus on this lawsuit. No offense, but try to stay on track."

"Do you pray?"

"I'm praying for patience right now."

"Seriously, Walt, do you pray?"

"I guess I pray."

"About things like this?"

"I think about problems and ask God to help me. Sometimes when things are going good, I sort of say 'thanks,' if that's what you're talking about."

"I wish I'd paid more attention to my mother's prayers," I said. "It sure doesn't come naturally to me. I spend a lot of time learning the same lessons over again."

Walt moved around the desk and sat next to me. "Have you prayed about this lawsuit?"

"I've tried to."

"And?"

"I'm so tired of it all. Who knows if it's God's voice or my own? I have other things I want to put my time and energy —and money—into. I don't know why I have to go through this lawsuit when I was trying to do the right thing."

"Lois, one of the things I've learned through the years is that God leads us through difficult times. I've seen it time and again."

"Does that include contentious lawsuits?"

"It includes everything," Walt replied.

"You'll probably have to remind me of that, Walt. I don't think I'm supposed to give in on this lawsuit. There are too many things at stake, too many people involved."

"If you're ready to go forward, I'd say we'd better get ready for a trial, probably in front of a judge, very likely a pal of the McCullers."

"You think it will go to trial?"

"Unless something changes drastically. We might be able to get a change of venue, but that's about the best I've got right now." He pulled out a legal folder and shuffled through it. "My dad says he'll help, but we're going to need another lawyer. I recommend this guy from Alexandria, Terrence D'Arbonne."

"Walt, we don't have that kind of money," I said. "There's no legal slush fund sitting around at the paper. This will cut into the profit-sharing plan. It's not the staff's fault we got sued."

"Lois, are you going to stand up for your paper or not? It sounds like you are. Dad will work pro bono. He likes you. He loved Aunt Helen. Despises Chuck and Dub. I'll do you right, too. I haven't contacted Terrence yet. He won't be cheap. I wanted to talk to you first."

"Go for it," I said, praying in desperation as I said it. "We'll borrow the money if we have to. But you can't keep working at discount rates. You have to pay the bills, same as everyone else."

I turned around a framed snapshot I had noticed on his desk. "Plus, Tammy must be a pretty high-maintenance girlfriend."

"I wondered when you were going to bring that up," he said, picking up the picture of Tammy on a pontoon boat, laughing, her hair blowing in the wind. She looked like a new person. "I wasn't quite sure how to mention it. Not like you and I had a hot and heavy romance or anything, but I enjoyed going out with you. Seemed awkward dating one of your employees."

"I'm happy for you, Walt. She's a special woman—feisty, but a special woman."

"She loosens me up," he said. "I think I calm her down. Good trade-off."

I didn't tell Walt that Chris and I were now officially dating. So far I had only told Marti—because she was a thousand miles away and unlikely to put it on the Green grapevine. "I knew it," she said when I called her. "I could tell something was about to happen."

Although I did not consider myself a superstitious person, talking about my new romance seemed a jinx of sorts. I still felt as though I were competing with a perfect person, Chris's wife who had died four years ago. It reminded me of when Kevin told me she didn't want to get her hopes up about Asa or when Katy was afraid to wish for the New York job.

"Go ahead and get Mr. D'Arbonne to Green," I said to Walt. "Or let's go down to see him. I intend to beat the McCullers, no matter what it takes."

I walked around downtown Shreveport when I left Walt's office, enjoying the tall buildings and the urban feel. I strolled through a public art gallery and checked out a nearby film center, studying the posters in the lobby and picking up a schedule. Maybe Chris and I could come up here one weekend. I stood before the giant downtown church, looking at its majesty and hoping for strength. And courage.

Suddenly I was eager to be back where I belonged. I wanted to see Chris and to sit at my desk. I hopped onto the interstate and barreled toward Green. As soon as I got back, I called the staff together and told them my decision, asked for their feedback and support. They were enthusiastic about going forward, but I could see my hint of fear reflected on their faces.

That afternoon, Iris Jo and Stan walked into my office and closed the door, about as rare as a cool front this time of year. "We're worried about the lawsuit," Iris said, "and what it might do to our bottom line—and to your future. We suggest contacting Major Wilson for help."

I slowly turned from the story I was editing and tried to keep my mouth from hanging open. "Did you just suggest we get in touch with the man you once described as lower than a snake's belly?"

Iris sighed. "I did. I hope you don't mind, but Stan and I have been talking this over. We've racked our brains, and we can't think of another way."

"Miss Lois, I know I usually work things from the other end of the paper," Stan said, "but Iris asked my opinion on this. I want to help out any way I can."

"I need all the help I can get. Why don't you two sit down and tell me where this is heading?"

Iris settled on the edge of a chair but Stan pointed to the ink on his coveralls and remained standing. I dug around in a cabinet, pulled out an old towel and laid it on the cushion. "Have a seat, Stan, and one of you tell me why in the world Major would help us."

"I've thought about this lawsuit and the fires from every angle," Iris said. "I've never known Chuck and Dub to do anything without Major. He may be the key to getting them to drop this suit. Or he might know something that will help us win."

"But why would he do anything for the paper? He's a liar and a thief, and we nearly got him thrown in jail with our coverage."

"When you mentioned seeing him in the park," Iris said, "I knew he was up to something. I've known Major since I was a kid. That man doesn't apologize. He wants something from you."

"He's trying to fool you somehow," Stan said.

"We've got to beat him at his own game, get in touch with him, try to pry it out of him," Iris said.

"I can't ask that man for help," I said. "I despise him. He despises me, for that matter."

"Lois, we have to try. Business isn't great, and we don't have the revenue to keep fighting," Iris said. "Before we go to court, we have to try it the Green way."

"The Green way?"

"Sometimes official channels don't work down here," she said. "You know that good and well. We're saying to go at this a different way."

While Iris and Stan waited, I placed a call to Walt on the speaker phone.

"No," he said. "Not only no, but absolutely not. This is a court case, and we can't give any ammunition to the other side."

"Let us try, Walt," Iris Jo said. "You and your father know I don't go off half-cocked. I know these men well, and they're desperate for something. I might be able to get information."

Reluctantly, to put it mildly, Walt agreed to let Iris place a call to Major on my behalf, suggesting we meet at the newspaper to restore our relationship with a former advertiser and local politician.

"You're smart women, and you know the future of the paper is on the line. Do not say or do anything that will hurt your case," Walt said.

Major surprised me with a polite return phone call the next morning. "Miss Barker, I'd be pleased to meet with you. I'd like to do it somewhere private, though. I'd just as soon the whole town not know my business."

I was pretty sure the whole town already knew his business. Alex wrote a thorough follow-up story after my encounter with Major in the park, and we had included the background and likely fallout of his plea agreement.

"I'd prefer to meet at the paper, sir."

He balked. "What I might have to say could be on the . . . sensitive side. What do you newspaper folks call it? Deep background, that kind of thing. You're the one who wants the meeting."

I would rather have eaten one of Chris's live catfish than admit I was more than a little afraid of Major and wanted our meeting to be on my turf. But I found myself in the hideous position of needing his help.

"I don't want to give fodder to the gossips in town," I said.

"I've been gossiped about so much that I'm used to it," he said. He seemed to think I was concerned about his reputation, not mine.

Finally, I let him twist my arm, agreeing to meet at his office. "I'm bringing someone with me, though," I said. "We do this my way or not at all."

He made what could best be described as a loud harrumph, among what I was coming to think of as his repertoire of odd noises. "That's the problem with you, Miss Barker. You don't understand the give-and-take of Green. Bring whoever you want—except for that Alex guy. I don't have any use for him. And don't forget, this is off the record."

The next day Iris Jo accompanied me to Major's, convinced we were doing the right thing. "I don't trust that man as far as I could throw him," she said, "but I'm certain he can provide information we need."

I looked over at her, surprised. My mild-mannered business manager acted as though she were a double agent.

"Once more, Iris, what kind of information are we looking for?"

"I don't know," she said, staring off into the distance, as though seeking an answer. "But he knows the McCullers better than anyone, and I guarantee he knows what they're up to."

"Why would he tell us?"

"Because he's the kind of man who likes to show off, let people see how important he is. By asking to meet with him, we gave him power—or so he thinks."

"Iris, I do believe you're an investigative reporter at heart."

She turned to me in the car. "You're much better at this than I am. How do you think he might help us?"

"I have no idea," I said. "You've known him for decades. I've only had the pleasure of his acquaintance for a year and a half or so. But I learned as a young reporter to go to the primary source. Maybe we'll learn something straight from the horse's mouth."

"More like the horse's rear end," she said. From Iris Jo, those were harsh words indeed. "Sorry. That wasn't a very nice thing to say."

I smiled, amused at her sudden fervor.

"By the way, Iris," I said as we pulled up outside Major's office. "I need to tell you something before we go in."

A rare look of worry crossed her face.

"Chris and I are dating."

"I *was* able to figure that out," she said, opening the car door with a smile. "Let's get this over with."

Inside the office, the desk where Linda used to work was vacant, the top cleared except for a phone, a tablet, and a pen. We yelled hello and walked on in, surprising Major. He sat behind his gargantuan desk in his paneled office. "I didn't hear you. I need to put a bell on that door or something."

"Is your secretary off today?" Iris Jo asked with what almost sounded like a dig in her usually even voice.

"I don't have a secretary right now," Major said. "Haven't filled that job since Miss Barker here stole Linder away from me. Still looking."

"We're mighty glad to have *Linda*," Iris said. "Thank you for letting her go."

My business manager was full of surprises today.

He gestured to the overstuffed sofa, asked if we wanted something to drink and walked to a large wingback chair, the same chair where I sat on my first visit to this office, with my former employee, Lee Roy Hicks. Last I heard he was still in jail for stealing from the paper and threatening me.

Major surprised me by sitting next to us. Usually he chose the huge desk chair, like a feudal king lording over the people sitting on the other side. "A new secretary's not in the budget at the moment," he said. "I've had a few financial setbacks. A slowdown, guess you could say. Some would say I got what was coming to me. Anyway, that's not what you came here to talk about."

I tried to look at Major without turning sideways on the couch, but Iris shifted completely, sitting knee-to-knee with him, her slacks almost touching his navy blue pants. As they settled in, I surveyed his office, my eyes widening when I saw a big black Bible, with a small pistol on top of it, lying on the credenza behind the desk.

I gasped, started to stand, and pulled at Iris Jo, but Major had seen my eyes and walked behind his desk with a quickness that surprised me.

"Didn't mean to shock you," he said. "That's my grandson's pellet gun. He left it at my house, and I've been meaning to give it back to him." He opened a drawer, dropped the gun in, and slid the drawer shut.

Returning to the chair, he crossed his legs. "Now, what can I do for you today?"

"We need information," I snapped. My irritation was obvious, and Iris shifted again.

"Lois does not mean to rush you, but we know you're a busy man. She wants to get to the point."

I looked at her, perplexed. *Had she apologized for my manners?*

"Ladies, as I've said, I want this visit to stay between us. I hope to regain the trust of the *Item* and get your endorsement for my re-election. But that is totally separate from this discussion. This is a meeting you called."

"Understood," Iris Jo said firmly.

Major looked at me. "Understood," I said feebly.

"We need your help with the lawsuit the McCullers have filed against the newspaper," Iris said quietly. "You're the only one who can set this straight."

I am sure I gulped at that moment.

"I see," Major said, drawling the words out and stretching back in the chair with his hands clasped over his head. "What could I possibly offer that would help you?"

From the smirk on his face, I knew Iris was right. This man knew something.

"Why would Chuck and Dub want the paper back?" Iris asked. She and Major ignored me, acting as though they were old friends having coffee.

"I can tell you that, but I'm not sure I should," he said.

"But think of your good name," Iris said, "your legacy, in Green, in Bouef Parish, throughout Louisiana."

Maybe she was laying it on a little thick, but Major obviously didn't think so.

"I suppose you're right," he said. "But people must never know this information came from me. I'll go to my grave denying it."

I started to stand up, hearing Walt's voice in the back of my mind. Iris Jo put her hand on my leg, subtly pushing me back onto the sofa and giving a nearly unnoticeable shake of her head. She knew how to work this man in ways I could not even imagine.

"Lord knows, I hope this is the right thing," Major said. His voice was lower now, and he almost seemed to be talking to himself. "If Chuck and Dub get wind of this, they'll probably shoot me and throw me in the lake."

"Why would they shoot you?" Iris had definitely taken over our side of the conversation.

Suddenly Major held court, sitting up straighter, his legs crossed at the ankles. You could almost see him judging himself against his friends and gaining status all the while.

"I've been friends with the McCuller family all my life. Grew up on the same street. Rode our bicycles all over this town. Downtown. Around the lake. Over to colored town." He stopped. "Sorry. Old habits."

"Anyway, the McCullers . . ." I prompted, while my brain raced to figure out what he was going to say before he said it. That old habit of mine had not been left up in Ohio.

"I've known them for years. Before my sister and I had our falling out, we all spent lots of time together. I used to think she might marry Dub one day, but that never came to anything. We spent a lot of time at Aunt Helen's house, too. The one you live in now, out on Route 2."

He rubbed his eyes behind his glasses. "She thought a lot of you, Miss Barker. Said you had smarts and a heart, a rare combination in her book."

"She was one of a kind," I said.

"But you made her nephews mad. You didn't treat them with respect. They thought you were a little too high-and-mighty for Green. Truth is, I feel the same way. You don't understand our ways, our town."

"But a lawsuit?" Iris asked, while I sat stunned by his words.

"They want that paper back so things can be the way they used to be. People come to them all the time, needing favors and telling how the paper has done them wrong. Mostly they don't want this woman to have it. Especially Chuck."

I stood abruptly, paced around the room and then rested against the desk that was nearly bigger than my condo in Dayton. My stomach churned.

I glanced at Iris Jo, knowing I was asking permission to speak. She gave a small nod.

"You're telling me I'm being sued because I don't do favors for people? Because my staff is ethical? Because I stepped on the toes of two rich men? Two hard-nosed businessmen?"

"I think what he's trying to say," Iris said, "is that this is personal to them."

"Personal?"

"That's right," Major said. "Like when you decided not to sell the newspaper to that regional outfit you were playing footsy with there for a while. Personal. You violated our code of behavior. Me and the McCullers have made things happen in this community, and you charge in here and act like you're smarter than all of us."

"Code of behavior?"

"You fired Lee Roy, and stirred things up at the Country Club with you and that black friend of yours becoming members, and the paper tried to send me to jail. All those things." Major nodded as he spoke.

I was glad he had put that gun away. He seemed shifty to me. "So you're saying I owe the McCullers an apology?"

"Correct," he said, making it into two words. Cor-rect.

"But they were wrong. They hurt people. They stole from their family business. They treated people unfairly."

"You don't know half as much as you think you do," Major said. "That makes you a dangerous woman to be running the town newspaper."

I returned to the couch and folded my hands in my lap, what I considered my Sunday school pose in meetings in Dayton. I looked at Iris, bewildered. "If I understand what you're saying, I have somehow wronged Chuck and Dub, who may or may not have deserved to be wronged, but I have wronged them nonetheless."

"Lois . . ." Iris Jo's tone of voice was one I had heard her use a time or two with Tammy, Katy, or Molly, but never with me. "Remember what Pastor Jean said Sunday? About treating people the way you want to be treated. About loving your enemies."

"I am not going to love the McCullers," I said, ignoring Major altogether. "I'll think about apologizing if that's the *Green* way." I put all my emotion into the word Green. "But I will not back down for calling them out on their racism. I can only go so far."

"Before you two get all tied up in that forgiving seventy times seven business, I'll tell you something else," Major said. He seemed pleased that I was rattled and that Iris was in charge. He was warmed up and ready to talk.

"Chuck and Dub have no grounds to sue you. They do not own *The News-Item*."

"We know that." My voice dripped with the intense disdain I felt. "I bought the paper from them more than a year ago."

Iris sat up straighter, picking up on something I missed.

"I'm sorry, Major," she said, apparently apologizing again for me. "What are you getting at?"

"I never understood that whole sale business in the first place. Chuck and Dub have not owned the paper for years. They sold it, lock, stock, and barrel, to Aunt Helen ten or eleven years ago when they had financial problems."

12

*Carrie Doler from the Ashland community was separat-
ing eggs to make her father's favorite Italian Cream Cake
when she got the shock of her life. "I heard a sudden
squeal of tires, then a loud crash behind the house.
A pickup truck had swerved into our yard, plowed
through my fig tree and vegetable garden and landed
in the middle of the workshop. On any other day,
Daddy would have been out there building birdhouses,"
she said. "Thank heavens he took the children fishing
that morning."*

—*The Green News-Item*

Alex burst into the newsroom and yelled for Tammy to come quick with her camera. "There is a bear in the Dumpster," he hollered. "A bear. A real, live bear."

For a moment, I wondered if Alex had been drinking.

"You're taking too long. Hurry. It'll be gone." Practically dragging Tammy outside, he kept saying, "I saw a bear in the Dumpster." I followed cautiously, torn between being fooled and afraid of confronting a wild animal.

"That's a trash bag," Tammy said, laughing when she rounded the corner of the building. Sure enough, a large black garbage bag blew across the parking lot and lodged in a tree. "That was em-*bear*-assing." She poked him in the ribs.

"Ha, ha." Alex flushed. "I could have sworn I saw a bear. I must be losing it."

"That bag looks like a bear," Molly said. "I can see it."

We all traipsed back into the building and settled into our usual spots. A pleasant late afternoon ritual had developed in the newsroom. By 5:00 or 5:30, work pressure eased. Alex was usually preparing for one of the many night government meetings he covered, and I was getting ready for some sort of civic gathering. Iris and Stan had started sharing a ride to work "to save gas," and they always checked in when they finished for the day.

Molly was in from school, had done a few of her composing room chores, and was eager to chat, quelling her impatience for Katy to return from New York. When "Kat," as she said her city friends called her, let us know she had permission to come back two weeks into the school year, Molly went into the bathroom and came out with a tissue. "My allergies are acting up," she said.

Linda began to call these afternoon visits *The News-Item* happy hour, and set aside a few minutes from her extra-busy schedule as both bookkeeper and police reporter. She cranked out more stories as a part-time beginning reporter than most of the veterans I knew in Dayton and had asked to share the court beat with Alex. She sent me two or three articles every afternoon. "Done," she would say. "Save. Send. Print. Finished."

"Why do you print those?" Molly asked one day. "You back everything up."

Linda pulled out the recycled tote bag she brought to work and stuck the papers into a manila file folder. "I want to become a better writer. I take them home and read over them." She dug around in the bag for a minute more and pulled out a plastic bag. "Pretzel, anyone?"

Alex almost always had a good story or joke to tell, often a farfetched description of a source who had to leave an interview to feed his chickens or who wore overalls with no shirt to a town council meeting. One day he told us a school administrator in the southern part of the parish spoke French to keep him from understanding what was going on. "What he doesn't know," Alex said, "is that I spent my junior year in France and am fluent. So I'm getting some really good tips."

Tom always finished his heavy work for the day at 4:30 p.m., starting the day at 7:00. You could set your watch by him. He would pour a cup of stale coffee, reheat it in the microwave—the inside of which looked like a crime scene—and scratch around on his desk till he found the crossword puzzle, faithfully torn from the Shreveport paper every morning. He hunkered over his desk, muttering as he read the clues and wrote his answers, wetting the lead with his tongue when he made an error. He saved a clue or two for us, sometimes I thought to humor us and sometimes because he was stymied.

When we casually gathered, we pounced on the words he did not have, competitive enough to want to be the one to solve the puzzle for him. Alex and Linda were especially ferocious, taking the same approach they took on news stories.

Molly and I, both missing Katy, sometimes went to the break area and talked, updating each other on a call or e-mail from Katy, communication that had lessened as the weeks passed. "She's having a great time," Molly said. "I don't think she wants to come home."

"She'll be happy to get back," I said, hoping it was true. "This has been a great experience, but she'll be overjoyed to see you and her family. She'll settle right back in."

"I miss her a lot at school." Molly assembled her backpack and the homework she had started earlier. "It was hard to begin a new year without her there. I don't have time to make many friends. I'm not part of the black kids, and I'm not part of the white kids."

Her remarks startled me. I never thought about the difference in the girls' races, although I had noticed it when they first became friends, when Katy floated around downtown, smoking cigarettes, and grieving her boyfriend.

"I'm sure you have lots of friends," I said, unsure what else to say. Only Marti and occasionally my old friend Ed had opened up to me in Dayton. Now every time I turned around, it seemed like someone threw me in deep water.

"I don't seem to fit in without Katy. I have fun playing with little Asa, though. Dr. Kevin lets me babysit when I'm free. She'd like to hire me when she's on call, but I can't give up my job at the store. I need the hours."

My heart ached as I watched Molly leave that day for her second job. She nearly always walked to the market, about ten minutes away, turning down the offer of a ride. "Katy says I need the exercise," she would say and head off, backpack on, head held high.

Today she ran back into the newsroom, backpack tossed aside, breathless.

"He's out there again. He's out there again," she said. "I thought it was a dog, but it's a bear. There's a bear climbing in the Dumpster."

"Yeah, sure," Alex said. "Real funny."

"Can't you see I'm working here?" Tom asked.

"No, I mean it. Come look!"

Tentatively we followed.

At first we could not see the animal, and I thought Molly was playing a prank on Alex. But sure enough a small black bear climbed out, stopping to stare when it saw us. Tammy grabbed the camera hanging around her neck and took pictures, and I gauged the distance between me and the door.

"Maybe we should call someone," Alex said.

"I'm calling my mom," Molly said, pulling her cell phone out of her pocket. It struck me as odd that Molly and Katy were always trying to scrounge up money yet were never without their phones.

"I meant someone like the police," Alex said. "Or Wildlife and Fisheries."

"Not a bad idea," I said. "Why don't you give them a call and get us a story on this?"

"Those bears can be dangerous, you know," Tom said. "He's probably looking for food. This hot weather puts them on the move." He was our resident expert on nearly any topic, an encyclopedia of knowledge both helpful and worthless. "Maybe we should call the radio station or post something online. Let people know to be on the lookout."

Every head in the parking lot—all seven of us—whirled in Tom's direction.

"But we compete with the radio station, Tom," Iris Jo said. "They sell ads against us."

He shrugged. "Maybe we shouldn't compete on this. It's a public service."

Tammy excitedly looked at her pictures and moved over to show Tom. He took his glasses off, squinted, and went through the images methodically. "Look at that rascal," he said. "He's eating my leftover chips."

"Tom's got a great idea," I said. "Why don't we post these online and let the radio station know they're there? We get publicity for the paper and let people know to keep an eye out. We can add any info Alex picks up, too."

So our daily online updates were born.

A group of excited game wardens came to get the bear, acting cool but with that undercurrent of people who love dealing with wild things. The capture created a spectacle of epic proportions.

Tammy recorded a video of the drama, our first to post instantly online. Tom pulled together facts about black bears in North Louisiana, and Alex wrote a short story about the sighting, capture, and release in a nearby national forest.

"Like it or not," Tom said, "I have officially been modernized." He started his walk home. "Katy will be so proud."

A relationship with Chris was not as easy as I dreamed it would be, but it certainly was fun and improved my cooking skills, which were weak by Green standards. His early season work as a football coach made my job as a newspaper publisher seem tame. He left his trailer as the sun rose and got home late and sweaty, usually still wearing his "Green High Rabbits" baseball cap and a coach's whistle around his neck.

Although I wasn't quite ready to put us on the front page of the paper, I was crazy about Chris and enjoyed every minute I spent with him. He didn't seem to mind keeping our relationship quiet either. By now I was certain I wanted this to work and tried to arrange my evening civic commitments around his astonishing number of parent conferences, meetings, and practices.

We made it a point to see each other almost every evening, sometimes at my place, sometimes his. The dogs were ecstatic when we came out after supper to walk with them or throw a tennis ball again and again.

"I think you're getting sort of fond of the mutts," Chris said one night, squeezing my hand and giving me a big kiss.

"Maybe." I leaned over to pet Mannix, my favorite. "I sure am crazy about their owner. He's growing on me."

"Their owner is wild about you," he said.

My cooking improved by baby steps, and I finagled a casserole or two from Pastor Jean, who never asked why I suddenly needed regular dinners, nor commented on my car in Chris's driveway after work.

"How're things going?" she asked one evening when I stopped by.

"Not bad," I said. "Not bad at all. I'm trying to pray every day, look on the bright side. Have some fun."

"Glad to hear it," she said. Without a word, she walked to the carport and lifted the lid on the big, old freezer. "How about a broccoli-rice casserole? And maybe some squash?"

I was particularly relieved when Chris pulled out food from his mother.

"She wants you to come over to eat," he said one night as we thawed purple-hull peas and a gallon bag of peaches. I had even worked up the nerve to make cornbread, referring repeatedly to a recipe from Iris Jo.

Intent on figuring out if I needed baking soda or baking powder, I didn't look up. "That sounds nice. Maybe we can do that one of these days when things settle down. First I need to learn how to make cornbread without a recipe."

"Not one of these days," he said. "It's time for us to let everyone know we're dating." He walked from the living room into his tiny kitchen and grabbed me from behind, lifting me off the floor and kissing my neck. "We might as well parade around town and get it over with."

"I'm not sure about eating with your parents," I said, turning to give him a hug and a kiss with the hope of softening the words. "I'm not quite ready for the cornbread competition."

"We have to go public sooner or later, Lois. But I'm a patient man. I'm ready when you're ready."

On the heels of the "bear scare," as it was now known around Green, I cajoled Molly into going with me to the football team's first scrimmage game. "I've never been to a Rabbit game," I said. "Iris says I've ruined my good name already. Please go with me."

Molly rearranged her schedule at the Pak-N-Go, and I picked her up at her rundown home, near Kevin's fix-up houses. I didn't see Molly's mom, but three younger children waved from the yard where they were swinging on a tire hung from a giant sycamore tree.

"I don't go to many games," Molly said, looking cute in blue jean capris and a sleeveless T-shirt. "But I suppose you have to now that you're dating the coach."

I smiled at her. "Looks that way."

The game was loud and fun. Cheerleaders unnerved me with their acrobatics, and a thriving nacho stand caught my eye.

"Coach is looking for you," Molly said as I scrolled through the program, wondering if we could pick up any of the advertisers. I looked up to see Chris scanning the crowd, a grin crossing his face when he spotted me.

I waved and leaned over to Molly. "He's really cute, isn't he?"

Her attention, though, was riveted on a player on the sidelines, who gave her a shy wave and ambled toward the water jug.

Chris and I boldly chose a big outing for our official coming-out date—the Labor Day Sweetheart Banquet, equivalent of the Valentine's Day parties held in the fellowship halls of many area churches. The odd party was a tradition at Green Community Chapel, although no one seemed to remember how it got started. Pastor Jean's theory was that it was on Labor Day weekend because "love is hard work."

Miss Ruth, an elderly church member, hosted it at her rambling farmhouse, rain or shine. I had skipped it the year before, in no mood for anything with the word "sweetheart" in the title and still not feeling quite at home at the little church.

This year was different.

Using my mother's recipe, I made cookies in the shape of hearts, with red sprinkles on top. I bought a new pair of bright-red jeans and a cute red-and-white shirt from Barbara Beavers, whose dress shop was one of our steady advertisers, and wore my hair in a ponytail with a red ribbon. I was going all out.

My stomach was jumping by the time Chris picked me up, looking quite handsome in khakis and a button-down collared shirt, starched and ironed.

"Washed the truck for you," he said, giving me a quick kiss as I climbed in. "Even threw out the Coke cans and catfish feed sacks."

I thought people might not notice we were *together* together, but I should have known better.

"Well, it's a sight for sore eyes, seeing you two together," Miss Ruth said when we walked onto her porch. "The quilting circle's been taking bets—no money, of course—on when you two would start dating."

She cackled as she took my cookies and Chris's grilled ribs. In Ruth's book, she had managed a social coup. "Look who's here, everybody. Lois and Chris."

People practically rushed us, as though we had just walked out of the church after a marriage ceremony. They hugged and gushed. A couple of older men told Chris it was "about time" he had "snagged this little lady." Chris squirmed slightly but held my hand and winked at me. I felt proud and happy.

Suddenly a silence fell over the room. It was almost as though the crowd took a step or two back, distancing themselves from us. A couple I vaguely recognized from church walked through the front door, Fran's parents on their heels. The former in-laws of my new boyfriend were here for our coming-out party. *Why had I not expected this?*

"Oh, my," Ruth said. "Let's get this food on the table."

"Hello, Chris, Lois," the Millers said, coming around me to hug their son-in-law. "Nice to see you."

After a few awkward comments, Chris, who at first seemed unfazed, made what appeared to be a gutless beeline to the den where most of the men congregated. I followed Pastor Jean into the kitchen, hoping I could do something helpful while waiting for the floor to swallow me up.

"It'll be OK, Lois," Jean said softly. "You're starting something new here. That's hard, but they understand. They want Chris to move on, and I happen to know they like you very much."

"They do?"

"Absolutely. One of the perks of being a pastor is that you hear opinions on most subjects before everyone else. That includes new couples and babies-to-be."

"They don't even go to our church," I said, glancing around to make sure no one was listening.

"Oh, the preacher's network is far-reaching," she said, wrinkling her nose and widening her smile.

"I like Chris so much," I said in a whisper. "But I feel like I can't live up to Fran. Everyone here knew and loved her."

"Lois," Jean said in her pastor voice, lowered a notch, "may I remind you that no one is perfect? I thought you had figured that out by now. Fran was a wonderful woman, but she's gone. Chris cares for you now."

"Another thing to pray about, I guess," I said.

"Good answer. Now, let's get these baked beans in the oven."

Moments later Iris Jo walked in with Stan, and all eyes shifted.

"A real date for you, too?" I murmured to Iris Jo.

"We try to keep it low-key," she said. "You know how things tend to get blown out of proportion in Green. If you and Chris are taking the bold step, Stan and I might as well, too."

"I must say it looks like the social life on Route 2 is improving," Pastor Jean said. "I even have Don here for the weekend."

Despite my early discomfort, the party was fun. I walked through the living room, trying not to look self-conscious. I studied the painting of the Lord's Supper over the couch, something that must have come from the grocery store in the 1960s. I examined doilies, placed with care around the room, even on the backs of chairs. I smiled at the plastic flower arrangement on the dining table.

Chris's parents, Estelle and Hugh, showed up as we sat down to eat and greeted me warmly, as though they saw Chris and me together every day.

"You look pretty in that red outfit," Estelle said. "Are you and Chris having a good time?"

"This is a wonderful party," I said, standing awkwardly by the couch. "Lots of good food."

"Well, we've got lots of good food at our house, too, Sugar, so you come on over when you can," she said. "We'd love to visit with you."

"Make that big old boy of ours bring you over for one of Estelle's famous Saturday breakfasts," Hugh said. He patted my shoulder and headed for the buffet.

Pastor Jean's husband, Don, brought his guitar, thrilling Ruth's great-niece, Jolene, who was learning to play and had her instrument, too. She opened with her signature song, "Jolene," of course. Then Don joined her in a remarkably good duet of "Love Lifted Me." Next they sang "Close to You," a romantic pop song I remembered listening to with my mother. The crowd joined in, horribly off-key, laying it on thick.

My favorite moment, though, was when everyone sang "I'll Fly Away," with Ruth banging it out on the piano. The older members of the group especially seemed to love the song, and I saw a person or two—not only women—dab their eyes.

Chris had joined me on the edge of the room when the singing started, and he put his arm around my shoulders. His mother looked at me and smiled. I felt as though I might fly away at that moment, carried off by happiness and the goodwill of these good people.

13

*The Green Elementary School Bunnies were victori-
ous for the third straight week Thursday, hanging on
to a narrow 21-20 lead over the Oak Ridge Spartans.
Unfortunately Star Defensive End Danny Zitto had to
be taken home after the third quarter because he ate
too much candy at half-time. "Danny's going to be a fine
high school player," his mother said, "but we need to
work on a few of the basics."*

—The Green News-Item

Katy returned in love with city life and an attitude worse
than Sugar Marie's.

"I'm home," she shrieked, dragging the word into two syllables and rushing into the newsroom as soon as she got to
town.

Everyone gathered around her, gushing over her new look.
She'd given up the punk hair for a sleek bob, in her natural
strawberry blonde. She wore a short, flared skirt and, despite
the warm weather, a smart, cropped jacket.

"Welcome back, Scoop," I said. "We've missed you."

She handed out souvenirs to each of us, including a designer
wallet to Molly, a giant pencil to Alex, a huge eraser "for big

mistakes" to Tom, and a fancy snow globe to me. "Because you like to shake things up," she said, giving me a hug.

Within a week, we all could cheerfully have killed her.

"At the magazine," she said, "we didn't do it like that."

"When I was in New York, people were more interested in national news."

"Have you seen those new Kate Spade purses?"

And on and on and on.

I put my money on Tammy to bring her down to size. But it turned out to be Molly.

"OK, *Kat*," she snapped one day, typing meeting announcements into the computer, no one's favorite job. "We get it. *You* went to New York for the summer. *You* had your dream job and your own blog. *You* got permission to start school later than everyone else. We get it."

The last three words came out through gritted teeth.

"Look who's talking," Katy shot back. "Ever since I got home you've been talking about 'this summer this, this summer that.' 'I was there for A.C.'s party.' 'I saw a bear in the parking lot.' 'I was the first to know that Lois and Chris were dating.' Well, la di da."

She stamped out of the newsroom with the drama worthy of any journalistic diva.

"Wait a minute," Molly said, jumping up and following her. "This is not over."

For the *Item*, this was a major brouhaha. My willpower was scarcely strong enough to let them go, but I knew they had to work it out. Forty-five minutes passed before both girls stalked back in and sat down at their computers, subdued and clearly ignoring anyone who walked through the room. I tried to ignore them right back, looking over page proofs for the upcoming Fall Festival section.

"Lois?" Katy popped into my office within a few minutes. "Have I been that bad?"

"Well, maybe a little," I said. I patted a chair, but she leaned against my desk.

"I didn't mean to be," Katy said. "I told everyone what an awesome editor you are, what a super paper this is." She paused. "When I came back, Molly was so close to everyone, like she had slipped into my spot while I was off playing clerk for the summer."

Now this was a twist.

"It's tough when you come home after an adventure," I said. "And it's tough when you're the one left behind. I can guarantee this won't be the last time this will happen. Might as well learn how to deal with it now."

"Couldn't you have at least called and told me about you and Chris? I hated being the last to know. Even some of the kids at school heard about it before me."

I tried but could not keep a straight face. "It just sort of happened, Katy. I wanted to keep it quiet, but I was no match for the Green grapevine."

"Is it serious?"

"I sure hope so."

"Me, too. Chris is such a nice guy, and you are perfect for each other. I'm sorry about that fight with Molly. She's my best friend, and sometimes I don't know how to talk to her. Do you think you and me and her could grab a burger before she goes to her other job?"

"Absolutely."

I was eager to tell Chris about the girls and their blowup, but he called to say he wouldn't be off work in time for a visit.

"Football is clobbering me, and if I don't get these tests graded, I'm going to be even further behind."

Early on, we had made the evening visits happen. But now my newspaper responsibilities and fall community meetings clashed with his obligations, conspiring against our visits.

"Good grief, Lois," he said one night as we sat in my porch swing at nearly midnight. "I meet you coming and going. Is your schedule ever going to settle down?"

Words of frustration, building for several days, flew out of my mouth.

"If that isn't the pot calling the kettle black, Mr. Dawn-to-Dusk. I wonder the same about you. Are coaches always this busy?"

"You're the one who has an event every night," he said, removing his arm from the back of the swing. "It's meeting here, meeting there."

"Me?" I spoke loudly enough that the three dogs ran to the steps to see what was up. "You're the one who doesn't have a spare minute for me."

He drew a deep breath. "It's both of us, isn't it?" He pushed the swing gently, moving us back and forth. "I want to spend more time with you."

"I want to spend more time with you, too."

"We'll have to work harder at this dating thing, try to make our schedules mesh," he said.

I pounced on that. "Why don't you come to the Chamber of Commerce banquet with me Saturday?"

"Saturday?"

"Saturday night. Free dinner at the Country Club."

"Do I have to wear a tie?" he asked. "Because I don't like tie events that much."

My anger grew like something out of "Jack and the Beanstalk."

"I didn't like high school football before I met you," I snapped.

"You don't have to be snide about it," he said. "I happen to be more comfortable in casual clothes. I'm not an important business leader like you are."

This had taken a nasty turn.

"It's definitely a tie event," I said. "Black-tie optional, to be more specific."

"You'll probably be busy, working the room, schmoozing your advertisers. I need to review game videos. Can we get together afterward?"

"It'll be late when it's over," I said. "We can see each other at church Sunday. Save me a spot." I wanted a playful tone to make this right but felt a far cry from lighthearted.

"We'll work it out," he said. But he didn't volunteer to go to the banquet with me.

The next morning, preoccupied and trying to back in next to the one car in the parking lot, I ran over the paper rack, the same one I had taken out during the ice storm.

"Got something on your mind?" I looked up to see Tammy getting out of the car next to me. *Could I ever get a break?*

"What *don't* I have on my mind?" I said, hoping my bad mood would shut her up. I knew better even as the thought crossed my mind. "Arson. A lawsuit. No profits at the paper."

"You and Chris having troubles?" she asked. "First fight?"

"No and no," I said, stooping to pick up the daily newspapers on the front steps and trying to keep from dropping my briefcase. "Don't see your boyfriend hanging around much these days. Troubles for you?"

Walt was wrapping up a big civil trial in District Court, so I knew that was a cheap shot.

"Well, actually," Tammy twisted her hair around her finger, a nervous habit I had not seen her exhibit in months. "I have some pictures to show you."

She pulled a strip of photo-booth shots out of her wallet, stopping me before I walked into the building. The first image on the strip was Tammy alone. The second was Tammy with a goofy-acting Walt. In the next, Tammy looked taken aback. In the fourth, they embraced.

"We're getting married," she said. "He took me to dinner and proposed in one of those photo booths at the outdoor mall in Bossier. Isn't that the sweetest thing you've ever seen?"

"Getting married?" My voice sounded squeaky. "I've had dishes in the sink longer than you two have been dating."

"Good line, Lois. I'll have to remember that one."

She tugged open the door, stepped into the lobby, and jumped over the counter, skirt and purse and all. "What can I say? I love the guy. He loves me. Not everybody's like you. We don't want to drag our heels."

"Ouch," I said.

Getting up my nerve, I laid down my briefcase and newspapers, took three steps back and made a running start. I jumped over the swinging gate, barely grazing it and landing on both feet.

"Wow," Tammy said. "You still have a surprise or two in you, Lois."

"I'm sorry I was a jerk." I hugged her. "You make a fantastic couple. Walt's a great guy."

"Too good for me," she said, shrugging. "He has more money in Starbucks gift cards than I have in my checking account. But I'll do my best to make a great wife." She stashed her purse and lunch bag and picked up the phone to take an obituary.

Striding into my office, I felt more like crying than I should have. Besides raising all sorts of questions about me and Chris, my conversation with Tammy steered me in another direction—doing something about the lawsuit. I had procrastinated by pretending Walt was too busy, but it was me who had stalled. I immediately called Walt's cell phone.

"Hey, Lois," he answered in a whisper. "What's up?"

"Why are you whispering?" I asked. "Where are you?"

"I'm in the lobby of the courthouse waiting for the session to begin. If the judge sees me on my phone, I'll be toast. Have you decided about the lawsuit?"

"I don't know." I waffled anew. "There's no rush, right?"

"Please let me get my paralegal digging on what Major told you. What could that hurt? Why are you dragging your heels? It's not like you."

"I want to keep this quiet, Walt, and figure it out on my own. Let me dig a little more down here first."

"Your call," he said.

"Why didn't you tell me you and Tammy are getting married?" I asked.

"Oops, sorry. They're summoning us to the courtroom. Got to go. Talk to you soon." The line went dead.

Walking through to Iris Jo's desk, I picked up a paper clip and fidgeted with it. An image of my former editor doing the same thing at my desk popped into mind. My job then had seemed stressful, but it seemed like a piece of cake at the moment.

"Morning, Iris," I said. "What do you think?" This must have been the hundredth time I had asked that question. "Any new ideas? Found our answer yet?"

"I've gone through old files, looked at notes from when the mystery sale supposedly occurred, sorted through every bank statement since time began. Tried to piece together who would be so mean to set fires like that. I don't get it."

"What are we missing?" I asked. "It has to be here."

"I was probably off track thinking Major could help us," she said. "Maybe he's trying to distract us. That's the conclusion I come up with."

"But he was so certain about the sale. What good would it do for him to lie?"

"Maybe he lies for the heck of it," Iris said.

"We'll figure it out. I will not let those horrible men win." I headed back to my office. Instead of starting on my day's editing duties, I pulled out the history of the paper again and went through it, searching for clues.

"Aunt Helen, what in the world went on here? Why didn't you tell me before you died?" I whispered. "Did Chuck and Dub own the *Item* or not?"

14

The town of Coushatta has decided to ignore the alligator seen under the bridge at the city park, according to a gator expert who works in the hardware store there. "He'll leave you alone if you leave him alone," Morris Fouche said. "Just don't give him people food, especially marshmallows." Is this neighborhood correspondent the only one who finds it odd that the "Don't feed the alligator" sign is posted next to the "All pets must be on a leash" notice?

—The Green News-Item

Movement near the Dumpster caught my eye.

Was the bear back?

I strained to see in the twilight.

Slowly the figure stood up and climbed into the bin. As he climbed out, I could tell it was a man—the produce man from out on Route 2.

"Good evening," I said, walking his way.

The man drew back. "I collect cans. OK? Recycle."

"Certainly," I said. "I'm Lois. We met at your produce stand." I held out my hand.

"Joe Sepulvado," he said, taking off a worn work glove and shaking hands. "Happy to see you again."

"We'll save the cans for you." I winced when I heard myself speaking loudly, as though that would somehow help him better understand. "Come get them anytime. We'll leave them by the back door."

"My thanks," he said and headed down the street. I watched him as the daylight faded. He picked up an item here and there and dug in trash set out for garbage pickup.

"I felt so ashamed," I told Chris later at my house. "I practically throw that kind of money away. He scrounges through garbage for a few cents."

"You offered to let him have the newspaper's cans," Chris said, pulling me down next to him on the couch. "At least you're helping."

"What kind of help is that?"

"It's a start. He's one of the regulars at the Spanish prayer service at Grace, by the way. Nice fellow. He and his wife haven't been in Green all that long. They send most of their money home to family."

I laid my head on his shoulder. "The other day at the grocery store the woman in front of me had to put back a carton of eggs because she didn't have enough money. I wanted to pay, but I didn't know what to do. We take it all for granted."

Wrapped in the warmth of my cottage and the nearness of this man I cared so deeply for, I wanted to forget about those who had less. But I couldn't let it go. "I don't get it. The poverty in Green is relentless. If God is as loving as everyone says, why does He let people suffer? And why some people and not others?"

"I ask myself that frequently, especially at school," Chris said. "Some of the students haven't had a new pair of shoes in who knows how long, and they barely scrape by with free breakfast and lunch. Their parents rarely show up for them. The best I can come up with is that we're to look for ways to help those who are put on our path. And we should always be thankful for what we have."

I asked Pastor Jean about it a few days later in the living room of her parsonage. "I cringe when I hear people say they choose to live like that, with next to nothing," I said. "Those little boys you take care of didn't choose poverty. Mr. Sepulvado and his wife didn't. I can't imagine anyone waking up one day and saying, 'I think I'll be poor.'"

"You may be trying to answer the wrong question," Jean said.

"What do you mean?"

"You're asking *how* this happened. Perhaps you need to ask what we can do about it." She picked up the worn Bible from her desk, the one she frequently thumbed through as she preached. "Want to know the scripture that haunts me most?"

"Is this going to make me feel even guiltier?" Jean's personal sermons always made me squirm.

"I doubt God wants us to feel guilty. I do think He wants us to act. Certain scriptures won't leave me alone. I figure that's God trying to tell me something I need to do."

"Lay it on me," I said, moving over to the spot Jean called her "prayer chair."

"Jesus pulls together this group of disciples, a ragtag band of men he has chosen to make the gospel real. He asks if they love him, and they are quick to say yes. Know what Jesus says?" She paused. "Feed my sheep."

She held up the Bible again. "Ordinary people, flawed, just like you and me. A basic way to show love."

"*Feed my sheep.*"

The words lingered in my mind as I wandered home. Once more I felt inadequate. Unsure. Selfish.

Kevin and I talked about it over dinner one night. She had become my best friend in Green and inspired me with her commitment to improve the community.

"I can't quit thinking about the poor people in Green, what we're supposed to do to help, what they have to do to help themselves," I said.

"Big hurts. Little resources. Every time I turn around I see it," she said. "You can't imagine the stories I hear in my office."

"Even driving over here I see the hardship," I said.

"It's not only the seasonal workers." She pointed to the quilt on the floor, where Asa was playing. "That boy, my gift, is a constant reminder. His mother and sisters died because they lived in a substandard house without a smoke alarm."

"But you're doing something about it. You help the neighborhood." I picked up Asa and walked to the front window, open to a cool breeze, and pointed down the street. "Look what your Mommy is doing. She's renovating those three houses right there. One-two-three. Isn't she wonderful?" The baby giggled and swatted at the window screen.

"Kevin, you've already fixed up a third of the houses you bought. The place looks different, feels different. And it's all because of you."

She walked over to the window by us and Asa immediately turned to her. "Your Aunt Lois is wrong," she said to the boy, kissing his tummy. "I planted a few seeds. Good people in Green give time and money to make this work. Aunt Lois even came out here with a hammer a time or two."

"Only because Chris made me," I said. "You do so much. You adopted A. C. You look after his grandpa. You help your neighborhood. I give away a few aluminum cans."

"You're doing a lot more than that," she said. "You bring Green together. You work to clean up downtown and this

162

neighborhood. You've given Katy and Molly jobs, and you help them see something in themselves. The problems are big. We can walk away overwhelmed, or we can do our little part. That's all we can do, Lois. Our part. Touch a life here and there and hope to make a difference."

I got down on the floor and made Asa laugh. "Yeah, but you're saving lives. I'm putting them in the paper."

Feed my sheep. The thought lingered as I drove home.

With fear and a little trembling, I took the topic of poverty to the Green Forward group. We had already planned the second annual Green's Gift to Green day for the Lakeside Annex neighborhood, a clean-up day and giant Christmas celebration for children. Maybe we could do more.

"Is there something for these newcomers?" I asked. "Some sort of fund-raiser or grant program or maybe even Spanish and English classes to help us communicate better? Anything?"

"We're biting off more than we can chew if we add another charity project," one member said. "To be blunt, if those people want to live here, they need to adapt on their own. It's part of being an American. Like Pastor Mali here." He pointed to the beloved foreign pastor of the downtown Methodist church.

"I'm an immigrant, like the people we're talking about," Mali said, his Polynesian accent slowing his words. "It is a very challenging life God has chosen for me, and I've had opportunities, for education, travel, steady work. The poor among us need such chances."

A member or two rolled their eyes. Another sighed and crossed his arms. Several nodded.

"I like your thoughts, Miss Lois," the Baptist pastor said.

Mayor Eva, a strong advocate of the association and a great contributor to local causes, was silent during most of the meeting. Often what she said brought us to action, and I was pleased when she finally spoke. "Maybe we need to broaden our Green

Forward Goals, tie our events to an ongoing program that goes a step further."

"Mayor," one of the bankers said, "I don't disagree with what you're saying, but it's hard to keep something going. We're all busy. Stretched." He was among a group of leaders in Green who would say they didn't disagree with you and then proceed to do just that.

"Citizens worked hard to get where they are, and they expect other people to do likewise," the town's florist said. "There are plenty of programs out there. We need to choose creatively."

"As a business owner, I'm hit hard by financial issues," I agreed. "But we need to help others, don't we?"

Rose, who had taken a vacation day from her mail route to attend the meeting and work on her antique store displays, moved her lunch box to the middle of the table. "We have always taken care of each other in Green. And we must find a way to do that with new folks. That's how our kinfolks got by. Your aunt made you a new dress when you started school, or your brother slipped you money for groceries, or you lived with a neighbor for a while."

Coming from Rose, that was a major speech. Postal worker. Antique mall owner. Farmer's wife. Activist?

"We could start small," she continued. "Offer seed money for tiny loans, like they do in foreign countries. Have some sort of community event to raise money. Not only for newcomers to our country. Homegrown folks, too."

"I'll be happy to look into what is involved in a micro-loan program," Duke, my banker and friend, said. "If each business puts up a hundred dollars, we could get something going."

Pastor Mali took out his wallet, dug through a disorganized collection of papers and pulled out a hundred-dollar bill. "I keep this for emergencies," he said. He placed it in the middle of the table.

The mayor, Sugar Marie on her lap with a sweater on, opened her tiny handbag and laid down a matching bill.

Rose counted out four twenties, two tens, and a five and put them on the stack.

Before we adjourned, we had raised $1,200 for our yet-to-be finalized micro-loan program.

I loved these people, I was even beginning to feel the slightest soft spot toward Sugar Marie, who licked my hand as she and the mayor were leaving.

Watching more closely, I noticed ways people in Green helped others all the time.

Pastor Jean clearly spent much of her spare time and cash on the three Mexican boys, babysitting when their mother worked.

Molly, who had less extra time than anyone I knew, tutored a neighborhood child on Sunday afternoons. Before long, she talked Katy into helping another child.

Kevin's parents, already serving the community in myriad ways, took Asa's grandfather into their home. "Until he's on his feet," Mr. Marcus said.

"He'll be such a help with the baby," Miss Pearl added.

Asa stayed with his grandparents at their motel on the lake while Kevin worked, and I sometimes stopped by for a quick visit during the day. These occasions were mostly excuses to play with A.C.

"He's growing like a bad weed," Papa Levi said. "And smart. That boy is smart."

"Kevin's already signed him up for preschool at the Baptist church downtown," Pearl said. "And he loves Sunday school. I think he might grow up to be a preacher."

"The good Lord spared him, that's for certain," Levi said. "God has a special purpose for this child."

This certainty about what God had in mind still made me uncomfortable.

"Why would God spare Asa and not his mother and sisters?" I asked Iris Jo on one of our lunchtime walks at the park. Louisiana days were beautiful in autumn, cooling off with a hint of fall color. We tried to get out of the building as often as possible.

"I wish I had an answer for you," she said. "I struggled with that more than anything after Matt was killed. I often wonder why God did not take better care of my son. Could I have prayed harder for his safety? Was I not a strong enough believer, a good enough Mom?"

"Iris, you were a wonderful mother, and your faith inspires me every day. It was an accident, a horrible car accident."

"Was God with Matt at that moment?" Iris asked, tears in her eyes.

I was in way over my head here.

"I'm not sure about a lot of things, Iris. But of this I'm sure. God was with Matt at that moment."

"So many people told me that God takes the best and brightest to live with Him in heaven. Do you know how that sounds when your child has been killed? I'm sure Mr. Levi feels that pain, too. He lost a daughter and two granddaughters. How does he bear that?"

"What if God does take the best and brightest?" I asked. "What if there is a greater purpose, something we are too limited to understand? Something that will be clear one of these days?"

I stopped and pretended to tie my shoe, completely uncomfortable with this talk, wishing someone else could take over.

"You're beginning to sound like Pastor Jean," Iris said, smiling and wiping away the last of her tears. "Thanks for listening. Sometimes the hurt is so intense I can barely hold it in. It washes over me at the most unexpected times."

"It's my fault," I said. "I always expect you and others to come up with answers I should be finding on my own. I dug all these feelings up in you today."

"You know what's strange?" Iris asked. "I needed to talk about Matt today. You gave me an opening when you asked why Asa survived when his family didn't."

She reached out and grabbed my hand as we walked.

"I know God had a plan when you came into my life. You've been a gift to me as I've searched for answers."

"I wouldn't have lasted a week in Green without you, Iris. I probably never would have gotten here in the first place. I guess God knew we needed each other."

Feed my sheep. Iris and I had fed each other, enabling each of us to go on.

Digging into my little backpack, I pulled out our bottles of water, the sugar-free drink mix we put into them, and two bananas. We walked to a picnic table and sat down to eat, both of us apparently ready to change the subject.

"Since we seem to be tackling tough topics today, I've got an idea I've wanted to run by you," I said.

"One of those famous Lois ideas? Are Stan and I going to have to paint another house? Or does this involve more home-made cookies?"

"Maybe cookies," I said. "Pearl was talking about little Asa and preschool and Sunday school. Ours is a smaller church, but why don't we start a Kids Club at Grace Chapel, maybe invite the children who live out in the country, the ones who need an extra hand? Do you think that's possible?"

"Lois, when I'm around you, I think anything is possible."

Unused to such comments, I dug in my pack and pulled out a couple of rice cakes. "Dessert," I said. "Not as tasty as your cookies, but better than nothing."

After we picked up our things, we quickened our pace, nearing the spot where I had encountered Major Wilson a few months ago. A large, late-model SUV sat where I had parked that day. A new pickup sat next to it. "Iris Jo, is that Major's Suburban over there?"

Iris squinted, making a visor with her hand. "I think so." She looked closer. "Look, there's Dub's truck. Now what in the world could they be up to?"

"Like you said, maybe Major is in cahoots with Chuck and Dub," I said, whispering even though the men were at least a hundred yards away.

A big, old car pulled into the park, slowed, and went to the remote parking area, next to the two vehicles. The helmet of black hair was obvious.

"It's Eva," I said and started to wave. Then I hesitated. "I feel like I'm spying or something. Like I've done something wrong. Maybe we'd better head back to work."

The mayor stopped by the newspaper within the hour.

"Good ideas at the downtown meeting," she said. "I've made some contacts. There may be city money to help out."

"I think we're on the right track," I said, feeling the slightest bit awkward.

"Speaking of tracks, Lois, I saw you and Iris Jo at the walking path today. Why didn't you come over and say hello?"

"You looked like you were in the middle of something," I said. "The journalist in me is wondering what business you could possibly have with your brother and Dub."

"It's personal," she said, picking up her keys and her phone. When she got to the door, she turned. "It's a very long story, but I wish I had stuck with Dub all those years ago."

15

Two Green men, brothers Jerome and Jeff Johnson, were detained by local police after their sibling argument spilled into the street in front of the Pak-N-Go. Jerome, 24, and Jeff, 22, tussled over who would ride "shotgun" on a trip to Shreveport. The two were passengers in a car driven by their cousin, Jacob Johnson. Green patrol officer Dwayne Perkins said he would have driven the inebriated men home but a local motorist had to swerve to avoid the brothers as they wrestled on the pavement. "We can't put up with goings-on like that," Dwayne said.

—The Green News-Item

The farm correspondent brought three large gourds, one made into a birdhouse, another shaped like a snowman, and the third intricately carved.

The reporter from the Cold Water community carried a blueberry pound cake. Her sister-in-law from Amos Cutoff was not to be outdone. She brought pumpkin bread and a Tupperware container full of what she called "country trash," a mix of nuts and dry cereal.

"Thank you so much," I said, taking the items. "You are the nicest correspondents in the world." *The Green News-Item's* future depended on its connection with its readers. These dozen awkward reporters were the thread that pulled all that together. The Community Correspondents Supper and Suggestion meeting was about to get going. I had decided the event was worth the money, even though our budget was tight.

The room buzzed louder when Anna Grace, the food correspondent, well into her eighties, walked in with a new laptop. "The kids gave it to me for my birthday," she said. "Thought I'd bring it to take some notes and wanted to show you a picture or two."

Tammy rushed to her. Before I could address the group, the two women—more than fifty years apart in age—compared notes on photography software.

"Thank you, Lord," I whispered. I was trying to notice the small blessings in my life, to be more aware of the little delights, instead of yielding to what seemed to be my general tendency to focus on the worst.

"Those things aren't worth a dime if they crash on you," farmer Bud said, killing my euphoria. "My sister, the librarian down in Lake Charles, says students come in crying all the time after they've lost their term papers."

"My nephew paid his credit card online, and they took out $3,447 instead of $347," the Ashland reporter said.

"We have lots of ground to cover," I said, not wanting the negativism to pick up steam. "I know some of you don't like driving at night."

"Thank goodness for daylight saving time," Tammy said.

"Don't get me started on that," Bud said.

"You want me to say the blessing?" Anna Grace asked. I still had trouble remembering that you rarely ate at a meeting in Green without "offering thanks."

After the prayer, as the food was served, I stood. "If you don't mind, I'll talk while you eat."

"Talk all you want," Bud said. "Not everybody gets invited to Oak Crest Country Club."

"Does this mean we're getting a raise?" someone said from across the room, bringing laughter.

"We can't afford raises right now, so we thought we'd try to buy you off with dinner," I said. "We wanted to do something special for you. Alex and Tammy keep reminding me how hard you work."

"Hear, hear," someone said, and nearly everyone raised a tea or water glass.

"We want more of your Community Items for the newspaper. Each of your personal voices is an invaluable contribution to *The News-Item*," I said. "We are adding regular items to our Web report, with special pages for each of your areas."

Murmurs rippled through the room, the kind you hear on soap operas during the verdict of a trial.

"I'm not doing any Web report," one person said.

"Told you so," Tom muttered to Tammy.

"I am," Anna Grace said. "I want to call mine 'Scene around Green.' Get it?"

"I'm willing to try," Bud said. "Don't want the world passing me by."

My role as owner and publisher made me want to pull my hair out and hug someone, often simultaneously. This meeting was a classic example. These ordinary citizens—"good folks," as Tammy called them—added something to the newspaper that could never be replaced by technology or full-time reporters.

"To close tonight's meeting," Alex said, "let's come up with story ideas. Miss Lois and the rest of us want to stress that while new media is important, we are not abandoning our traditional format."

"I think he's finally growing up," Iris said quietly.

Tammy listed the suggestions on a flip chart, keeping up with the suggestions in an organized way.

"The best door decorations for Christmas," a veteran correspondent said.

"Favorite family recipes for Thanksgiving," someone else called out. I could tell that did not sit well with Anna Grace.

"Personality profiles on school secretaries, before they close all the country schools," the woman from Cold Water said.

The list grew.

"Did you say purple martins, Mr. Bud?" Tammy asked.

"Yes, when they come, how to get your martin houses ready. A reminder that you need to paint the roofs green."

"That's nearly six months from now," Alex said.

"It'll be here before you know it," Bud answered.

"What about the hummingbirds?" Anna Grace asked.

"The story ideas are flying tonight," Tammy said, and everyone laughed.

In minutes we planned contests to see whose purple martins came earliest the next year, whose clematis vine bloomed first, and who had the cutest Christmas card photos. Each of those would be conducted online, with the top winners published in the paper.

I did my best not to jump in. "Their enthusiasm reminds me to relax and trust them," I said to Iris.

"You say that now," she said with a smile. "Wait till the first time you get an irate call about something 'cute' they wrote."

"One last thing," Bud said. "I'm trying to help the 4-H club decide on a community service project, and the *Item* could work with them. I suggest a book fair at the library downtown. We can ask the citizens of Green to donate used books, a way to recycle and help others." He thought for a second. "We'd be making Green even greener."

"Did Bud just make an environmental joke?" Alex said.

"We can get that downtown group involved," Anna Grace said. "Raise money to give laptops to high school students who can't afford them."

Tom jumped in. "We can have an essay contest. Print the winners in the paper." He looked a bit sheepish. "And post all the entries online."

"I can take pictures of the students," Tammy said.

The group continued to throw out ideas, when a waiter walked up to where I sat, leaned over, and whispered in my ear. "Ma'am, the mayor's on the phone for you. Says it's important."

I quietly excused myself and picked up the phone in the foyer.

"There's another fire at the newspaper," Eva said. "Seems to be contained outside."

"Not again . . ." My spirits, so incredibly high a minute ago, plummeted. "At least I don't have to start calling people. Everyone's here with me. We'll be right there."

The meeting broke up dramatically, with correspondents yelling their best wishes as I ran to my car, grabbing the keys from the valet and peeling out. In my rearview mirror, I saw the stream of cars falling in behind me, like a loose-knit funeral procession.

This time it was the Dumpster.

"It took longer to hook up the fire hose than it did to put that one out," the Fire Chief said. "It was a good practice drill, more or less. It's awfully dark back there, though. Easy for someone up to no good."

The now-familiar young deputy walked up. "Mayor, Miss Lois," he nodded slightly. "Good news. We finally have a perp."

"Perp?" Eva said, frowning.

"Perpetrator. We know who has been setting the fires. We've made an arrest. Caught him red-handed, right by the Dumpster, around the corner there."

"Oh, thank you," I said. "Now maybe we can move past this."

The deputy pointed to the squad car where the Police Chief talked to someone, the car doors standing open.

In the back seat sat Mr. Sepulvado. It was nearly dark, but I thought I saw him wipe a tear from his face.

"You can't be serious," I said. "That's the produce man. Mr. Sepulvado has been setting fire to the paper? He burned down my garage?"

"He's guilty as sin," the young officer said. "Not talking. Hasn't said a word in his defense."

"Because he hardly speaks English," I said.

I looked at Eva. "What possible reason would he have to set those fires?"

"Criminal mischief, pure and simple," the officer said before Eva could answer.

"I thought you were going to call me when you had trouble," Chris said from behind me.

I whirled around. Somehow seeing Chris made me believe everything would be all right.

"I'm so glad you're here," I said. "They've arrested Mr. Sepulvado, the man we were talking about the other night. They say he set fire to the trash bin tonight. Set all the fires."

"Impossible," Chris said. He hugged me. "You OK?"

"I guess so," I said, feeling an urgent need to run. "I'm not sure how many of these 'not too bad' fires I can take. This seems to get worse and worse. It can't be Mr. Sepulvado. You said yourself that he's a nice man, a good man."

"Don't worry. We'll figure this out." He gestured toward the police car. "Let me talk with Doug."

Getting the matter resolved took more than a talk with the chief, and Chris returned with a grim look.

"He says Mr. Sepulvado was by the bin, had matches in his pocket," Chris said. "Someone called in the fire, just like before. When they got here, he was back there."

"He was getting cans," Linda said, walking up as we talked. "Everyone knows he makes extra money going through the garbage. Since when is that a crime?"

The Chief wanted to make an arrest in the unsolved fire cases more than he wanted to let the alleged arsonist go. "I'll release him to you," he told Chris. "First we have to take him over to City Hall and book him. Collect bail."

"You'll have to get an interpreter if you do that, Doug." Linda stepped up again. "It's the law if your suspect can't speak English."

"This guy should know English by now. No interpreter. No coddling just because you do-gooders don't want to believe he might be guilty." The chief looked slightly less certain as he spoke.

"Before you haul him off, Chief," I said, "let me get a few things straight." I took the reporter's notebook from Alex. "On the record. For the paper. And for my attorney."

"Your attorney?"

"The one I intend to hire to prove an arsonist is terrorizing the town while we waste valuable time and energy on a produce salesman. Who, by the way, has permission to be on my property."

Chris stopped my tirade. "Lois and her crew want to find the person setting those fires more than anybody," he said. "But we find it hard to believe this is your man."

Someone was harassing me. It was not Mr. Sepulvado.

The next few weeks felt scrambled, as though the parts of my life were a dozen eggs cracked and stirred. Marti's wedding was close, and I needed to leave town. The newspaper was barely making enough money to meet the bills. Mr. Sepulvado had been charged and released on bail, which Chris had put up. The Green Rabbits were on a historic winning streak, thrilling Chris and making me hoarse from screaming. Dating the coach made me something of a hero, much more glamorous to most citizens than owning the paper.

With so much going on, I could not relax. I thought about going by to see Pastor Jean or walking over to Iris Jo's desk for a heart-to-heart, but Kevin rescued me with a call to say she had splurged on a babysitter. "We'll have girls' night out at a place with glassware and tablecloths, no drooling allowed," she said. "My treat."

When I arrived at the restaurant, Iris, Jean, and Kevin greeted me with surprise birthday wishes and big hugs. "Surely you didn't think your friends would miss your birthday two years in a row," Kevin said. "We know we're a few days early, but since you're going to be gone . . ."

Last year my birthday had gone unnoticed. I hadn't mentioned it, not all that keen on getting ever closer to forty and not sure what my future would bring. This year, in the midst of all the hubbub, nothing had been said of my turning thirty-eight.

"You women are the best." The words came out with a squeal, a sound that felt odd coming from me. "How did I get so lucky to have you in my life? How would I get through all my crises without you?"

Before we ordered, they insisted I open the gift, sitting in the middle of the table. It was a gorgeous green leather tote bag, "Lois" stitched on it, with an outside pocket to carry a newspaper in.

"For the trip to Ohio," Jean said.

"Like the one in that catalog you've been looking at," Kevin added.

"For all that stuff you carry everywhere you go," Iris said. She passed the breadbasket my way.

"I love it," I said, "and I love each of you."

"So what's wrong then?" Iris asked. "You've been stewing over something all day. You're not acting like the carefree bridesmaid-birthday-girl."

"Is it that obvious?"

"It took us a while, but we've pretty much got you figured out by now," Kevin said. "You share our cares, we share yours. What's the problem?"

"For one thing, I'm getting too close to forty. I'm still waiting for that divine road map you three keep hinting at." They laughed. "Then there are the fires. I don't like things I can't figure out, and those are a scary mystery."

"There's something else, too, though," Jean said. "Something different."

"Go ahead and confess, friend, or we're taking that present back," Kevin said.

"This trip to Marti's wedding has me freaked out, and I don't know why. I hate that feeling."

"Your best friend's getting married. That's always bittersweet," Kevin said. "Don't you think it's going to be hard on us when you and Chris get married?"

"Me and Chris married? Did I miss something?"

"I know you won't let yourselves go there yet," Kevin said, "but I'm already there in my mind, planning what I'll wear. Why do you think we didn't have your initials monogrammed on that tote? And when it happens, we'll be happy and sad. Admit it. That's how you feel about Marti."

"You're uneasy about going back to Ohio, too," Iris said. "It's hard to leave home, but you'll be glad when you come back."

"That's the weird thing," I said. "Till recently, Ohio was home. Now I'm leaving home to go home to leave home to come home."

"Your life is here now," Jean said. "You face big decisions, but you'll know how to handle them when the time comes. You always do. Enjoy the wedding, and come back to Green refreshed."

Leaving the restaurant with my new bag and my three friends, I felt happier about the months to come. Whatever life threw at me, they'd be there to help.

———

The police department halfheartedly agreed to Eva's request to increase patrols near the paper. They were certain they had their man and were ready to move on to other matters, such as teenagers cruising on the south side of town, playing loud music, and littering. They lectured us again on installing better lighting, and Stan apologized and ordered a fixture that put out as much light as midday sun. No one would wander back there unnoticed.

"I hate to leave Green to go to the wedding," I said to Chris, wishing things were more definite between us. We had not discussed our relationship since shortly after football season started. "Everything seems so unsettled. What about the paper? What about you?"

"I'll be waiting for you when you get back. So will the *Item*. Go and have fun. See your old friends. Do whatever it is that bridesmaids do. I'll take you to the airport and be waiting for you with open arms when you get back."

Saying good-bye to Chris up in Shreveport was much harder than I expected. I was used to being with him nearly every day.

"I'm going to miss you," I said.

"Ditto," he replied. "Come on home as quick as you can."

⸺⧂⸺

The wedding in Dayton was on a beautiful fall day—well, beautiful in Green, according to Chris by phone. In Ohio, it fell into the awful category. "It's raining up here, a cold rain," I told him.

Marti certainly was not bothered.

"Isn't this the most wonderful day?" she asked as we adjusted her dress. "I can't believe I'm getting married. I'm so blessed to have Gary."

"You're going to be a great wife," I said. "Wife! Think about that." The twinge of regret I had felt when the two started dating was entirely gone.

"I hope it works out for you and Chris. You think it will?"

"I'm not sure he wants to marry again. It's complicated since he lost his first wife. He has family and so many friends and his Green Rabbits."

"But those don't take the place of you," she said, picking up her veil.

"Sometimes I'm not so sure. The paper gets in the way, too. It would be hard to be married and run *The Green News-Item*. We both have such time-consuming jobs."

"You'll figure it out," she said. "There's someone special for you, and I think it is Chris. Love is on the way. I feel it."

"All brides think that for their bridesmaids," I said. "Let's get this show on the road."

Perhaps it was the gray drizzle that made the church seem so much warmer, or maybe it was the certainty with which Marti and Gary said their vows. The ceremony was serene and hopeful.

The next day I drove by my old condo, past the *Dayton Post*, and finally to the cemetery where my friend Ed was buried. I found it almost impossible to believe two years had passed since his death.

"They are so happy," I said at his grave, wishing he were there to hear, hadn't died so suddenly. "Marti was syrupy. You would have hated it."

Glancing around to make sure no one else was out in the nasty weather, I moved closer to his grave. "It scares me sometimes to think I might have lived my life without the gift of Green. I don't get it, though, how this plan and purpose stuff works."

I leaned over, reached into my new green tote bag, pulled out a rolled-up copy of the latest edition of *The Green News-Item,* and placed it next to the tombstone.

"Thanks, friend."

16

*A week after a Logansport family unearthed bones along-
side their personal pond while planting a garden, a sister
and niece in Eastern Oklahoma were struck by lightning
and killed. The area family admitted worries over being
cursed for "unsettling possible sacred Indian grounds."
Their pastor and friends from the Beulah Methodist
Church have stepped in to help.*

—The Green News-Item

It was a handshake deal."

Knocking but not waiting for Iris Jo to answer, I barged into
her house, talking as I went.

"It was a handshake deal."

She turned down the burner on the stove and wiped her
hands on a faded towel. "What in the world are you talking
about, Lois?"

"It hit me when I turned onto Route 2. Chuck and Dub sold
their share of the paper to Aunt Helen with a handshake. They
didn't have a written contract."

I watched Iris try to get her mind around this idea. "You
may be right."

"I'm sure of it." I was disappointed by her lack of enthusiasm. "What else could it be?"

"Talk to me while I cook." She gestured from the table to the stove. "I'm frying chicken and can't leave it. Stan's coming over for supper."

"I have figured out the answer to the problem we've wrestled with for months, and you're worried about fried chicken?" I said. "Didn't you tell me you were eating healthy?"

"Stan likes fried chicken. I like Stan. So, fried chicken it is. Tell me what you've come up with." Iris moved about the homey kitchen with the ease of a pro.

"I guess I went a bit overboard, rushing in like Nancy Drew," I said. "I'm desperate for everything to settle down, the lawsuit, the fires, the mystery Major threw at us."

"Stan and I want the lawsuit taken care of, too, so we can all move on with our lives. I'm not sure about something as simple as a handshake, though."

"It makes sense if you think about this being a family deal. Helen didn't need anything in writing when Chuck and Dub sold her their part of the paper." I rocked a salt shaker back and forth on the table. "Is that too far-fetched?"

"Maybe not. Most of the time Helen trusted those boys," Iris said, "although she handled them cautiously. She wouldn't need anything official. And she wouldn't be worried if she lost money in the deal. Money didn't matter that much to her."

Together, with grease popping on the stove, we pieced together a possible scenario.

"They needed money, and money mattered a lot to them, especially to Chuck, who has a family and what you might call expensive tastes," Iris Jo said. "Helen knew they would inherit the paper anyway, so she went ahead and let them borrow against their future. I guess it didn't affect the shares of their brother and sisters." She boiled water to make iced tea, something no Green meal was served without.

"Why not just give Chuck and Dub the money? If she knew it was going to be theirs anyway, why tie the paper into it?" I asked. "Why would she take their shares of ownership?"

"Because she didn't trust them *that* much," Iris said. "Nobody understood those boys better than Helen. She knew she had to have something to hold over their head. Especially Chuck."

"So why let them handle the sale of the paper to Ed and then me? If they didn't even own it anymore?" I stood up and walked over to look out the window over the sink. "Am I making more of this than I should?"

"Helen was at an age where she didn't need to fool with the paper anymore," Iris said. "Chuck and Dub didn't want to do much heavy lifting, but they sure liked the clout the *Item* gave them."

"When Helen died, they inherited back their shares of the paper. Right?" My thoughts were racing. "But I had already bought the paper by then. They got the money from Aunt Helen's estate, so they didn't get the paper."

"Looks that way," Iris Jo said.

"They can't win the lawsuit because they haven't owned the paper for years. When Ed and I bought the paper, we were in actuality buying it from Helen. Now I have to prove that without mentioning Major's name."

"You want to stay and eat?" she asked, but I was already on my way out the door.

The answer was in Aunt Helen's history of the paper, in a messy envelope in the back of the binder. Stuffed among a collection of papers, the plain envelope looked like something you would pay a utility bill in. It was not sealed.

"More history," it said on the outside in Helen's handwriting.

"*Item* sale complete," the handwritten piece of paper said. "Chuck and Dub to Helen." The date and all three of their signatures were accompanied by one witness: Major Wilson.

I had my proof, unofficial, but proof nonetheless. This was family business, done Green style. Now I had to figure out what to do with it.

When I called Walt, he wanted to take it to Chuck and Dub's attorneys immediately and put it into the court record with a motion to dismiss. Terrence, who had been formally retained to help us, came to Green with Walt to convince me. "There's no alternative," he said.

"I want to do right by Aunt Helen," I said. "Maybe that means settling this mess informally."

Walt was quicker to see where I was going than Terrence was.

"Lois wants to use a handshake deal to get them to drop the lawsuit," Walt said. "Keep this from escalating."

"I don't get it," Terrence said. He was a handsome, formal man, and all business. "We have the proof we need. They filed suit against her. We have reason to suspect they have been trying to intimidate her with a series of fires. If you ask me, this has already escalated."

The two lawyers seemed to have forgotten I was there.

"But what would we lose by trying?" Walt said. "Maybe meet casually. These family deals don't always follow the standard rules. You know that as well as I do."

"I thought Lois Barker was a hard-nosed newspaperwoman who took on corruption and shook things up," Terrence replied.

"She is, and she does," Walt said, finally catching my eye and smiling. "But she does it in her own Lois way."

"It's worth a shot, if that's what the defendant wants," Terrence said. "Let's make it happen."

We met the McCullers at a conference room at the newer motel on the edge of town, the most neutral site we could come up with. Terrence and Walt coached me on what to wear, what to say, and how to act.

"I understand," I said. "Quiet Southern woman, dressy dress, apologetic."

"Aunt Helen, I'm doing this for you," I said under my breath when I got out of the car. Four attorneys were present, along with Chuck, Dub, me, and Iris Jo. The meeting was to be off-the-record, no court reporter present.

"This is highly irregular," Terrence said, "but I don't suppose we have anything to lose."

"Chuck, Dub," I said as we got started, "we asked for this meeting today to resolve the dispute over *The Green News-Item*."

"What's this all about?" Chuck nearly snarled the question. "Get to the point, Miss Barker."

Terrence frowned and looked as though he might stand up, so I plunged in, not looking at the notes the attorneys helped me write.

"I want to apologize if I was rude about my ownership of *The News-Item*," I said. "You built a good newspaper, and I want to help it get even better. To make a difference in Green, in Bouef Parish. What progress can our community make if it doesn't have the strong presence of its newspaper?"

Chuck started to interrupt, but Dub nudged him.

"I had the greatest love and respect for your Aunt Helen and can't imagine she'd approve of the way we've been handling this," I continued. "I ask you to drop the lawsuit, and I will do my best to address the differences you have with me."

"This is a crock," Chuck said, standing up.

"Why don't you hear her out?" Dub asked.

"I'll tell you why. She snowed everybody—you, Aunt Helen, the mayor." He looked at Iris Jo as he said those words and then pointed to Terrence. "She comes in here with her high-faluting black attorney, thinking she can change my mind. I would rather see that paper boarded up than have her run it."

Chuck stormed out of the room, followed by Dub and his attorneys, who were mildly apologetic.

"See you in court," Terrence said to their backs.

"Well, we tried," Walt said.

I stood abruptly, stung. "I swallowed my pride, and this is what I got? Take this forward. You two do whatever we have to do to win." I looked heavenward. "Sorry, Aunt Helen."

The experience hardened my heart. Those arrogant jerks would get their comeuppance. If they didn't want to settle the matter personally, I would humiliate them publicly. They chose how this game would be played. That was not my fault.

I went directly home, too angry to go to my office, and frustrated I had agreed to help with the new Wednesday night program at church. I picked up the phone to call Jean and tell her I was under the weather, dialed four numbers, and slowly put the receiver down.

Feed my sheep.

I grabbed a book on the coffee table and threw it across the room. For good measure, I threw another. Then I picked them up and put them back on the coffee table and walked down the gravel road to church, my head still feeling as though it might explode.

The instant I stepped into the noisy room at Grace Chapel, my attitude shifted. The sweet children who gathered made it hard for me to stay upset, and I felt ashamed and calmer as I stepped into their area. The evil McCullers of the world would not overcome the goodness of these little ones.

"Miss Lois, Miss Lois," the kids shouted. "Look what we made." They so clearly felt at home in the class, listening intently to stories about Bible characters and blurting out funny answers to questions from Iris Jo, tonight's teacher.

"They make trusting look so easy," I said to Pastor Jean.

"They've discovered what you haven't figured out yet," she said with one of her small smiles. "It *is* easy."

Only a dozen or so in number most weeks, the children were as noisy as a church full, rushing to the Wonderful Wednesday Supper line and shoving each other to get the first spot. "They're taking all the rolls," I overheard a woman say, and my heart sank. "Their mothers should provide food. This isn't a free cafeteria."

"Children," Pastor Jean stepped up. "Quiet, please. There's plenty for everyone. Let's have our prayer, and we'll help you fix your plates." While it seemed as though she were addressing the children, I knew she also spoke to the adults.

Feed my sheep.

After that night, I brought more food to the suppers, stretching my culinary skills. The potluck was a cooking competition of sorts, a collection of homemade food that made me want to push in line, too.

"Getting pretty fancy, aren't you?" Jean asked one Wednesday evening. "I used to think I needed to pray for a cooking husband for you. Maybe that's not necessary after all."

The number of children grew each week, with various church members picking up a carload here, a vanload there.

Disruption of the services also grew, while the patience of a few outspoken members shrank.

"They're tearing up the lawn," one deacon said. "We've worked for years to get that grass to grow."

"Someone's got to supervise them," an elderly woman snapped. "They are running wild. They're going to hurt somebody."

Others were more charitable, or at least willing to wait and see.

"They don't know any better," an older woman said. "They'll learn."

"They're happy to be in church," someone else said. "We can show them how to behave."

As Chris and I cleared up the classroom, Iris pushed a hand through her hair with a heavy sigh. "Some people plain don't like Pastor Jean," she said. "'Ever since that woman preacher got here . . .' If I've heard that once, I've heard it two dozen times."

"They turn their backs on needs," I said.

"Give them a little time," Chris said. "They'll come around."

"I don't want to give them time," I said. "It's wrong what they're saying. They would rather write a check to some mission overseas than help children right here on Route 2."

"Don't you think you're being a little hard on them?" Chris asked. "You know how tough change is. People have to get used to the idea that our church is different than it was."

"I thought churchgoers were supposed to love other people, be kind, all that stuff it says in those Bibles they carry around with them," I said. "They're a bunch of hypocrites."

"Sure they are, in certain ways," he said. "We all are. Most people try to do the right thing. If it becomes us against them, we've got a big problem."

Iris picked up the clutter that littered the room, juice cups and paper thrown everywhere, tacking a drawing to the wall. A giant sun dwarfed three small children, standing in flowers.

"It hurts my heart, when I overhear ignorant, cruel remarks," she said. "But don't overlook those who are serving. Consider how far we've come."

Pastor Jean appeared at the door as we talked.

"Whatever we do, we have to do it with love," she said. "Without love, there's nothing."

"This is hard for me," I said. "Somehow I've got to learn how to love other people, people like Chuck and Dub and Major and some of those little old ladies who I want to . . ."

"Maybe you'd better stop while you're ahead," Chris said.

We headed into the parking lot.

Marti's words at her wedding came to mind. "Love is on the way."

I had thought she meant romantic love. But something deeper was going on here.

17

Mrs. Paralee Ross, from the Godley Prairie commu-
nity, relates that the former husband of her great-niece
Barbara Ann has been reincarcerated after his trial on
charges of illegal squirrel hunting ended abruptly when
he jumped through the window of the City Court
in Tyler, landed in the bushes, and fled.

—The Green News-Item

Hundreds of books were donated for the first Green Book
Fair, lining every inch of spare space in the newspaper building until they could be priced and sorted.

With Tom mounting a vigorous editorial crusade, people
cleaned shelves, attics, and garages of boxes of old books.
Paperback romances poured in, along with tattered church
hymnals, cookbooks, and self-help guides. "This could be the
most fun I've ever had at my job," Tom said. "I'm getting paid
to go through books."

In a surprise move, Dub brought two boxes of Aunt Helen's
books. "These might as well be put to use," he said, bumping
into me in the lobby, his arms full. "Aunt Helen would have
been your first customer at the Book Fair."

"I can't wait to see what she read all those years," I said, trying to be polite. "Thank you, Dub."

As he walked out, the mayor walked in, looking smart in a fall pantsuit, luminescent pearls at her ears and her throat, Sugar Marie on a rhinestone leash. "Good to see you, Eva," Dub said, nodding his head. "You look pretty, as usual." He pulled a tiny dog treat out of his pocket and handed it to Sugar. I'm fairly certain I gasped.

"What brings you down here?" the mayor asked, fidgeting with the dog. I wondered again what they had been talking about that day in the park with Major.

"Book Fair." He pointed to the boxes on the counter.

"Glad to hear it. It's a very worthy cause," Eva said. "Take care of yourself."

Worn out from moving books, editing stories, and going over the next week's potential advertisements, I shuffled my feet to the car that evening. My cotton shirt was wrinkled, and my knit skirt had a big smudge on it. A piece of paper caught my eye, under the edge of my tire. Not only was I a mess, my parking lot was trashed, too. Litter was one of my pet peeves in Green, and I snatched the paper up, wondering why people couldn't throw their garbage in cans.

This was a page torn from a puzzle book, and I crumpled it up and tossed it into a container on the edge of the parking lot. As it went in, I realized it had my name written on it.

The reporter in me could not let it go.

Sighing, I gingerly reached down to pull the paper out, avoiding a fast-food hamburger wrapper and a soft drink cup.

"Trying to encroach on Mr. Sepulvado's territory?" Linda's voice made me jump.

"I'm looking for something."

"I noticed. Want me to help?"

"Here it is." I held up the small sheet.

"Would it be out of line for me to suggest you buy your own, unused puzzles?" she asked.

"This is weird. Look." I held it out to her. "It has my name on it."

"And?" She looked as confused as I felt.

"It isn't mine." I studied it more closely. "I've never done one of these in my life."

"Let me see. I love them," she said, snatching the sheet from my hand. "Difficulty Level: Medium. Time: Ten months. Ten months? That's crazy."

I looked over her shoulder. "Why?"

"This, see . . ." she pointed at the paper. "This is where you enter the time it took you to do the puzzle. Why would someone write ten months on there?"

She started figuring in her head. "These numbers don't make sense. They're wrong. Whoever did this is lousy at it. To top it off, they did it in different colored ink. They might want to stick with pencil."

The words "whoever did this" reverberated through my mind, a regular refrain this year, what I thought of now as the year of fire.

"Why would that have my name on it?" I asked.

"Maybe someone jotted a reminder to give you a call or something."

"Maybe," I said, taking the paper back and squinting at it. I thrust it back at her.

"Linda, look at those numbers again. Could they mean something?"

She studied the sheet intently, her look one I often saw when she was reporting or working on our budget. "I don't know what you're getting at. In fact, you're not making sense at all."

"I'm going crazy. I keep expecting us to figure out who set the fires. I look over my shoulder constantly, expect clues everywhere I turn. Before long I'll be interrogating people in the grocery store."

As I spoke, Linda studied the sheet once more. "There is something a little odd about this," she said. "Look at the first one in red. And this one in blue." She held the puzzle toward me again. "This has to be a coincidence."

She pulled out her reporter's notebook and referred to notes on the inside back cover. "I've got the details of the fires written here." She pointed with a stick pen. "The numbers on this puzzle are the months, dates, and times of each fire."

Panic hit first. Then befuddlement. Ten minutes ago this was an annoying piece of litter. Now it might be an answer to who was hassling me.

"How peculiar," Linda said. "Why would anyone go to all this trouble? It doesn't tell us anything."

"Maybe it does," I said, my brain thawing. "These other numbers—the ones in green—what are they?"

Linda wrote a note or two, took out a tiny calculator and figured and then scratched everything out and started again. She did that three or four more times before looking up.

"They could be phone numbers, or birthdays. Maybe even social security numbers, I guess, or a drivers license number or street number."

We got into the front seat of my car; the fall breeze had a bite to it. "Well, I'll be darned," she said after a minute more of rewriting the numbers, her lips thinned. "That's Chuck McCuller's phone number there, his house address there."

"You've been watching too many detective shows," I said.

"Lois, I'm sure," she said, a determined note in her voice. "I dialed that number plenty of times when I worked for Major. I know that address. When they built the subdivision, Chuck insisted his house number be his birth date. It was a big joke and a pain to the people who laid out those streets."

She handed the sheet to me, frowning. "Maybe I sound like a rookie reporter, but somehow this implicates Chuck in the fires."

"I don't get it," I said. "Who would do this, leave this?"

"It sounds ridiculous, but anybody could have been trying to warn you," she said. "Nearly everyone in town comes to the paper at one time or another. Maybe you need to sleep on it. Think about anyone unusual you've seen around."

"Should I call the police?"

"Doug would probably put you on the first plane back to Dayton if you told him this theory," she said with a small laugh. "I'd hold off on that until you know more."

After hours of figuring, referring back to my calendar and checking and double-checking Chuck's address in the phone book, I went against every piece of advice anyone had ever given me.

I went to Chuck's house. Alone. At night.

"Miss Barker, what an unpleasant surprise," he said, when he opened the door. He wore a pair of dark Levis and a long-sleeved plaid shirt and held a glass in his left hand. "Have you come to your senses and decided to hand the paper over?"

"Why do you want to run me out of town?" I asked, boldly stepping into the beautifully decorated hallway, an Oriental runner partially covering the oak floor.

"I don't like you," he said. "You know that. You don't belong here."

"You dislike me enough to set fire to my desk and my garage . . . and my Dumpster." I practically sputtered the last word. "To sabotage the paper you claim to love?"

"Of course not," he said. "You're crazy if you think I would go to such juvenile lengths to get rid of you. I'm doing it the grown-up way. With a lawsuit."

His smugness irritated me almost as much as the fire on my desk.

"You and your brother have not owned *The Green News-Item* for years," I said, bluffing for all I was worth. "You merely managed it for Aunt Helen."

"You don't know what you're talking about. Now get out of here before I call the police and have them haul you out."

"You broke into the pressroom and caused that fire, and you set all the others, dirty work meant to get me to leave. You know schedules and entrances and ways in and out. You're slippery. You stole from your family while running the paper. You ruined Dub's life with your manipulation, dragging him along with your schemes, even kept him from the woman he loved." I was making this up as I went along, and my voice rose.

"Quiet down," he said. "My wife's in the back. I don't like to bother her with my business life."

"You don't want her to know you're an arsonist and a liar? She already knows you're a thief after that whole Lee Roy mess. Might as well add these new qualities to the list."

"Get out," he said through clinched teeth. "You have no proof. That's what you're best at, throwing out accusations with no proof."

"You and I both know I have proof. I can assure you it will be front page news." I didn't have hard evidence, but I had intuition, a note from Helen, and a love for Green.

"Get out," he said, sloshing his drink onto the carpet.

"I have proof. Aunt Helen left me what I needed," I said softly and slammed the door loudly.

I drove fast all the way home, looking in my mirror to make sure he wasn't following. I locked every bolt at my house, including the bedroom door, and wished I had a dog to sound the alarm if someone came near.

I knew Chris and others would be furious when they found out what I had done—and all apparently for naught. But I felt better. I had handled it as I thought Helen would have wanted me to.

The next day I foolishly handed Linda a brown envelope that contained a copy of Helen's "newspaper sale" note, the puzzle sheet, and a short account of my theories. "Take this home with you and put it somewhere safe. Don't ever mention it to anyone unless I turn up in a burning Dumpster."

"And just yesterday you said *I* was watching too many detective shows," she said.

Middle of the morning, Tammy popped into my office with a grin.

"That good-looking lawyer from Shreveport is here to see you, Lois. And his buddy, too." By now Tammy was sporting a big diamond engagement ring and planning "an apple-and-pewter theme" wedding in the summer.

The sight of Walt and Terrence together early in the morning instantly made me nervous. "What did you two do," I asked, "synchronize your watches to meet in Green? Not fair to Terrence. He has further to drive." I hoped my tone covered my jitters.

"We've come to celebrate," Walt said. "Chuck and Dub told their attorneys this morning to drop their suit. Chuck placed the call at seven a.m."

"No explanation. Just 'drop the lawsuit,'" Terrence said. "Might I add that my jaw dropped right along with that news."

"Thank heavens! I can't believe that actually worked," I said, regretting the statement immediately. I shifted slightly, avoiding eye contact.

"What worked?" Terrence asked.

"Lois, did you have something to do with this?" Walt said.

I looked at him directly. "I prayed."

The news spread immediately through the small building, and everyone gathered in my office for a telling and re-telling of Chuck's early call. No mention was made of my visit, although Linda had a smirk on her face when she brought me a cup of coffee.

Walt and Tammy wandered off for an early lunch together, and Terrence made a few calls and tried to get me to admit I had meddled.

"No comment. No comment. No comment," I said.

"I'd better head back to Alexandria," he said. "I've enjoyed working with you and wish you the best. You've got a fine little newspaper here."

"Terrence, I need you to come back to Green."

"No problem. Shall I call Walt?"

"This isn't a legal matter. I hope you'll speak to the Kids Club at my church about being an attorney. We're having a special camp Thanksgiving week. You'd be great."

"Not unless you tell me what you did to get the suit dropped," he said with a smile on his handsome face.

"Let's just say it could only have happened in Green." I picked up my calendar. "Now about Kids Club."

———

At the book sale a week later, I bought at least half of Aunt Helen's books, including two church cookbooks and a notebook full of handwritten recipes. Tom had placed it on the collectibles table, and I paid top dollar for it, knowing it was worth every cent.

"Look at this." I waved my latest find at Iris Jo, who was flipping through a paperback of some sort. She laid the book down quickly.

"What have you got there?" I glanced over her shoulder. "Living with Breast Cancer," I read out loud. "You buying that for someone?"

There was an awkward silence. My heart skipped a beat before she spoke.

"I have breast cancer, Lois."

"Maybe not," I said stupidly. "Maybe it's a scare."

"Not a scare," she said. "My surgery is in two weeks. Linda's all set to take over for me in the office. You've had so much on your mind with this lawsuit and the fires that I dreaded telling you." She picked the book back up. "To be honest, I've dreaded telling anyone. The only people who know are Stan, Linda, and Pastor Jean. I thought maybe this book might have some tips."

Dozens of people milled around the book tables, but no one paid attention to us. "I don't want people looking at me funny," she continued. "You know that 'she's got cancer' look. They already give me that 'she lost her son' look. I don't think I can take any more pity."

My heart was heavy, but I was determined to show optimism.

"Hmm . . ." I pretended to hesitate. "I believe my friend Iris Jo would tell me I need to let people care, allow them to help me. She would say it's in the Bible somewhere."

"Second Timothy," she said, laughing. "The apostle Paul wrote to his young friend for help."

"I knew it," I said. "We'll talk about this more later."

"Lois, Lois," someone called my name, and I turned around to see Anna Grace and Bud sitting at cash boxes, Anna Grace waving. Iris Jo and I walked over to the money table. "We've already raised nearly three thousand dollars for our laptop scholarship fund," Bud said. "Can you believe that?"

"What a great idea you had," I said. "What would we do without our community correspondents?"

"I want to donate a thousand dollars more," a voice behind me said. I turned, face to face with Major Wilson.

"I thought you were broke," Bud said. Iris Jo winced.

"Not too broke to help a good cause," Major said. "I checked with the parish, and your Go Forward Green group or whatever you call it can have Spanish lessons in the workroom at the courthouse." He shook hands with Bud and kissed Anna Grace on the cheek. "You'll have to come up with a teacher, though."

By closing time, I had a pretty good idea what most people in Green liked to read. The turnout was astonishing, and I loved watching the recycled books leave for new life. "I can see these used books on coffee tables and bedside stands and bookshelves all over Green," I said to Tom.

"I'm taking a few home with me," he said, pointing to a stack teetering at close to two feet high. "I even got a new crossword puzzle dictionary."

I walked across the room, dodging to miss Katy and Molly, who carried books for older customers. As I moved out of their way, I bumped into Dub McCuller, and his armload of books toppled to the floor.

"I'm so sorry," I said, bending to help him pick up the books. "Good to see you. I haven't had a chance to thank you for dropping the lawsuit."

"My pleasure," he said and grabbed a familiar-looking puzzle book right before I could pick it up.

18

Sunflower Girls leader Annie Roberts, mother of Melanie, age 6, held a tea in honor of Sunflower Moms last Saturday. She used her beautiful silver teapots and trays as she served finger sandwiches and cookies, prepared by the little Sunflowers. What a delight it was to see each girl dressed in their best Sunday school dresses and gloves, such a rare sight these days. All of the ladies agreed that this made for a wonderful weekend. "I feel so blessed today," Annie said.

—The Green News-Item

Katy's college entrance scores were lower than she had hoped.

Molly's were much higher than she had expected.

"I've got to bring these up," Katy said, waving them as she ran into the newsroom one Friday afternoon. "I want to go to a good school. My parents are going to kill me." Her mind raced as fast as her body. "Did you like my feature story on Page One today?"

"Great job. Her daughter's already been by to pick up extra copies," I said.

"I write good stories. I make decent grades. Why didn't I do better on my test?" She was whining, rare for Katy.

"These results are not that bad." I studied them again. "You may have to take it again, but you're a smart girl. You can do it. Don't forget test scores are only part of the requirements. Go back and look at the entrance packets. Someone told me the essay is one of the most important parts at most colleges."

"I want to be recruited," she said. "I want to be on the staff of the college newspaper and work up to editor. I want to go somewhere big and interesting."

Molly was oddly silent, hanging back when Katy headed out.

"What about you," I asked. "Did you take the test too?"

"I did."

"So how'd you do?" I could not figure out why she was so reticent. She was a somewhat shy girl but had been part of the *Item* family long enough that she usually jumped right in.

"I did OK. Better than OK. Good. Very, very good." She grinned.

"Congratulations!" I jumped up to hug her. "Katy stole your thunder."

"College means a lot more to her," she said, twirling one index finger around the other. "She gets carried away."

"Your scores confirm what we've always known—how incredibly smart you are. You don't seem very excited for someone who got that kind of news."

"It's not a big deal," she said, shoving her things into her backpack.

"Of course it's a big deal. Most kids would kill for those kinds of scores. You've got good community involvement and work experience. You're an admissions office's dream."

"Miss Lois, my mother works full time as an aide at the nursing home and still has to sell meat pies to make enough money to buy groceries. You really think I can go to college?"

"Those good scores can go a long way toward helping you get a scholarship. I have lots of contacts, too."

"It's not only the tuition money," she said. "I help around the house with my brothers and sisters. And some of the money I make goes to, you know, my family. We barely get by."

Once more I realized how very much I took for granted.

"I can't stay and talk about college because I've got to get to my job at the Pak-N-Go," Molly continued with an unusual sarcastic tone. "Don't you think that just about sums it up?"

"We'll come up with something. At least let me give you a ride to work to celebrate."

That evening Chris and I went out to eat, our rare Friday night date when a sporting event did not get in the way.

"I want both girls to go to college," I said. "They don't have to go to an Ivy League school, but they need to go somewhere. I've got to figure out what to do."

"Here we go again. Another Lois Barker crusade. What are you thinking this time? Bake sales?" Chris smiled, reached across the table and laid his hand on mine. "For a woman who claims to have a hard time loving others, you sure stick your nose into their business a lot."

"Are you scolding me?"

"Not at all. I'm proud of you."

I shrugged, half embarrassed, half pleased. "Those girls mean the world to me. I want to help them in any way possible. Thank goodness we have a few months to figure it out."

"There's not a doubt in my mind that you will," he said. "Not one single doubt. Do you keep a list?"

"A list?"

"Of the people you're helping at any given moment," he said. "You must have about a dozen right now. I know you're worried sick about Mr. Sepulvado, too."

"Until they drop the charges, there's a black mark against his name," I said. "You and I both know the McCullers were behind the fires. Ever since I confronted Chuck, everything has been quiet. Just because he didn't confess doesn't mean he didn't do it."

"I'd rather not bring that up," Chris said. "It still gives me high blood pressure. Don't ever do something like that again."

"I know it was stupid, but I was desperate. I thought if Chuck and Dub dropped their suit that somehow the police would figure it out and drop their charges against an innocent man."

"That's what I'm here for. You've got to let me help fight your battles. Deal?"

"Deal," I said.

"I'll talk to Doug again," Chris said. "See what he's come up with."

On that evening, Chris invited me again to join him for Saturday breakfast at his parents' house. He seldom missed the family gathering, but I'd never worked up my nerve to go, even though we were clearly a couple. I was a coward.

"It's high time you took part in this Craig family tradition," he said. "My mother cooks a mean biscuit."

"I don't know, Chris. I usually go to the office on Saturday mornings, catch up, clean off my desk . . ."

"Go to the office after breakfast. You know we start early. Leave when you need to. That's the way this works."

"Are you sure?"

"Sure I'm sure. We wouldn't have invited you if we didn't want you to come. Is there a problem?"

"I see your parents at church and out and about, but . . ." I took a large drink of water. "Are you ready to bring a girlfriend home?"

"Oh, I get it," he said. "This is about Fran, and my having been married before." He touched my hand across the table-top. "Let's put it this way. If I don't bring you home soon, my mother is likely to come get you herself. She likes you."

"Likes me? She hardly even knows me."

"She likes whoever makes her boys happy. And you make this boy very happy."

"I'll be ready at seven," I said. "I'll try not to wear pajamas."

His mother was as delighted to see me as Chris said she would be. The rest of the family acted as though I came every week.

"Good article yesterday on that woman who makes the purses," his sister-in-law said. "I think I might try to make one of those."

"I liked the feature on the basketball player," one brother said. "Seems like school sports might be getting a little more coverage these days."

"Give her a break," Chris said. "Surely you can come up with something better than that lame joke."

"Try my mayhaw jelly," his mother said. "You've never had better."

"Best jelly and cathead biscuits around," his father said.

I did not even know what a mayhaw was before I moved to Green. The weird little fruit didn't grow in Ohio. I guessed the oversized biscuits must be catheads, another new one on me.

As the group scattered, I volunteered to help Miss Estelle with the dishes.

"I'm going to look at daddy's new leaf blower," Chris said, leaning over to kiss me. "I'll be right back."

I was so startled by his affection in front of the family that I drew back, as though I'd touched a hot pan. "I'll visit with your mom," I said. "No rush."

Estelle and I chatted while she washed and I dried. "I don't use my dishwasher all that much," she said. "There is something satisfying about cleaning up after a good meal. Besides, it gets me out of sitting around listening to all that talk about hunting and fishing."

"I like to wash dishes, too," I said. "I'm not the neatest person, but I appreciate a clean kitchen."

"It's so good to have you with us today," Estelle said. "I've been hounding Chris to bring you over."

"We're both busy." I hesitated, trying to decide how much to say. "I guess, too, he wasn't ready."

"He thought you weren't ready," she said, putting the biscuit pan, which she wiped out but did not wash, in a cabinet with a loud crash. "He was a little intimidated at first with you being the owner of *The News-Item* and all."

"You think so?"

"I know so. He's been serious about you for a long time. It took him weeks to work up the nerve to ask you out." She stacked the old, chipped plates into the cabinet. "It was time for him to get on with his life. I was scared he might never find someone." I liked that she did not say "someone *else*," as though I were a follow-up act.

"I felt that way when I moved down here," I said. "I told my friend Marti I was never going out on another date."

"Heard you dated that lawyer fellow from Shreveport when you first moved to Green."

"We went out a few times. Nothing serious." Now the conversation was making me perspire.

"Chris didn't like that very much," she said. "I think that's about the time he decided he needed to spend more time with you."

I practically ran to Chris when he walked back into the house. "Guess I'd better be going. Have some work to do," I said. "Thank you so much, Miss Estelle, Mr. Hugh, for the breakfast."

"Come anytime," they said at the same time.

"Mom giving you the fifth degree?" Chris asked as we climbed into his truck. "Asking you about your intentions and all that?"

"Pretty much."

He kissed me tenderly when he dropped me at my house. "See you tonight, sweetheart. Thanks for going to breakfast."

⌘

Iris Jo was at the church cemetery when I pulled in a little later. My presence seemed to rattle her.

"I came to tell Matt about my surgery," she said, pointing to her son's grave. "I know he's not here, but it comforts me."

"It's like standing on holy ground," I said.

She wrapped her arm around my waist. "If you don't watch it, Lois, you're going to make a preacher."

"Make a preacher?"

"Something my mother used to say. What are you doing here anyway?"

"Between you and me?" I asked.

"Always."

"I came to visit Chris's wife's grave." Iris waited for me to continue. "I like him so much it scares me. More every day. As a matter-of-fact, I love him."

206

"Finally," Iris Jo said. "Hallelujah! It's clear he feels the same way about you."

"Thank goodness back at you." I was warmed by the exuberance of the usually serious Iris Jo. "I sure hope so, but he doesn't say much about his feelings. I haven't told him yet. I'm trying to get used to the idea myself."

"I've known Chris a long time," she said. "He's not a big talker. But there's no doubt in my mind he loves you."

"I don't know if it's all right. The timing." I pointed to the tombstone. "'Loving wife. Devoted daughter. Generous friend.' How's a woman supposed to compete with that?"

"You're not competing. You're making Chris happy. Fran would be OK with it," Iris Jo said. "She never wanted Chris to spend the rest of his life alone. She told me that." Iris squatted and traced Fran's name on the stone. "She would have pre-ferred to live, but she didn't. Chris did. Life goes on. That's one of those lessons I learned the hard way."

"I don't want to ask her permission to love her husband," I said. "But if I go on without her blessing, I feel guilty. So many people knew and loved her. I want them to be OK with it."

"You don't need her permission, or anyone else's," Iris said. "This is about you and Chris, not about all those other people you seem worried about. Listen to your heart, and do what is best for the two of you."

"Iris," I walked over to her son's grave, a few feet away. "Do you struggle with doing the right thing?"

"Every single day. I make choices and hope and pray they're the right decision at the right time. Especially now with this cancer. I don't want to lose a day."

"You always seem calm, content."

"I have faith that things are going to work out all right—even when I can't imagine how. Most days I feel like I'm doing what I'm supposed to do." She adjusted the silk flowers on Matthew's grave. "You're the same way."

"Me? Not at all."

"You make it harder than it sometimes needs to be, Lois, but you leave the rest of us in your dust."

"Me?" I asked again.

"You, you, and you," she said. "You do what needs doing, help whoever needs helping, find a way around whatever gets in your way. That's probably why this Chris thing is hard for you. You're used to running things. You have to give up control. That scares you."

"Have you been watching Oprah?" I asked and sat down on the cold ground. "I love the paper so much, and it takes a lot of my time. Chris was deeply in love with a woman who died. That took so much of his heart."

"He has made peace with that," Iris said. "I suspected it for more than a year. When he came over here and buried his wedding ring, I knew it for certain."

"Buried his ring?"

"He put it there. See." She pointed to a tiny patch of dirt. "I happened to walk up as he was leaving. 'It was time' was all he said. I think in his own way he was telling Fran he had found you."

"Oh. My." I couldn't stop the tears. "Really?"

"You're way too tough on yourself, Lois. Accept the fact that there was someone before you but you're the person Chris has chosen now."

I looked at Iris. I looked at Fran's grave.

"I do," I said.

19

Addy Thompson won the Rodeo Days pickup giveaway at a radio station in Shreveport, driving home a brand-new Ford F-150. "I was just about going to have to buy me a new truck," Miss Addy, 92, said. "If anyone wants to buy my old truck, I'll throw in the bed liner and one of my chocolate pound cakes if you don't want to haggle. It runs great and doesn't quite have 100,000 miles on it."

—The Green News-Item

The name on the window could not be right. Surely I would have heard.

I unlocked the door and rushed in, wondering who the Saturday clerk was. No car was in the lot, so it might be Katy, who often caught a ride, or Tom who usually walked from his old house around the corner.

"Tom? Katy? Tammy?"

I glanced at my cell phone, as usual unreliable. Three missed calls.

Katy was at her desk, earplugs in, transcribing a tape. I tapped her on the back, and she jumped.

"What's the deal with the deaths?" I asked. "Who told you Chuck McCuller died?"

"Tammy said that one would shake you up," Katy said. "She's gone out to Route 2, looking for you. Tried to call you at home and on your cell."

"Are we sure?" I asked.

"He's dead all right. The funeral home has already called. The Police Chief confirmed it," Katy said, digging around on her desk. "They faxed this 'statement' a few minutes ago." She used air quotes as she talked, one of her favorite devices. "I already wrote the obit for Tuesday. Made a few calls. Figured you might want to put it on the website."

"Apparent heart attack, this says. Died at home during the night. Well, I'll be." I was stunned. "Do the others know?"

"I think Tammy talked to Iris Jo. I called the mayor for a comment," Katy said. "She hadn't heard it yet. That wasn't cool. Seemed pretty upset. Said she'd call me back."

"Any word from Dub?" I asked.

"Not yet. I thought we might wait till later or you might want to call him yourself. To be respectful, you know."

Impressed with her initiative, I nodded. "Some college is going to be so proud to snag you."

I went to my office and called Walt, who had already heard from Tammy.

"How are we going to clear Mr. Sepulvado's name?" I asked. "I should have gotten on this sooner, forced Chuck's hand."

"Lois, you did force his hand," Walt said. "You somehow, I'm still not quite sure how, got him to drop the suit. We don't have proof he set the fires."

"I know he did," I said. "It was all part of his hate campaign against me."

"Well, he's dead now. He won't bother you anymore," Walt said.

I rushed over to the high school, where Chris was working on a football fund-raiser. "I won't have to fight that man again,"

I said when I told him, suddenly sobbing against his chest. "I feel bad for his family but I'm sure not sorry he's gone from my life." Relief flooded me.

Over the next few days, the details of Chuck's death remained veiled in secrecy, and Alex was convinced a conspiracy was afoot. "The cops usually tell me tons about cases like these," he said. "They had to go out to the house since he died at home. They're tight-lipped on this one."

"Do you think he killed himself?" Tammy asked, the day after the funeral.

"No way," Linda said. "Way too vain. Probably drank himself to death."

"I never saw him take a drink." I then remembered the glass he held the night I visited him. "Guess he hid that."

"He was a mean drunk," Linda said. "Saw him lose it a time or two with Major."

"Maybe he's not dead," Alex said, enjoying the speculation. "The coffin was never opened. Maybe he ran off to Mexico or something."

"That'd be ironic since we know how much he loves Mexicans," Tammy said.

"He's definitely dead," Katy said.

"And you would know that how?" Alex asked.

"My mom played the organ at his funeral. She sneaked a peek in the coffin."

"Your mother?" Tammy said, a look of admiration appearing on her face. "I never would have figured her for the type."

"She wanted to see it with her own two eyes. She never forgave him for giving Lois such a hard time—and the rest of us, too. But don't you dare mention that. You'll be attending my funeral if that gets out."

The coroner's report showed Linda was partially right. Chuck died of heart problems and a combination of too much alcohol and prescription painkillers. His dark side apparently had run deeper than I suspected.

Dub's appearance at my house late one evening after the funeral was completely unexpected. I almost didn't let him in, but I decided I owed it to Aunt Helen.

"I waited for your boyfriend to leave," Dub said. "Would like to settle this between you and me if possible."

Chris was going to throw a fit when he learned about this, but Dub did not seem like an evil person, only sort of clueless. I looked around for something to use as a weapon, just in case.

"Are you sure this is a good idea?" I asked.

"I'm not sure of anything except I need to get that produce man's name cleared," he said. "I have evidence that he did not set those fires. I should have done something sooner."

"Of course it wasn't Mr. Sepulvado. But who was it? You? Your brother?"

Dub held up his hand as though trying to stop my questions. "I hoped to wrap this up without dragging Chuck's family through it, but I see now that will not be possible."

"You weren't so worried about Mr. Sepulvado's family, were you?" I asked. "Nor the people at the newspaper, good, hardworking people."

Dub shook his head slowly.

"I was weak," he said, taking his white handkerchief from his pocket and wiping his face. "No man wants to admit to being weak."

"You set the fires?"

"No, oh no. I didn't know about them until after the Dumpster fire. I swear I didn't. Chuck said something about that man getting arrested, like he was happy about it. Then I realized my brother was behind the fires, all of them. He wanted to scare you. Run you out of town."

"Why didn't you report him? Do the right thing for once?"

"At first I thought he only started that one fire. I told him I'd go to you if he didn't stop. He hated you so much that he threatened me when I said that."

"Did you leave that puzzle page?" I demanded.

"I did," he said, laying the handkerchief on the arm of the couch. "It was another example of my foolishness. I figured you were smart enough to work it out."

"Talk about taking the weak way out," I said.

"Next thing I know, Chuck called me, said I was right. 'Too many people know too much,' he told me. He acted like he had seen the ghost of Aunt Helen. Said she would never have wanted us to file suit and that he would talk to the chief about the charges against that guy."

"But Chuck dragged his heels and dropped dead," I said.

"Yes." Dub's look was grim.

"If you didn't know about the fires, who called them in? Someone was always conveniently in the neighborhood when the fires started."

"Wasn't me. I would guess Major, but I'm not sure. He and my brother were pretty tight. Major hinted at it that day Eva and I met him at the park, but I had no idea what he was talking about."

"Why'd you meet him in the first place?" I felt as though I were back in Dayton, doing a big investigative project, but this time the subject was my life.

Dub closed his eyes and took a deep breath. "For Eva. She wanted us to talk. There have been misunderstandings through the years. We used to be close, Eva and me and her brother. Watching you change so many things for the good of Green made her want something better for us."

Facing Dub, I leaned over the back of a rocking chair. "Why would you agree to file suit against me in the first place? You and Chuck hadn't legally owned that paper for years. Why would you do that to me . . . and to Aunt Helen?"

"You weren't from here," Dub said. "We weren't open to your outside ways. I let Chuck convince me you didn't live up to the deal. My poor judgment has cost me more than I can ever say, but I'll clear things up. I'm meeting the chief of police when I leave here."

He didn't try to shake my hand when he left, and I was relieved. I did not want to touch him or have anything to do with him.

"I was wrong," he said, walking off my porch like a much older man.

When I turned around, the handkerchief, like the one he had given me when Sugar Marie bit me on New Year's Day, was still on the couch. I picked it up and threw it away.

Facing the staff, I outlined the events of the past few weeks in tedious detail, from the puzzle page to my late-night visit to Chuck's house. "Alex, I need you to get on the story. Tammy, go back over every one of your photographs for evidence about the fires."

"Linda, pull out that puzzle and the rest of the information," I said. She followed me to my office. "Mr. Sepulvado's name could have been cleared days ago if I had gone forward."

"I can't see Doug tearing up the charges based on a puzzle page found under your car," Linda said. "This was no ordinary case."

"If there was *any* chance I could have helped sooner, I owe Mr. Sepulvado an apology."

The developments played out pretty much as I expected, except more quickly.

Dub was charged with withholding information about a criminal investigation and immediately pleaded guilty to a reduced charge and received probation.

"I take responsibility for my actions and will pay my debt to Green," he said in an interview with Linda. "My life will be different from now on."

Charges against Mr. Sepulvado were dropped. "I am grateful to have my honor restored," he said to Katy, with Pastor Jean as interpreter.

Major Wilson pleaded not guilty as an accessory to starting the fires and to illegally carrying a concealed handgun. A search of his office found cell phone records identifying calls made on the days of each fire.

Alex attached himself to the story, fascinated at Major's motivations. "He didn't want to betray his pal," the reporter said. "Instead of turning Chuck in for the fires, he called the Fire Department every time."

Alex flipped through his notes. "He said the strangest thing to me: 'I hope this doesn't foul up the Spanish lessons at the courthouse.'"

"He wanted to do the right thing at some level," I said. "He couldn't quit crossing the line."

The Police Chief didn't know whether to be perturbed with me or not. "He took one look at the puzzle page," Walt said, "rolled his eyes, snatched it out of my hand, and told me to get out of his office."

My column about the situation ran on Page One, an attempt to explain what had happened. It was the hardest thing I had ever written.

Iris Jo was at home recovering from her surgery, and I went by for reassurance that I hadn't acted, in the end, like the Big Boys.

"Was I underhanded?" I asked. "I went over to Chuck's and bluffed him into dropping that lawsuit, and I was relieved when he died. I didn't turn that puzzle over to the police. When it comes down to it, am I just like them?"

"If my arm weren't so weak, I'd punch you," Iris said. "I'd like to see someone else get in that briar patch and do any better."

"You could," I said. "You could have done better."

"Lois, I've sat here these past few days thankful for my surgery so I didn't have to be in the middle of things."

"You're our foundation at the paper, Iris. You've kept me on track and kept the *Item* in the black through very hard times."

"Barely in the black," she interrupted.

"In the black nonetheless. We've paid all our bills, and next year you'll come up with a way to make more money. You always do. The paper seems lonely without you. We'll be glad when you get back."

"Lois, let's wait a few weeks to think about next year. Get back to work. You're giving me a headache."

Her teasing tone reassured me that she was indeed feeling better. As I left, I stood in her yard, next to the fake windmill and her new plastic birdbath, and gave thanks for her healing and her wisdom.

Mr. Sepulvado was pleased when Chris and I visited his weather-beaten travel camper after the charges were dropped. He insisted we have cake and coffee with him and his wife.

"Lo siento mucho," I said as I entered his home, hoping my apology was correct.

"Bad situation," he said. "Not your fault." He looked me right in the eye. "I forgive."

Chris turned to me in his truck as we left. "Now you have got to learn to forgive yourself."

20

*A double golden wedding anniversary celebration
was held at the Senior Center on Saturday afternoon.
Longtime Route 2 residents Lawrence and Elizabeth
Bradley and Donald and Fain Bradley of Catahoula
Parish, who became high school sweethearts at Green
High, were married one week apart, fifty years ago.
Lawrence and Donald are brothers, and Elizabeth and
Fain are sisters. The celebration included a sit-down
lunch. The Senior Center was also the setting for the
First Baptist Young Marrieds, who met later on Saturday
for a covered dish dinner and game night.*

—*The Green News-Item*

The land clearing started in mid-November. Trees were bull-dozed, large piles of brush burned with ugly efficiency. Within what seemed like a few hours, large patches of dirt replaced little areas of woods I had come to love.

"They've started the highway project," Pastor Jean said. "You knew it was coming."

"I thought they were going to hold off at least till next summer," I said. "The last word was they would wait for dry weather."

"This is preliminary work," she said. "Not the real clearing. These roads take years to finish."

I put my hand to my forehead. "Then I don't want to see what the real clearing looks like. I'm not sure I can bear it. I wish they would have chosen the other route."

"So it would be in someone else's neighborhood?" she asked gently.

"Yes. No. Oh, I don't know. I hate the way it looks. Route 2 won't be the same with all those trees gone. I love our little country road."

Pastor Jean looked at me with a knowing smile and went back to copying the bulletins for Sunday's services.

"What was that look for?" I asked.

"A year ago you were ready to sell your paper and leave this place. Now you're ready to throw yourself in front of a log truck."

"When you put it like that . . ."

"Change happens," she said. "Isn't that what you're always telling me when the church is too slow for you?"

"That's different," I said. "Those are good changes. Needed changes. This is a big ugly interstate."

"Interesting how 'good change' is in the eye of the beholder," Jean said. "A lot of people around Green are plenty happy to see this interstate come through. Makes us more accessible. Some people are getting rich off the sale of land. Lots of construction jobs, too."

"I don't know why I bother coming to see you," I said. "All you do is make me see the error of my ways."

She handed me bulletins to fold. "We'll have to figure out what we're going to do about this building, sooner or later. And the cemetery. And the parsonage."

"I thought they decided to bypass Grace," I said. "Merely needed that land where the parking lot is now."

"I'm not so sure. It's going to be awfully close. With all the kids in and out and the older people, it may not be safe." She sighed. "We'll tackle that one later. First we've got to finish getting ready for the Kids Club Camp."

"I heard back from that lawyer, Terrence," I said. "He's coming Wednesday to speak at the career program. So is Kevin. Chris will take care of the games, and Tammy's going to teach the kids to take photographs and let them look at their pictures on her laptop." I rattled off the other details from my mental list.

"You're good, Lois Barker," she said. "Now be off with you. I have to write a sermon."

———

At the last minute, Tammy called to say she was running late for Kids Club because of a "breaking news story." Pastor Jean picked up the phone in the corridor by the fellowship hall and signaled for me.

"I think someone's having a baby," she said, a perplexed look on her face.

"You won't believe this in a million years," Tammy said when I took the phone. "Wilma Palmetto Starks, that woman from the dry cleaners, just saw her own grandchild for the first time—at the Cotton Boll Café!"

"Tammy, that's sweet, but I need you out here now," I said. "The children are expecting photos. And Terrence hasn't called today, and Kevin got delayed at the clinic and is picking up little Asa."

"The pictures are fantastic," Tammy said, as though I had not spoken. "These might even be worth a contest or the wire services . . . that tiny baby in a turkey pan."

I shook my head, took a deep breath, and propped myself against the green linoleum countertop. I opened the cabinet over the sink, looking for an aspirin. I knew Tammy didn't expect me to speak until her story was finished.

"Wilma's son-in-law rushed in and said they weren't going to make it to the hospital. Wilma's daughter had a baby right there in the diner! John Joseph Jones, seven pounds five ounces, wrapped in the cook's towels and kept in a turkey basting pan until the paramedics arrived."

"At the Cotton Boll?" I asked, trying to decide whether to get drawn into this tale or fret about Kids Club. "And you got it all?"

"More than you want to see, I guarantee. Well, gotta go. I'm locking up at the paper and heading your way."

Lord, help me, I thought as I walked into the parking lot to look for my missing guest speakers.

Kevin arrived first, apologetically pulling A.C. out of his car seat and looking her normal gorgeous self in her tan jeans and burnt orange jacket. Asa wore a tiny football jersey and jeans, part of what appeared to be an endless wardrobe for tots. "People give him something everywhere he goes," Kevin told me once. "It's so sweet."

Chris helped carry her things in, and Tammy zoomed in next, while a large group of children played on our make-shift playground, many wrapped in ratty sweaters or hooded sweatshirts.

Terrence arrived twenty minutes late, driving a late-model BMW convertible. The children flocked to him as he stepped out. They might not know what they wanted to be when they grew up, but they definitely knew they wanted a fancy car.

"Some crowd you have here," the lawyer said, surrounded by eager kids, all trying to get his attention. "Impressive."

"They obviously think you're impressive, too," I said, escorting him into the "clubhouse" we had decorated. Chris had made a rocket out of cardboard boxes, and I had lettered a sign saying, "Shoot for the stars. God has great plans for you."

The idea was mine and surprised everyone.

After shaking hands with Chris and greeting Pastor Jean, Kevin, and Tammy. Terrence sat in a small chair, looking every bit the successful professional. I knew some child would be changed by this day.

"Good afternoon, children," he said, in a deep voice, one you could imagine booming in a courtroom.

"Good afternoon," the children echoed loudly, still pushing each other to get closer.

"My name is Terrence D'Arbonne, and I like cars and soccer and music. Do any of you like those things?"

The children squealed loudly, and one boy ran for the corner where we kept the soccer balls. "We play soccer," he said shyly, handing Terrence the ball.

Terrence briefly twirled the ball on the tip of his finger, much to the delight of the group. "Today," he said, "I want to talk to you about school and why you should study hard and learn a lot. I got a bad grade once. And you know what happened?"

"Did you get in trouble?" a little girl asked, her eyes big.

"My grandmother held my chin in her hands, looked me straight in the eye and told me I could do better than that."

"Did she whip you?" one boy asked.

"She didn't hit me," Terrence said, patting the child's shoulder. "But she sure whipped me into shape."

The squirmy group was rapt as the big man spoke.

Kevin leaned over and whispered to me, trying to keep Asa from scooting away. "You've been holding out on me. You didn't tell me Terrence was so cute."

"You told me you weren't interested in dating, as I recall, but I happen to know he's single, and he sure seems to like children."

Later that afternoon, I saw her chatting with the lawyer while he played with little Asa.

"Good fellow," Chris said as we straightened up in the tiny church kitchen. "And a great program. I've never seen those kids sit so still. You are amazing."

"That Terrence is amazing," I said, tossing used paper plates and collecting a few dishes. "You think he and Kevin . . ."

"Now, Lois, I don't do matchmaking." He handed me a dish towel. "I'll wash. You dry. Get us in practice for the big Turkey Day feed at Mama and Daddy's tomorrow."

I took the towel and meticulously dried a bowl.

"Are you sure?" I asked.

He gave an exaggerated sigh and kissed me. "We're not going to start down that road again, are we? I thought we were past that."

"But Thanksgiving," I said. "That's a big family deal."

He looked at me oddly. "Surely you know by now, Lois Barker, that you are family."

When we arrived the next day, Estelle was pulling a huge turkey out of the oven and Hugh was setting up extra chairs. I gave each of them a kiss on the cheek and settled in to set the table, knowing automatically where the utensils and napkins were kept.

The chaos of children and conversation delighted me, and I beamed at the compliments my fruit salad and corn casserole got. My Ohio-style white-bread dressing was not much of a hit.

"Interesting," Estelle said when she took a bite.

"You're good with cornbread," Chris said. "Next Thanksgiving, can we stick to cornbread dressing?"

Next Thanksgiving?

By the time December came, my Christmas plans didn't get a second thought. Shipping gifts to my brothers and their families, I felt a twinge of sadness. But my home and Chris were in Green.

"I've got a great idea for the special Christmas paper," Katy said, as usual running into the newsroom with the force of a Mack truck. "Little Asa and Sugar Marie."

"That darling boy and that sweet dog?" Tammy interrupted. "I get to take the pictures."

"You take all the pictures, Tammy," Molly said, plopping down next to Katy. "But you're going to love this one. We'll put A.C. in the manger down at the live nativity scene. Sugar Marie will have a fleece sheep outfit on."

"Then we can blow it up to be the whole front page, with a gigantic headline that says 'Merry Christmas,'" Katy continued. She sat back, clearly pleased with herself. "Pretty good, eh?"

"We'll have to convince Kevin," I said. "She's a very private person. Doesn't want to call too much attention to herself and her son."

"We already did," Molly said. "She said yes."

"We reminded her that Asa is her precious gift, and that Christmas is about God's precious gift, that kind of thing," Katy said. "Mayor Eva loves the idea of her dog in that photo, too."

The poster page was a big hit, and the newspaper quickly sold out, our last edition before the holiday.

Chris seemed especially interested in it, asking a dozen questions about whose idea it was, how we did it, and when the next paper would come out.

"You thinking of a career in journalism?" I asked.

"I realize sometimes I don't know much about your business. Want to talk about the basketball team's man-to-man defense?"

The next day Eva called and invited me to lunch at the Country Club on Christmas Eve. "Let's have a real Christmas visit," she said. "Haven't seen much of you lately."

On December 24, I wrapped a few gifts and stopped at the office to clear off my desk, happy to be planning a nice Christmas break, a luxury not experienced in my job as city editor in Dayton. I was surprised to see Tom, Katy, and Tammy, all working in the newsroom. "I thought I gave you the day off. What's up?"

"Someone had to post the obits," Katy said.

"I'm sorting the mail, looking for payments," Tammy said. "Won't be here long."

Tom closed his computer screen. "Checking my e-mail. Came to pick up the Shreveport paper."

"Don't work too hard." I headed off for lunch. "Merry Christmas!"

Eva pulled into the club's circular driveway right after me, in her boat of a car.

"Nice wheels," I yelled, waiting by the front door. That car got on my nerves for some reason.

As the driver stepped out, the woman handed her keys to the valet. I was mortified. "Sorry," I said. "I thought you were the mayor."

"Of course I'm the mayor," she said, turning. "What do you think?"

Her dyed-black, teased hairdo had been replaced with a light brown bob, short and cute, not all that different from Katy's. She looked twenty years younger.

"I love it," I said, unable to resist the urge to touch it. "You need a better lunch date than me."

Our meal was filled with interesting chitchat and a quick reference to her brother. "Major's probably headed to jail this time, but he feels badly about what he did to you," she said. "I hope he may be reformed. I guess time will tell."

"I hope so," I said. "Have you talked to Dub?"

"Several times." She looked almost coy with her new hair-style. "We're trying to figure each other out after twenty-five years of ignoring each other. We've both made big mistakes. But that's a story for another day. I must tell you my biggest news!"

"A new hairdo. An old flame. What else?"

"Sugar Marie's a mother," Eva said. "My sweet baby had one little girl puppy about a month and a half ago. Things have been so crazy I forgot to mention it."

I put my hand up to my face, no evidence of the bite still there. "Congratulations, I think. You're not expecting a baby gift, are you?"

"I've noticed the way you've started spoiling Sugar Marie. You even put her on Page One of your newspaper. She's got you eating out of her paws." The mayor fidgeted. Was it the hair or Dub that made her seem almost giddy?

"As a matter of fact, this is for that sidekick of yours." I handed Eva a tin of fancy dog treats I had ordered online. "Tell her all is forgiven and forgotten."

Eva set the gift on the floor, fumbled around under the table for her purse and glanced at her phone. "Sorry. Wanted to make sure I didn't have any messages. I have more news." She set her purse in her lap. "I'm giving myself a new Cadillac for Christmas. Picking it up this afternoon."

"You don't mean it. Has the Auto Museum called for your old car yet?"

"Aren't you the funny one?" She glanced at her watch. "We better get going."

"But we haven't had dessert," I said, surprised at her sudden haste.

"It's later than I thought. I told the dealer I'd be there early afternoon." She stood up.

"Go ahead," I said to her when we got to the valet stand. "I'm not in a hurry."

"You go on. I've got to run to the restroom."

While Eva was inside, the attendant hurried back from where my car sat, apologizing profusely. "I'm so sorry, Miss Barker." He shook his head. "I locked your keys in the car when I parked it."

"What?" I snapped, and then softened. "Are you sure?"

"Unfortunately so. We can call a locksmith, but it may take a while." He looked at the old-fashioned clock on the outside wall. "With it being Christmas Eve and all."

Just then Eva strolled out, glancing at the valet.

"Eva, little problem here," I said. "My keys are locked in the car. I know you're in a hurry, but can you drop me at the paper? I have a spare set in my desk."

She glanced at her watch. "Well, I guess so, but won't you need a key to get in?"

"Someone will be there. Half a dozen people were milling around when I left. If not, I'll run down to Tom's house, grab his key, and ask him to bring me back over here."

I noticed she tipped the attendant fifty dollars. "Have a Merry Christmas," she said.

Instead of driving me up to the front of the building, Eva stopped on the street and leaned over to give me a little hug. For a brief moment, I thought she might open the door and push me out.

"Enjoy the holidays," she said. "I'll bring the new car by soon." Then she handed me two quarters. "In case you need to make a phone call."

I tried to hand the coins back to her. "Are you OK? Has that new hairdo affected your brain?"

"Couldn't be better," she said. "Now scoot. I'm running late."

Walking through the parking lot, I glanced at the news-paper rack I had twice run into with my car. The large photograph caught my eye, and I smiled. Stan must have added a few more copies of the Christmas edition.

As I got closer, jingling the change in my hand, I realized it was not the Christmas paper at all. What in the world? Had someone vandalized the rack? I stepped closer. *The Green News-Item* masthead was in place. But the huge headline was different.

I peeked around but saw no one. I jerked the rack handle to no avail. Then I looked down at the two quarters in my hand and smiled.

I dropped the coins into the newspaper box and pulled out the single copy of the paper, labeled "Special Edition" in red letters at the top.

"Will You Marry Me?" asked the banner headline.

"Local Coach Hopes to Wed Newspaper Owner," the smaller headline read.

I slowly opened the page to its full length. Tammy's cute photograph of Chris and me, taken at Kids Club Camp at Grace Chapel, took up almost the entire space. A small enve-lope was securely taped to the bottom of the space.

My hands trembled as I fumbled with it.

Inside the envelope was a beautiful engagement ring, old-fashioned and utterly charming.

I slipped it on my finger, and ran up the stairs to the paper.

Chris stepped through the lobby, opened the door for me and paused.

"So will you?"

"Goodness gracious, yes!" I said, hurling myself at him.

"I love you, Lois Barker," he said, pulling me into a deep kiss.

"I love you, Chris Craig."

As we kissed again, the entire staff of the *Item* spilled out into the lobby, laughing, whistling, and giving each other high fives.

"We did it," Tom said. "We really did it."

"I knew we could pull it off." Katy jumped up and down.

"Were you surprised?" Molly asked.

Tammy snapped dozens of photos and hugged Walt, who stood nearby, smiling. Iris and Stan held hands and grinned.

"How?" I sputtered. "When?"

Chris patted the men on the back and hugged the women. "Lois and I are getting married," he said, a dazed look on his face. "She's going to be my wife."

"Look at this ring." I held my left hand out to the women who huddled over me instantly. I kissed Chris again. "Isn't it gorgeous?"

With the merriment in full force, my arm securely around Chris, Mayor Eva walked up the stairs, dangling my car keys from one hand and cradling something in a small blanket with the other.

Chris opened the door, never letting go of me. "She said yes! Thanks for helping pull it off."

"I never doubted it," Eva said. "I was so certain that I brought your first wedding gift."

She held up a ball of wiggling fur not much bigger than my hand, a tiny copy of Sugar Marie.

"Holly Beth, meet your new mother."

The End

Discussion Questions

1. *Goodness Gracious Green* opens as Lois Barker begins her second year in Green. How does the start of her year differ from what she expected? Have you ever had a similar experience, where things did not turn out as you thought they would? How did you respond? What surprised you about Day One of Year Two for Lois in Green?

2. What do you like best about Lois as she settles into her second year in Green—and what does she need to work on? How is she struggling and how is she blossoming? Have you had periods in your life when you felt as though you were growing but weren't always sure what to do?

3. Deciding to stay in Green was a tough decision for Lois, and she wonders at times in *Goodness Gracious Green* if she made the right decision. Do you think Lois did the right thing when she kept the little newspaper? In your life, do you wrestle with making decisions and wonder about them afterward? What advice would you give Lois?

4. Occasionally Lois finds that her former life as a big-city journalist in the Midwest clashes with her life in Green. In what ways does she see this happening? How well does she deal with it? In what ways is it good and in what ways might it be bad?

5. Lois wants the staff to help run the newspaper, but battles her own desire to be in control. Did she make the right decision to start the profit-sharing program? How can she handle this wisely? What part do the employees play in making this work? How are they handling it? If you were on Lois's staff, what suggestions would you have? Have you battled the issue of

changing technology in your personal or professional life? How have you approached this?

6. Community correspondents are an important part of *The Green News-Item*. What do you think of their reporting? Why are their voices important? In what ways do they capture the personality of Green? Have you seen similar situations or news items in your life? How can a newspaper best represent its community?

7. In her daily life in Green, Lois interacts with a variety of characters who count on her for advice. How well does she handle this challenge? Who do you most like among these characters? Among the meaningful people in the changing life of Lois are young Katy and Molly. What do they symbolize in *Goodness Gracious Green*? In what ways are they alike and in what ways different? How might Lois help them in the future? Have you had an opportunity to mentor or coach a younger person? What did you learn from that experience? Do Katy and Molly remind you of anyone in your life?

8. The McCullers and Major Wilson continue to be part of Lois's life in *Goodness Gracious Green*. What roles do they play? How do they complicate things for Lois and the newspaper? What doubts do they raise for Lois, and how do they help her grow? What part do Aunt Helen's lessons play in these relationships?

9. The poverty in Green and on Route 2 troubles Lois and brings up a variety of issues in the community. Why do you think Lois is particularly bothered by this? How does she respond? Have you ever faced an issue that troubled you deeply, one that rose above others in your heart and mind? What was the issue and what actions did you take?

10. Green continues to face a host of changes—from an influx of immigrant workers to the new highway to

the economic woes the paper and other businesses face. How do these changes affect Lois and the newspaper? What impact do they have on Grace Community Chapel? Do you find it hard to deal with change? How might Lois and the residents of Green learn to handle these changing situations?

11. Chris Craig plays a large part in *Goodness Gracious Green*. His relationship with Lois seems complex. Why is this? What are the biggest challenges they face as they grow closer? In what ways are they alike? In what ways are they different? What is Lois learning from Chris?

12. Life for Lois in *Goodness Gracious Green* is filled with transitions. What are some of those? How does she handle them? Have you had a time in your life when friends took different paths or when you had to handle a tough transition? How did you approach it?

13. The deep friendships that Lois has built in Green continue to grow. In what ways is she enriched by Dr. Kevin, Iris Jo, and Pastor Jean? What does she learn from them? List a few of the times these friends help Lois in *Goodness Gracious Green*. How have your friends helped you through life? Can you think of a particularly meaningful lesson you've learned from a friend or a friend who is available when you need him or her?

14. Lois continues to be on a journey in her life, and this includes trying to develop spiritually. Why is this a challenge to her? In what areas does she falter? How does she move forward? In your own life, have you wrestled with growing spiritually? What advice might you give Lois as she continues to ask tough questions about faith?

15. What thoughts do you have for Lois as her life moves forward? What do you think the future holds for her in Green? What changes do you think she will face?

16. List a few words you think Lois would use to describe her life in the months ahead. Make a similar list for your life. What steps will Lois have to take to make her dreams come true? What steps might you take to live the life you long for?

**Bonus chapter from book three in
The Green Series**

Coming in February, 2011

The Glory of Green

1

*A neighbor in the Ashland community wants the hoodlums
who took his U.S. flag from the pole in the front yard
and replaced it with boxer shorts to return his flag.
However, the perpetrators should not expect to get
their shorts back. "The red hearts aren't my style, but
Martha Sue seems to like them," he told this correspondent
with a wink. 'If you ask me, it's a sad day when
Old Glory gets undermined by underwear.*

—*The Green News-Item*

For the past couple of years, my number one talent has been second-guessing myself.

I had fussed over my move to Green. Fretted over whether to keep *The Green News-Item*. Debated how to fight for the little newspaper. Wondered if I could settle in small-town Louisiana.

But I never once doubted my decision to marry Chris Craig.

This man was so kind and fun—OK, and good-looking—that I could scarcely believe he would be my husband in less than a month.

I *was* having a hard time, though, believing what he had just said.

My bridegroom was supposed to give away his catfish collection. Instead, he wanted to give his mobile home to a single mom who attended church across the road.

"Don't you think that's the perfect solution?" he asked, a big smile on his face. "We don't need this place, Lois, since we'll be living in your house."

Here I sat, at his kitchen table, with woven, ceramic, and stuffed catfish everywhere. And there he stood, drinking coffee out of a mug with a fish handle, tossing out a suggestion that made my selfish streak feel bigger than his heart. And Chris had a big heart.

"It hit me last night after I dropped you off," he said. "Those boys deserve better than that shack out in the middle of nowhere. This trailer isn't worth much, but they'd have room to run and play, and the roof doesn't leak."

While Chris talked about changing lives, my thoughts strayed back to that darned catfish collection. Getting a husband at age thirty-eight was one thing, taking all his things was something else. My cozy cottage, with its mix of antiques and modern art, was arranged the way I liked it.

I looked around the paneled room and wondered who thought the catfish pillow on the couch had been a good idea. Just because Chris raised the whiskered fish part-time didn't actually make him a fan of the creatures as art objects. *Did it?*

"So, what do you think?" he asked, and I pulled myself back to his brainstorm.

"It's a generous gesture," I said and paused.

"Why do I feel like there's a 'but' coming next?"

"I assumed we'd rent or sell it to bring in a little money," I said, squirming inside as I heard how the words sounded. "I thought you were going to have a garage sale and get rid of a few things. Then we would decide about the trailer."

"There's no need for a garage sale," he said. "Let's move everything down the road. Your house is plenty big for all this."

He swept his arm around, sloshing coffee onto the gold linoleum. Holly Beth, my four-month-old puppy, scampered over to lick it up.

"Holly, stop that," I snapped, grabbing a paper towel with one hand and scooping her up with the other. "You're way too young for caffeine."

She licked my face and burrowed under my chin, and Chris laughed. I wasn't quite sure what to do with the dog, our first wedding gift, a surprise from Mayor Eva Hillburn.

Chris leaned in to kiss me, but Holly Beth moved between us, licking him on the cheek. He stroked her soft white fur, still focused on his grand plan.

"I can get a couple of buddies to haul my stuff a few days ahead of time. That way Maria and the boys could move in here before our wedding. Mama will be thrilled if I stay with her and Daddy for a while."

"It's all happening so fast," I said. "I see now why they recommend a year to plan a wedding."

Chris placed Holly gently on the floor with her favorite toy, a squeaky rubber newspaper, and pulled me over to the tweed plaid couch, similar to one my friend Marti had when we first met twenty years ago.

"You're not getting cold feet, are you?" he asked, wrapping his arms around me. "I'll get rid of some junk. I love you much more than my wagon-wheel coffee table."

"I just didn't realize all the decisions we would have to make. Maybe we should have eloped."

"No way am I running off to marry you," he said. "I intend for all of Green to be there when Pastor Jean pronounces us husband and wife. It'll be a day to remember."

"No doubt the locals will talk about it for years," I said and cuddled next to him, his arm draped around my shoulders. "They'll tell how that hussy from Ohio stormed in here and took the town's best catch."

"Are you snuggling or stalling?" Chris asked after a couple of quiet moments.

"Both," I said. "Let's talk about this house business later. I need to check on Iris Jo. Will you take care of the little princess for a few minutes?"

"Of course I will," he said, picking the puppy up as he helped me into my jacket. He lifted my dark ponytail over the collar and kissed my neck.

"She likes you better than me," I said, opening the door while Holly licked Chris's face and yelped as though she had never been happier. "I was afraid that was going to happen."

"Surely you're not jealous of your own dog," he said and made a big smooching sound, pretending to kiss the puppy and then giving me a little peck on the cheek.

"Don't be silly," I said.

When we stepped outside, his three dogs jumped around us, and I reached into my jacket pocket for treats. "But I'm not above bribing your dogs to love me more."

As I walked the short distance down the gravel road, my steps slowed, and I savored the sweetness of a day on the cusp of spring and worried about Iris, undergoing chemotherapy for breast cancer.

A key employee at the paper and a woman who had become my confidante in a short time, she lived between me and Chris, our places spread out on Route 2. Tiny Grace Community

Chapel sat across the road, with Pastor Jean's parsonage adjacent to the old-fashioned building and cemetery.

The winter air was chilly but the signs of early spring were evident, a flock of robins migrating through, the tiniest of green leaves on trees, and jonquils budding in the shallow ditch. Spring was definitely about to burst forth, and everything would be new and fresh for our wedding day.

This was the symbol of my new life in Green and the roots I had begun to put deeply into the red Louisiana clay.

When Chris had proposed on Christmas Eve, we wanted a short engagement, egged on by family and friends who had tried to push us together for more than a year.

"Don't you think you've dragged your heels long enough?" asked newspaper clerk and photographer Tammy. "You're not exactly a spring chicken."

"Speaking of spring," Iris Jo, the peacemaker of the group, said, "how about March or April? You love North Louisiana in springtime."

"Don't plan it too close to the Easter cold snap," Katy, a high school intern, said. "Spring dresses look silly under coats."

"Katy's got a good point," Tammy added. "The weather's pretty freaky that time of year."

"When's the weather not weird around here?" I asked.

Before the New Year had rolled around, my mind had turned to planning a spring wedding, a beautiful late March day, the perfect time to become Lois Barker Craig, an honor I did not take lightly. I could see flowering quince in big urns at the front of the church, mixed with mock orange and early dogwoods, and maybe a redbud branch or two. I would carry tulips and jonquils and ask Miss Barbara, a cranky advertiser who owned a clothing store, to find me a dress.

A journalist for more than two decades and owner of *The Green News-Item* for more than two years, the deadline of a wedding seemed easy.

Little did I know.

My mental to-do list added item after item. I woke up in the middle of the night and jotted notes on a tablet I kept by my bed, and taped notes on doors at home and work. With less than a month to go, I needed to finalize my family's travel plans, empty a closet for Chris, and plan coverage to fill the upcoming editions of the newspaper, not completely trusting anyone else. Tammy called me bossy, but I preferred to think of it as leadership.

Now I had another issue to consider. I had spent months looking for ways for our community to serve people in poverty. *Was I too stingy to offer shelter to a precious family?*

The mobile home was not much by the standards of many of the people I knew in Dayton, nor in the eyes of those who lived in fancy houses on Bayou Lake in Green. I had judged Chris when I met him, wondering why a man who taught school and had land with ponds would not choose a better house.

"I like it out here," he told me when we started our evening walks, the strolls that turned into romance. "The bright stars. The open space. I'm not a fancy guy, and I don't need a fancy house." We had never spoken of it again.

As I drew near Iris Jo's home, Stan—all-around production guy at the paper and recent public boyfriend to Iris—backed out in his giant blue pickup, his window whirring down when he saw me.

"I brought a little breakfast, but she's still puny," he said. "Thanks for coming. You always make her feel better."

I waved and walked around the house, tapping on the door into the den, a room made from an enclosed carport. "It's me," I yelled, going in without waiting for a reply.

Iris, who was only slightly older than me but seemed wiser and, well, more mature, was propped up in the overstuffed recliner she had bought before her surgery. She gave a small smile when I entered.

"I'm here to hold your hair back as needed and ask for marriage advice," I said, leaning over to give her a careful hug.

"I'm past the throwing up stage today and thankful to still have a little hair, so I'll pass," she said. "But I'm happy for your company."

I sprawled on the couch, at home in her small ranch-style house. I tried not to wince when her cat, Earl Grey, appeared from the kitchen, climbed up on the back of the sofa, and swiped at my hair. What was it with me and animals?

"Early, baby, leave Lois alone," Iris Jo said. "You know she's not a fan of yours."

"She's OK," I said, scooting over slightly. "Just as long as you don't give me a kitten for a wedding gift."

"Holly Beth still wreaking havoc?"

"I never knew how much work puppies were," I said. "I'm trying to house-train her, but I'm gone so much it's hard. You've seen what happens when I take her to the office. Tammy and Katy spoil her rotten, and she cries at night to get out of her crate. Don't tell Chris, but she sounds so sad that I've let her up on the bed some."

"Have you taken Mayor Eva off the guest list for springing a dog on you?"

"It's hard to hold it against Eva when Holly's so sweet," I said. "She's definitely more lovable than her mother." Sugar Marie, the mayor's Yorkie and Holly Beth's mother, had bitten me on the face last year and still had a bit of an attitude problem, if you asked me,

"You mentioned marriage advice," Iris said. "What's up? Since you've only been engaged three months, isn't it a tad early for trouble?"

"My loving husband-to-be thinks we should give his trailer away," I said. "I'm not so sure."

"Does he have a recipient in mind?"

"Maria, from the Spanish service at church, and her sons."

"That sounds like something Chris would do," Iris said.

"So you like the idea?"

"He's not going to be my husband," Iris said. "Your opinion is the one that matters."

"Chris says if they lived closer, the church could help more. Doesn't that seem a little over-the-top?"

"What's over-the-top?" Tammy waltzed through the door right as I spoke. Iris and I waved and said hello, and Earl Grey jumped down to rub against Tammy's leg. She picked him up and tickled him on the throat, the cat purring as loud as the hum of an old refrigerator.

"Traitor," I muttered.

"Are you planning a big wedding maneuver?" Tammy said, sitting next to me with the cat on her lap. "She's not trying to outdo me, is she, Iris?"

Tammy had grown up in Green, worked at the front counter of the *Item* most days, and was used to being in the middle of everything. If she wasn't the center of the action by happenstance, she put herself there. Engaged to Walt, the newspaper's lawyer and an almost-boyfriend of mine, she was planning a summer "apple and pewter" wedding on the beach in Florida.

"Apple and pewter?" copy editor Tom had asked when she whirled into the newsroom one day with the decision. "Would those be the colors formerly known as red and gray?"

"You clearly have no idea what makes a beautiful wedding," she said, flinging a bridal magazine on his desk. "Maybe you ought to study up in case you decide to tie the knot one of these days."

In his mid-fifties, Tom had never been married, and I had a hard time imagining him on a date. He looked a little rough around the edges, with a beard in perpetual need of a trim. He planned his few social activities around when his library books were due.

"What's over the top?" Tammy repeated, looking from me to Iris. Today, the budding photojournalist seemed closer to Katy's teens than her own late twenties, sitting on the couch in tight jeans and a long-sleeved chiffon shirt.

"Chris wants to give his trailer away," I said.

"Wow," Tammy said, her eyes widening. "I hope Walt doesn't do that with his house, because I'm not sure where we'd live. My apartment's tiny."

It pained me to consider Tammy's move, so I ignored the comment. It was unlikely she'd commute from Shreveport, about an hour away, and it was as though the staff had taken a vow not to speak of it. Even though Tammy occasionally made me want to strangle her, she often helped me see the world in a different way. A couple of years in Green had attached me to my employees in a way I never felt as city editor in Dayton.

"It's possible I'm not all that excited about my groom's give-away idea," I said. "I should be. I have a great house that will be perfect for Chris and me."

"A house that Aunt Helen *gave* to you," Tammy said. "You can help someone the way she helped you." Twirling a big bracelet on her arm, she played with the cat, unaware that she also played with my emotions. My beloved house on Route 2 had been a gift from Helen McCuller, deceased former owner of the newspaper, and it anchored me in the little community. Chris and I could do the same for Maria and her children.

"How dumb can I be?" I asked after a moment.

Iris and Tammy looked at each other and smiled.

"That's a rhetorical question," I said.

"You're the smartest person I know," Tammy said.

"I'm a hypocrite. I've preached to everyone for months to help newcomers, and now I'm miffed that Chris wants to do just that."

"Welcome to engaged life," Tammy said. "You aren't used to Chris making decisions that affect you. That's hard, especially for someone like you."

"Someone like me?"

"You want to call the shots," she said.

I looked at Iris, a quiet woman with a gentle manner. I could tell she was trying not to laugh.

"I *do*, don't I?"

"Lois, you help everyone you cross paths with," Iris said. "But most of us like being in control. That's what I hate most about this cancer. It wasn't in my plans."

"Marrying Walt wasn't in my plans either," Tammy said. "What a cool surprise that was. We never know what's around the corner."

"Somehow all the twists and turns work out," Iris Jo said. "You and Chris will make the right decision."

"He already has," I said. "I've got to go."

I headed for the door and turned back to give Iris a kiss on the cheek.

"I'll tell him his idea is brilliant. Then I'll suggest he donate his decorator items to charity."

Chris and I met the next afternoon with Maria and Pastor Jean in the parsonage next to Grace Chapel. Jean, still dressed in the skirt and blouse she had preached in, settled the trio of boys in front of a cartoon DVD and returned to the kitchen, where we sat.

"¿Hay algo mal?" Maria asked Jean, looking tired and a little worn.

"No, no," Jean said and patted her hand.

Once more frustrated at my lack of Spanish skills, I glanced at Jean and Chris, both of whom were learning the language at a pace that surprised me. My studies were interrupted by impatience and a decided lack of devotion to vocabulary words.

"Maria wants to know if something is wrong," the pastor said. "She's had so much bad news these past few months. I told her this was a good thing." She smiled at the younger woman as she spoke and touched her hand softly.

One of Green's many Mexican immigrants, Maria looked about thirty and was the mother of boys ages four, five, and seven. Her husband had been killed on a gas well in a nearby parish, and she struggled to make ends meet, working as an aide at a nursing home.

Trying to learn English, she alternated between the two languages and was one of the regular attendees at the controversial Spanish-language service Pastor Jean had started.

"Lois and I have a gift for you," Chris said.

"A gift?" Maria asked, and then smiled, her white teeth beautiful against her dark skin. "More clothes for my boys?"

"Una casa para sus chicos," my wonderful fiancé said in his new Spanish. "A house for your boys."

"We want you to have it," I said.

"For me?" Maria asked.

"For you," Chris and I said at the same moment.

I turned to Jean, inspired by her relentless efforts to meet the needs of her flock, whether spiritual or physical. "Let's have a party and give items for the house. No hand-me-downs."

"A new kind of bridal shower," Jean said. "As always, I like the way you think, Lois. I'll spread the word while you show Maria the place."

Maria seemed almost dazed as we escorted her across the road and into the trailer, the boys more interested in the dogs than the tour.

"How much?" she asked after we looked at bedrooms and pointed out closets and cabinets.

Chris and I looked at each other, puzzled.

"How much the rent?" she asked. "I don't think I can afford."

I engulfed her in one of Green's famous hugs, tears flowing down my cheeks and Chris's eyes glistening.

How much?

How much courage it took for her to build a better life for her children.

How much energy to make decisions every day without understanding the language.

How much?

"Gratis," I said in one of the few Spanish words I had mastered. "Free. Our wedding gift to you."

Looking at the trailer through Maria's eyes, I was reminded how much a home of your own mattered.

How incredible it would be when Chris moved into *our* home on Route 2, the simple old house that would be filled with love.

Up Close and Personal with Judy Christie

Q: When writing this novel, what was your inspiration for the challenges that Lois would have to overcome?

A: As I've watched Lois and others in Green develop, I realized anew that rarely is life a neat little package with challenges settled once and for all. Trials come at us from unexpected directions, sometimes from outside forces and often from internal worries and fears. Challenges that Lois faces come as she grows and realizes that life is bigger than herself and that serving others is important. Lois begins to think she has life all figured out at the end of *Gone to Green*, but in *Goodness Gracious Green* she realizes again that life is a journey, with roadblocks and detours—and spectacular joys.

Q: Are you finding that book clubs and reading groups who are reading through the Green series are connecting with the characters just as you have?

A: Oh, my, yes! What an unexpected joy book clubs and reading groups are in my life! Sometimes readers connect with characters in ways I never expected, and they talk about Lois and Katy and Chris as if they know them. My heart beats extra fast when that happens. I cherish memories of sitting around a living room with a group of readers, standing in the front of a small Louisiana church answering questions, or visiting with a club at a public library, chatting about the town of Green and what's going on, knowing I'm surrounded by people who love reading and appreciate Green. Readers have favorite characters and favorite scenes and love to talk about Green. Could there be sweeter words than a reader asking when the next book will be out . . . and trying to talk me out of an early copy?!?!

Q: When you write, what kind of environment are you usually in?

A: The Green novels are written from my wonderful writer's cottage at our home in North Louisiana, with occasional jaunts to Camp Slower Pace, a fishing cabin on Lake Bistineau. Both places allow me to go to Green in my mind and help me fight my love of a good distraction. In my cottage, I write at a great corner desk, looking out into our backyard, and edit manuscripts in a big comfy chair or in the little porch swing, a gift from my husband who encourages me and my writing career every step of the way. At the camp, I stare out a big window at the lake, and ideas tumble out. Wherever I am, I'm surrounded by big note cards, preferably colored, with details, ideas, and questions on them. I keep a Big Picture journal handy, with lots of pens and markers, to map what could happen next and to organize my thoughts. I usually have a how-to-write book nearby and will pick it up for inspiration along the way. Long walks at a Louisiana state park or a city park near our house are also part of the writing process. I laugh and cry and think about the plot, which I'm sure makes others at the parks wonder about my sanity.

Q: Everyone has something that they like to "treat" themselves to as a reward when their work is accomplished! Is there anything that particularly motivates you when you're facing a serious deadline?

A: Give me a great flea market with chipped green pottery or primitive antiques and a couple of girlfriends who appreciate such finds, and I'm instantly renewed! My treats after I finish a manuscript almost always involve antiques, a good meal, or a fun trip with my husband—and often a combination of the three.

Since I was a journalist for many years, I tend to be obsessed with meeting deadlines, so I hibernate when finishing a project. Afterwards, it's fun to emerge and reconnect with family and friends.

Q: What spiritual elements and lessons do you think readers have drawn and can continue to draw from the Green series?

A: One of the blessings of writing fiction is that readers bring different perspectives to the stories and take away different lessons. I'm deeply moved when a reader is touched spiritually by something that happened in Green. I believe we can all change the world for good with our lives, and I hope that Lois and her story will help readers consider their own paths and what they were created to do and be.

My prayer is that the stories will encourage and entertain and educate readers in whatever way they need in their unique wonderful lives.

Lagniappe (a little something extra) *from*
Judy Christie and her friends in Green

Mama's Tea Cakes

An example of the many desserts dropped off for Lois at the newspaper in Green. This recipe comes from author Judy Christie's mom, who got it from an old family friend who had a beauty shop in her backyard. They are delicious with a cup of coffee!

Mix 1 quart plain flour, 2 teaspoons baking powder, 1 teaspoon soda, 2 cups sugar, 2 whole eggs, ½ cup buttermilk. Cut in ½ cup shortening as if making biscuits. Use extra flour to make stiff dough. Roll out very thin, then cut. Place in shallow pan. Cook in 450-degree oven. You can add any flavoring, generally nutmeg.

Way down in Louisiana...

Lois learns a lot about Louisiana in a short amount of time. If you'd like to know more about this unique and wonderful state, go to http://www.state.la.us/Explore/About Louisiana/

A wonderful town to visit in North Louisiana is Natchitoches. The oldest town in the Louisiana Purchase, it has brick streets, a great little bookstore, other neat shops, fantastic food, and charm galore. Famous for its Christmas celebration, it is also a great place to visit in the cooler days of fall and the gorgeous days of spring. To learn more about Natchitoches, see http://www.natchitoches.net/index.php

For more on the author and tips to enjoy each day more, see www.judychristie.com

Homemade Chocolate Syrup

Members of Grace Community Chapel regularly bring Pastor Jean homemade food, which she shares with Lois during some of their therapeutic visits. This recipe for chocolate syrup is a favorite—and can be saved and used as needed. It came from author Judy Christie's Aunt Jean, who died of breast cancer. Pastor Jean is named in her memory.

½ cup Cocoa   1 cup Water
2 cups Sugar   ⅛ tsp. Salt
¼ tsp. Vanilla

Mix cocoa and water in a saucepan; stir to dissolve cocoa; heat to blend the cocoa and water. Add sugar, stirring to dissolve sugar. Boil for 3 minutes; add salt and vanilla.

Pour into clean sterilized pint jar.

About the biscuits Lois ate at the home of
Dr. Kevin's parents in Gone to Green *and then with*
Chris's parents in Goodness Gracious Green . . .

Those delicious biscuits, made from scratch, are a key part
of a great Southern meal, served at breakfast, lunch, or
supper. It's hard to find a true recipe for them because a
great cook makes them from memory.

This account of how such biscuits are made was shared
by dear friend Sarah Leachman, who grew up in Ashland,
Louisiana, and watched her mama, Estelle Bumgardner,
make these for decades.

Mother didn't have a recipe. She first melted oil
(preferably leftover bacon grease) in her round biscuit
pans that had been seasoned from many years of use.
She used an old large round bowl (not very deep because
you didn't want to have to reach down very far) with flour
leftover from the day before lining the bowl. She sifted self-
rising flour (had to be self-rising) on top of the leftover flour
from the day before.

Mother never measured, just sifted until she knew she had
enough flour and then made a large hole in the middle of the
flour with her fist and filled that hole with fresh buttermilk.
To that mixture she added a large pinch of baking soda

(not baking powder) and a pinch of salt and then poured
in some of the oil from the pan. All this was mixed carefully
and lovingly with her hands (never with a spoon).

I can see her now swirling that mixture of dough around
in that bowl. With every swirl a little more flour was added
to the mixture. When she had gotten just the right amount
of flour mixed in, she carefully pinched off a large portion
of that dough and rolled it in her palms (very lightly).
She would carefully place that biscuit in the greased pan
and get grease on that side of the biscuit and then turn the
biscuit over so the other side would get oiled.

These were baked around 375 degrees for probably
20 minutes. You could just look at them and tell when
they were done.

When I was home, it was always my job to butter the
biscuits. Every biscuit in both pans was buttered (never
skimping on the butter). Those biscuits were so delicious they
could be eaten just by themselves right out of the oven.

In my mind, I can see Mother now in that old, cold kitchen,
making those biscuits at the kitchen cabinet. How I would
love to have another one of those hot biscuits and sit
down at the table and visit with Mother and Daddy.

Want to learn more about author
Judy Christie and check out other great fiction
from Abingdon Press?

Sign up for our fiction newsletter at
www.AbingdonPress.com
to read interviews with your favorite authors, find tips
for starting a reading group, and stay posted on what
new titles are on the horizon. It's a place to connect
with other fiction readers or post a
comment about this book.

Be sure to visit Judy online!

www.judychristie.com